Danny King was born in Slough in 1969 but spent his teens in a Hampshire backwater called Yateley. He left school as soon as he could and has worked as a hod carrier, a shelf stacker, a painter (kitchens not portraits), a postman, a sub-editor and a porn magazine editor (answers on a postcard if you can guess which one he's asked about the most). He moved to London in 1992 to study journalism at The London College of Printing and has been here ever since. He lives and drinks in Crystal Palace so if you see him in a pub, buy him a beer and tell him you liked his book, that'll cheer him up (short hair, big nose, fat face, squinty eyes, creased clothing, looks hopelessly out of place wherever he is). He's currently working on *The Pornographer Diaries*.

The Hitman Diaries
Danny King

This book's for my best mate Brian McCann. It's safe to say that Brian is without doubt the funniest man I know and the only person who cracks me up all the time (even when he's desperately trying to be serious). I've nicked so many lines and expressions from Brian and given them to my characters that really he should be given a co-author credit... but he's not. The only difference between my characters and Brian is that Brian actually means all the outrageous and unbelievably offensive things he says. So, here's to Brian McCann, the funniest and most ridiculous man I know. (Brian wanted me to put 'hardest' but everyone knows I could smash his face in if I wanted to, no problem.)

Library of Congress Catalog Card Number: 2002115465

A complete catalogue record for this book can be obtained from the British Library on request.

The right of Danny King to be identified as the author of this work has been asserted by him in accordance with the Copyright, Designs and Patents Act 1988

Copyright © Danny King 2003

First published in 2003 by Serpent's Tail, 4 Blackstock Mews, London N4 2BT

website: www.sepentstail.com

Printed by Mackays of Chatham plc

10 9 8 7 6 5 4 3 2

The Hitman Diaries

ACKNOWLEDGEMENTS

As ever I'd like to thank my Editor and the only Welshman I know, John Williams, for helping me shape my final draft with phrases like 'chapter six is a bit fucking boring, isn't it?'; to Pete Ayrton, Jenny, Ruth, Deirdre, old whatsisname, this week's publicist and everyone at Serpent's Tail for making all my non-sexual dreams come true; to the incredibly sexy nurse Jo Frost from St George's in Tooting for talking me through how to bump someone off with a jab (wow, she was great and I nearly asked her out, but then I sobered up and remembered the considerable age and beauty gap between us); to Andrew Emery and Nat Saunders for subbing my subbing and ding ding ding; to my new neighbour Clive Andrews for living close by so that now I have someone to go to the gym (chuckle chuckle) or the pub with; to the rest of the McCanns – Paul, Tom, Joe and Greg for being like the brothers I always wished I'd had; to my actual brothers Robin and Ralph… you guys; to Cliff Harrington, Simon Kempthorne & Nigel Gosden for being a couple of years older and telling me what aches and pains I can expect next (actually, Cliff's younger than me – much achier though); to David Crow for threatening to tell everyone I'm a bender if he didn't get a mention this time around (I'm not actually, but I believe he is); and finally to all the Wednesday night Borough football lads for giving me a stage on which I truly stink: Derby Matt, Tom, Wayne, Sam, Pete, Martin, little Ben (all alone in the big city), mental Daz, the two Macs – fat Muggle Paul and his younger-looking but surprisingly older brother Mark, the senior citizens Joe, Matt, Sean & Keith, to Barrie, suddenly married with a kid (how did that happen?) and everyone else whose face I couldn't put a name to while writing this, though a special mention should be reserved for Ollie Scull for using my towel to dry his ass and nuts with while I'm in the shower every week for a joke. Just gets funnier and funnier.

1. Sweet talking

You know, it's a lonely business being single.

Anyone that says otherwise is a liar. Old grey-haired tankard drinkers who block the bar and regale their fellow pullover-wearers with tales of youthful manly mischief and hell-raising are about the only ones who ever talk about bachelorhood with misty eyes. But then, that's just because that's what tankard drinkers do. In reality, most of them are secretly praying that they die before their old ladies so they won't be left alone to cook, clean and fend for themselves.

Of course, you do get young guys trying to tell you that women aren't worth the effort as well. 'You're better off without them,' I think is the popular expression, though again this is merely an angry self-rebuke for being made to beg, plead and grovel humiliatingly with a pair of high heels as it walked out the door in search of better sex.

See, men are meant to be with women just as women are meant to be with men. It's part of Mother Nature's grand plan. And it's fucking annoying when you're left out. If you allow yourself, you can become very bitter, and that doesn't do anyone any favours, least of all yourself. Girls can smell desperation, and it's not an attractive cologne. I've often found myself lying awake at night wondering if the girl of my dreams was out there somewhere waiting for me to find her. I've thought about her a lot. I'd wonder what she was doing at that moment; if she was lying in bed thinking about me, or if she was rowing with her husband, dreaming of the day when something better would come along. Sometimes I'd think of her making love, enjoying herself, abandoning all her inhibitions, becoming intoxicated with lust. Suddenly she's in the arms of her lover. She's making love to him while I'm here all alone, yet I'm the one that could really love her and she doesn't even realise it. Why doesn't she know? Why is she staying with that arsehole when I'm out here…?

…I have to stop myself there. It's hard not to get jealous and work myself up into a temper. Yes, I know, she might just be a figment of my imagination, but I still love her. I know it sounds silly, but I've lived my whole life with her a dozen times over. I've met her, wed her, settled down, had children, grown old and died with her all in the space of a sleepless night. It's a sad state of affairs to be in love with a phantom. You end up doing all manner of strange things to her in your mind in an effort to prove to her how much you love her. I've given mine leukaemia and brain tumours and all sorts before just so I could bowl her over by shaving my head as a mark of solidarity while she went through the chemotherapy. She loved me for that! And it's not just illnesses I've inflicted on her. I've taken her through wars and back to show her just how much she means to me. I've had her stabbed, shot, beaten up, crippled, horribly burnt and even gang-raped before now, all in the name of love. Anything, just so she had a rotten time of it and I could prove my worth to her by standing by her, taking care of her and avenging her. I remember the night I had both her legs off underneath a bus.

That was one of my favourite fantasies.

You know the funny thing though, despite all we've been through together, I've never actually known her face. She hasn't got one. Well no, that's not right. She's got one, I just haven't seen it yet. And until I do, my fantasies will always remain just that, fantasies. And that is where the desperation comes in, because you look for her everywhere. The checkout girl in the supermarket, the woman opposite you on the train, absolutely any girl who wanders within talking distance of you in the street. Everywhere.

I was staring across the table and looking for her in Janet when she took time out from shovelling food into her face to give me a grateful smile. Was Janet my leukaemia girl? I'd been a bit pissed off when she'd reached a fork across and tried some of my starter without asking so what chance did she have when the chemotherapy started?

'This was very nice of you to take me out,' she simpered.

'That's quite all right,' I replied.

'This is a rare treat for me,' she said, prompting me to run my eyes over her fourteen-stone bulk and wonder if she was referring to using cutlery.

'What's that?' I asked.

'Steak,' she told me. 'I normally don't touch anything like this. I usually try and stick to salads.'

'Of course,' I murmured, glancing down at the garnish and peas that had been pushed to the side of her plate.

To say Janet was unattractive would've been deeply uncharitable. She was a big girl for sure, but she had beauty too. Some people think that if a girl is fat, she is automatically ugly. I've never agreed with this. Janet had sparkling eyes, a spotless complexion and a childlike naivety and warmth that filled the room. I would've even gone so far as to say that if she ever shed about six stone she would've been a real babe – well, maybe that's pushing it a bit. Still my point is she was a nice woman. I just wasn't sure whether she was my cup of tea. But then, it'd been so long since I'd had any tea, I couldn't remember just how many lumps I had with it.

'That was absolutely lovely,' she said mopping up the last of the juice with a bread roll. 'Shall we have a look at the sweet trolley?'

I dropped my knife and fork on to my half-finished meal and said: 'Sure, let's take a look.' I motioned to call the waiter over when Janet stopped me.

'Erm, Ian,' she started sheepishly. 'Are you not going to eat the rest of yours then?'

I looked down at my food and then across at the desperation in those sparkling eyes and pushed across my plate. 'No, please, be my guest.'

'No point in wasting it,' she said, cheerfully tucking into my sirloin.

'Yes. No point in starving yourself,' I replied rolling my eyes. I suddenly saw it was going to take all of my guile keeping my dinner around Janet. Oh well, I supposed I didn't mind too much. I mean, you have to let the woman have her way in the evening, don't you, if you're to have yours later. Mind you, that was looking like less and less of a treat as the date progressed.

She finished the last of my steak juice with my bread roll then gave me a smile and a nod to tell me it was time to get the sweet trolley motoring over here. The waiter wheeled it to our table and Janet quickly went into a 'supermodel in chocolate crisis' routine again. 'Oooh, I feel like being absolutely wicked tonight. Oh no I can't, it's too much, but it looks so scrummy. Do you think I should? Ian, please don't tell anyone will you?'

About tonight? You must be fucking kidding! I thought to myself.

'Go on then, I'll have a small slice of gateau with… is that vanilla ice cream? A tiny scoop full of that. Well, maybe just a bit more, it looks so small once you get it on the plate doesn't it?'

When the waiter finally got round to me I just asked for coffee.

'Are you not having any?' Janet asked me all sorrowfully.

'No, go on, you can have my pudding as well if you want, I just haven't really got a sweet tooth that's all,' I told her.

'Haven't got a sweet tooth? What about all the Mars bars? You like them.'

I'd slipped up. I'd gotten to know Janet through buying Mars bars and forgotten to keep up the pretence. That was thoughtless, where was my head? See, Janet worked in a newsagent's a couple of miles from where I lived, and I'd gone in there one day a couple of months back and she'd really taken my eye. She'd seemed friendly and pretty, a little bit lonely perhaps like myself, though, in my memory, definitely thinner (my own romantic subconscious at work there no doubt). Anyway, I'd caught her eye that first meeting and she gave me a nice smile and I'd ended up thinking about her all day. With that one pleasant handing back of the change she'd endeared herself to me so much that I had wanted to know more about her. So, I'd started popping in every now and then to pick up a Mars bar or a paper or a trigonometry set or something, anything just to get her to hand me back my change, give me a little smile and leave me feeling good for the rest of the day. I'd gone in there so often we'd gotten to know each other by name and even exchanged a few words and a little polite laughter over our transactions. It was hardly the romance of the decade, but it was nice, comforting and warming. And then last week, I'd finally got round to asking her out. I'd followed her home to find out where she'd lived then 'bumped into her' on the bus the next day. We'd had a cosy little chat, I'd helped her with her bags and she'd agreed to come out for dinner and a drink.

And you know what, now that she was here in all her glory, I don't know why I'd bothered. Sometimes, when you get what you want, it's never the same as sitting at home wanting it, is it?

'Sweet tooth? Me? Oh yes, I like Mars bars and Kitkats and that. What I mean is, I'm just not a big fan of pudding. I don't really like it. A little too rich for me.' I could see the confusion in her face as she tried to work out what the words 'I don't like pudding' meant before she laughed it off and changed the subject.

'So Ian, what is it you do for a living?'

'I work with computers,' I told her.

'Ohhh,' she cooed. 'That sounds very exciting!' which it clearly didn't. 'What do you do with them?'

'I build websites,' I replied.

'Ohhh,' was all the interest she could manage that time. We sat for a moment or two while I waited to see if there was a follow-up question. There wasn't. After another moment or two's silence she just went: 'Ohhh,' again.

'So how long have you worked in the newsagent's for?' I decided to ask.

'Since I was a little girl. Fifteen. I got a part-time job in there after school and when I left the year after that Mr Wilson took me on full time.'

'Do you like it?'

'Oh yes, it's the best job in the world. I mean, it's every girl's dream to work in a sweet shop, isn't it?' she boasted.

'Is it?' I exclaimed wondering why I'd never heard that before. 'I thought all girls wanted to be actresses or supermodels or something!'

Janet looked a little hurt by this.

'No they don't,' she muttered into her cake. 'It's to work in a sweet shop. That's what they really want to do if they're honest.'

I could see that. Kate Moss, who got paid millions of pounds every year and flown around the world to have her arse kissed by the swanky jet set, was really secretly dreaming of being in a position to pocket a few Bounty bars when the security camera was having its tape changed.

Janet stared at her pudding, sliced off the littlest corner of ice cream and lifted it to her mouth like it weighed ten tons.

I'd hurt her feelings.

I hadn't meant to do that and I suddenly felt rotten. Why shouldn't it be every girl's dream to work in a sweet shop? If Janet wanted to cling on to this nonsense then why shouldn't she? What business of mine was it to shoot down her fantasy? I mean, we all did it to a lesser or greater extent, didn't we? I knew I did. In a world where glamour and beauty are taking over as the number one quality, everyone needs a little reassurance. Let's face it, at a time when even soap stars – traditionally the ugliest bastards on the box – are good-looking enough to model clothes and release records, what chance have the rest of us got? So, how do you salvage a little self-worth? Well, you end up telling yourself that Brad Pitt or George Clooney or the like might be every woman's fantasy, but how good are they at... then you name something fairly hum-drum that you're quite good at (e.g. driving a coach, playing the fruit machines, prescribing glasses, etc.) to make yourself feel better about not being Brad Pitt or George Clooney.

That's all Janet was doing, propping up her own self-worth by telling herself that she was the envy of other women. Nice of me to knock her down. I quickly tried to make amends.

'How many of those supermodels could do the hours you work and still stay lovely and bubbly as you, hey? Tell me that,' I said as she gathered a few gateau crumbs up on her spoon. This astonishingly empty compliment about staying cheerful in a dismal, dead-end job seemed to do the trick because Janet quickly perked up in agreement and made a few choice remarks about how Jordan wouldn't even know how to sort out the papers in the morning and suchlike.

We spent the next few minutes talking about the merits and drawbacks of having supermodels working in the retail industry before she revealed her real cross.

'And just look at them, they're like sticks aren't they? What fella would want a woman like that? It's not sexy. No, you want something to get hold of, don't you? A proper woman, who's all lovely and snuggly in bed.'

I didn't want to shatter her illusions twice in such quick succession so I played along and made a few positive noises, though I fell short of expressing my undying love for all things ample.

'And what about you then Janet, what sort of man do you go for?' I asked.

'Ohhh, ohhh,' she started up, making me think she was about to order more cake. 'I'd love to be ravished by a hunky, sweaty backwoodsman,' she said and giggled. This was a little insensitive on her part considering I clearly wasn't the sweaty backwoodsman type, made all the worse when you considered I'd gone out of my way to express an appreciation for bloaters.

'Or Pierce Brosnan. He has got it all hasn't he? Tall, dark, handsome... dangerous. The sort of man that makes women weak at the knees.' Oh yeah, very fucking fair. You have James Bond or

Nanook of the North while we get Fatty Arbuckle's greedy sister! I was half-tempted to make some comment to Janet about how the last thing she needed was weak knees, but decided to let it slide. It did wind me up though. I don't know why it should. I'd finally come to the conclusion that she wasn't my long lost love and so therefore didn't particularly want her fancying me, but it was just a question of manners. I was taking her out, paying for the meal and being nice to her, she could've at least made the pretence of finding me manly and attractive. I shouldn't let trivial little things like this get to me but I've had it all my life. 'Don't worry about it, it's only Bridges, he don't matter.' Cunts.

She was still drooling over sixpacks and hairy chests while I brooded over my own shortcomings when the waiter came over to clear the plates.

'Ohhh, you know, before you take mine away, maybe I'll just have another little slice of gateau,' she said picking up her cutlery again.

'Oh, help yourself, after all it's only me paying for it,' I jeered and immediately felt like the biggest bastard in the world. I dropped my face into my hands and apologised a couple of dozen times before I dared look up.

Why was it that when she said something that hurt my feelings she didn't feel like this?

Don't think about it, don't think about it, it'll only wind you up again, I told myself. Clear your head, no one matters but you.

'I'm so sorry,' I said again. 'Please go on, have whatever you like.'

And you know what, to my absolute astonishment she did as well.

There's just no putting some people off their grub is there?

2. A few more fish in the sea

There are two halves to any evening and the evening of my date with Janet was no different. We'd just finished our meal, or should I say, she'd just finished our meal, and we were leaving the restaurant. Janet dropped a few hints about going for a dance somewhere but I'd already made up my mind that I didn't want to see her again so I pretended to miss them all. We left the restaurant and walked across the car park to where I had parked and Janet asked straight out if I wanted to go back to her place then. 'It's all right, I live alone. I have done since mum was taken.'

The way our date had gone, and in the light I now saw Janet, I really didn't feel myself attracted to her in the slightest.

'Okay!' I said.

I'd asked her out in the first place because I thought she might've possessed hidden beauty and a good heart, but now I no longer cared. A quick shag was about all she was worth, if for no other reason than just to clear my head. Well, I'm only human, I need sex just as much as the next man. Much as I didn't fancy her any more, a quick roll around with her in bed would tame my libido for a fortnight or so and let me think about one or two other things for a change.

I ran a careful eye over Janet's arse and made a quick recalculation. Seeing that milky white backside first thing in the morning, I reasoned, might even fill me with enough self-loathing to put me off sex for a month. Which, when you're not getting it regularly, is a good thing.

I was just about to open the passenger door for Janet when I heard, behind me, the sound of an angry man's voice. It was being directed at me.

'Yes you, you fucking snotty-nosed little cunt!'

I turned around and caught sight of this enormous gorilla and his white trash wife storming across the car park in our direction.

'Are you talking to me?' I asked and he slammed me up against the side of my car.

'Yes I'm talking to you, you big-nosed cunt. Who the fuck d'you think you are, looking at me like that?'

'What?' I asked in confusion. 'What do you mean? Who are you?' He pressed his arm across my throat and leaned in so that his face was only a few inches from mine.

'Don't give me that! I'm the poor cunt you've been screwing all night.'

'Screwing?' I said, not taking his meaning.

'You've been staring over at me, giving me and my girlfriend the fucking evil all fucking evening, haven't you, you fucking little... fucker!' He was clearly upset about something.

'Sorry?' I asked again not knowing what he was talking about.

'It's too late for that,' he said taking me to be apologising, which annoyed me.

'He's not sorry at all Frank,' shouted his wife at the pair of us. 'Him or his fat wife, they've both been staring at us all dinner-time.'

'She's not my wife,' I said and thought about adding: 'And she's not fat either' but then I figured that would've just embarrassed us all.

'Leave us alone,' Janet finally piped up to my defence. 'Go away or I'll get the police.'

'I've never seen you before in my life,' I told Frank. 'Let alone been staring at you.'

'You fucking liar! All fucking dinner-time you were looking at me.'

'I don't know who you are,' I said to him. 'This is the first time I've ever seen you.'

'Did you hear that Mand'?' he said bringing his missus back

into proceedings. 'The fucking brass front.'

'He's a cunt!' she ventured.

'Get off me!' I said trying to pull his hands away.

'Don't fucking start with me,' he said pushing me harder into the car. A bit rich that!

'Fucking hit him,' Mand' urged and he did, right in the ribs, before slamming me up against the car again.

'Not staring now then, are you?' he said then clouted me round the head with his free hand, sending me to the ground. I landed painfully but wasn't given a chance to dwell on it because Frank started laying into me with the boots. Somewhere off behind his size elevens I could hear Janet crying and Mand' orgasming as car park justice was dished out. I sensed Frank wasn't finished with me by a long shot and I was trying to make the best of defending myself when something just snapped inside me and instinct took over.

I can't even clearly remember doing it but before I knew it I had my Glock out of its holster and pointed at Frank's throat. The move, compared with his clumsy assault, was so quick he didn't even see the weapon until it fired, ripping through his voice box and opening up his arteries.

Suddenly I was up and aiming the gun at Mand's face. She had no chance of screaming, or no realisation as to what was taking place. All she knew was one second she was going out with a tough nut, the next minute the lights were out. I'd taken her out so cleanly that there was no sense risking a second head shot, even if my Glock was silenced. Frank, on the other hand, was still hanging on to this life with annoying determination so it was he that I awarded possession of the contents of the third chamber.

I swung round once more and immediately found my final target. I was just about to pull the trigger when I suddenly remembered she was my date.

'I'm sorry,' I told Janet, the gun a bare three inches from her forehead. 'I'm a hitman.'

'I won't tell anyone,' she blubbed and covered her mouth with her little chubby hands.

'I know,' I said, 'I know you won't,' then blew her brains out. People always say they won't tell anyone when there's a gun at their head but they always do. I lowered the automatic and took a moment out to let what I had just done sink in.

Then I panicked.

I was standing a few yards away from a busy restaurant with three dead bodies at my feet and the murder weapon in my hand. Not only that, earlier on in the evening I'd been seen dining with one of the victims.

Whoever the lawyer was that was going to get me off this little lot was certainly going to earn his legal aid.

I quickly ran over the plus points in my head: it was dark; we were standing at the back of the car park… I had a hatchback.

No matter how bleak things might look at first glance, you've always got a chance. Never throw in the towel. The game's not up till the fat lady sings – sorry Janet, no offence – so I quickly got to work. I dragged the three bodies further into the shadows and between parked cars, unlocked the back door of my car and reloaded my Glock with a full clip – just in case.

Let me tell you about my car. In my line of work a hatchback is a lot more practical than a Ferrari. I could probably afford a Ferrari if I wanted one, but then how many bodies are you going to get in that? Always be prepared, that's my motto, and five doors and a lot of space sometimes proves to be the most useful weapon in a man's armoury. Don't get me wrong, this sort of thing didn't normally happen to me when I went out on a date. But then, by that same token, I'd be lying if I said it had never happened to me before.

I folded down the back seat, but left the parcel shelf in place to provide a little cover, then I loaded in Mand' first. Mand' was the lightest and fitted in nice and snug against the rear passenger door. I was about to reach for Frank when I heard voices. I looked around and saw a good dozen people of differing ages and levels of ugliness exiting the restaurant and walking towards the car park. Munsters family outing no doubt.

I had to keep my head, there were way too many of them to try and take down so I had to play it calm. Funnily enough, I did have a machinegun concealed in the car, but this was getting silly enough as it was. I'd need a skip to take that lot away. I stood up in clear sight, took my bucket and scraper and casually wandered around to my front windscreen and began giving it a wash. The Munsters divided themselves up into three cars and slowly drove off, still chattering about the food, the service, the bill and all those other little things people who've just left a restaurant talk about. No one afforded me anything more than a glance and for the time being, the danger had passed. But my car was surrounded on all sides by other vehicles and it wouldn't be long before one of these diners would be out.

I manhandled Frank in next, pushing him in against his girlfriend and tucked his feet in behind him, before addressing the problem of Janet. Only now did I realise just how big she was. Frank had been heavy, but he'd been all muscle and sinew, easy to get hold of and lift. With Janet, everything was soft and loose, I couldn't seem to get a firm grip on any part of her except her wrists and ankles. I also saw the error of putting Mand' in the car first, as loading an awkward, heavy weight was hard enough but trying to load it into an already full area just amplified the problems. I should've saved the lightest for last, but I wasn't going to start unpacking now.

I managed to swing her legs up and in, then get her under the arms and lift so that she was up in the car, then I pushed her back with all of my might until finally she'd cleared the back door. I closed it down then looked at my clothes and saw that the three of them had leaked all over me. The sticky scarlet didn't show up too badly on my black jacket and trousers, but my white shirt was a mess. I quickly stripped out of it and chucked it in the back with the bodies. There was actually more room in there than I had at first thought, it was merely cramped at the back where Janet lay.

One or two more things needed doing before I was off. I tore up a couple of black bin-liners I had in the car with me and covered Janet, Mand' and Frank. Then I grabbed the two-litre bottle of mineral water from the glove box and did what I could to wash away the worst of the blood from where it had pooled on the tarmac. It wasn't very effective, all it really did was dilute it down a bit, but that would have to do as I could hardly knock on the kitchen window and ask for a bucket of soapy water. ('You don't happen to have a stiff broom I could borrow as well have you?' 'What's it for?' 'Er…' BANG! BANG! BANG! followed by a machinegun noise which I don't know how to spell.)

I pulled out of the car park nice and carefully and headed for Kent. Why Kent? Well, moored up on the Thames Estuary, in a little out-of-the-way harbour, I had a launch. Nothing flash, nothing fancy, just a bashed-up old boat with a little cabin and a bit of storage space I used from time to time. It was parked among a dozen or so pleasure boats, nice and anonymous, though mine wasn't for pleasure, mine was a working vessel – as Mand', Frank and Janet would soon find out.

Some killers like to bury their victims, plant them like little acorns up in Epping Forest, but from my experience there are certain drawbacks that go with that method. Firstly, you really have to scout your burial site first. Britain is a pretty small country and very little of it is untouched by ramblers or dog walkers or game keepers, farmers and so on. If you're getting rid of somebody, presumably you don't want that person popping back up again to land you in the dock, so your choice of location is really important. Secondly, you have to dig the fucker, and that's hard work! It's also noisy, if there's anyone around while you're doing it, you'll attract their attention and if you've got a dead body lying next to you and they see it, soon you find yourself having to dig two holes. If your heart's set on burying your body then it's always best to dig the hole the day before and cover it over with bracken. And finally, there's the problem of access. Ideally you'd like to stick your man miles out in the middle of nowhere, but the problem with that is that you have to be able to reach your hole. That means using a car most of the way then a very short walk through bushes and scrub to your grave. It has to be a short walk because remember, you'll be carrying a dead weight of possibly ten, eleven, twelve or thirteen stones with you, and if you're going to get into the killing business, it's really something you have to do alone. Of course the ideal solution to the problem is to get your victims to walk to the holes themselves then kill them out there, but then this presents its own set of problems.

We'll be looking at these in a later chapter.

For my money, I'm a 'drop them in the drink' sort of guy. It's easier, there's a lot more places to leave them (two thirds of the planet is your oyster) and there's less chance of Barratt Homes digging them up whilst turning Watership Down into a few hundred semi's.

I was taking it nice and easy on the way down to my boat, keeping just above the speed limit, mirror, signal, manoeuvre, all nice and safe and sticking, where I could, to B-roads and country lanes. I was pondering to myself on the way down whether or not I'd have to get rid of the car now or whether it was possible to salvage it after having so much forensic splashed around it. Ditch it, definitely. No point in taking any chances. I'd find a nice quiet spot and burn it out, it was the professional thing to do. Besides, I really didn't want to have to get in on my hands and knees and scrub up all that horrible goo. That was one horrible, nasty job, and it never did the trick anyway. Cleaning a blood-splattered car up so that it would pass a forensic test is almost impossible. No, only fire cleanses it thoroughly.

It seemed a shame though, I hadn't had the car that long and it was nice and comfortable. I had a lot of cars, or at least, the use of a lot of cars, depending on what job I was called upon to do. Fast cars for quick getaways, vans to dress up as commercial vehicles, motorbikes for city centre work (which were my own personal favourite), we even had a couple of black cabs somewhere, which I never got to use, all with false plates, phoney log books and erased serial numbers. In fact, even the car we were driving in on the way down to Kent was registered to some long dead cot death case, with driver's licence and papers in the side door compartment to match. You know, it's odd, but I don't think I've been inside anything that could actually be traced back to me since my mum wrote 'IAN BRIDGES, AGED 13' inside my school blazer – two weeks before my fourteenth birthday.

But this wasn't a jobbing car, it was my everyday runaround, the car I drove to the shops, to the park. This was typical, just when I'd found a car I liked, I had to go and burn it. I'd see Logan in the morning and ask him to get me a new one but I knew he'd make a big deal of it and be unable to get me the same model. I'd have to take what I was given.

I was brooding on this point as I waited by traffic lights on a little country crossroads just outside of Gravesend when a Range Rover pulled up behind me. I twisted the mirror so that I could keep an eye on the driver while we waited for the green.

He was looking around, into the moonlit field on our left, down at his radio, a quick glance at the lights, over to the trees on our right, then into my car and at the twisted blood-covered arm that stuck up from beneath the black bin-liners... then very, very, very quickly away again.

The bastard must've come loose after I went over a bump or something!

I jumped from the car and in the blink of an eye had my gun pointed straight at his head.

'British secret service,' I said. 'Get out of the car now please sir!' The guy looked shocked and confused, which was the idea, giving me a chance to yank open his door and pull him out. I often use this ploy in situations like these. It stops a person from reacting instinctively and gives you a second over them to get close enough to take them out. Let me explain. Supposing this was you and you'd just seen a dead body in the back of a car. The driver jumps out and suddenly you see a gun. What are you going to do? You're going to step on the fucking accelerator probably, aren't you? But, if he says British secret service or CID or police or doctor on call or something, then you might hesitate. After all, the British secret service might have a good reason for having dead bodies in the back of their hatchback and you don't want to go and blow James Bond's cover by shouting murder when there's national security at stake like some typical bungling civilian. They are on our side, remember.

Wrong. In the second or so that it's taken you to mull this over in your head, I'm in control of the situation now and you're dead.

'Charles Parnell,' he said introducing himself as I made some pretence at patting him down. 'I'm an accountant.'

'This way please Mr Parnell,' I told him, keeping the gun in his back. 'My guv'nor wants to have a word with you. Through here, this way.'

I quick-marched him through a gap in the hedge and whacked him over the head. Parnell went down cold and it took just another second for me to open his throat up with my knife. I ran back to his Range Rover and pulled it up on to the kerb, as if it had been parked, locked it up and chucked the keys into the field where Parnell lay.

In the time it took to kill a man and park up his car, the traffic lights had changed back to red but there were no other cars about so I sped on through them. Parking the Range Rover would buy me a few hours. Anyone who passed by it would probably think it had broken down or not give it any thought at all. Parnell himself might not be found until someone realised he was missing and by that time, hopefully I'd have got rid of my current crop of casualties.

I was pushing the pedal a little harder now, trying to put as much distance between the crossroads and myself before the next car came along. Happily the lane was black as I sped towards Chatham. I checked my rear view mirror, but where I had positioned it to keep an eye on Mr Parnell, I could no longer see the whole of the road behind me.

I was just repositioning the mirror when there was a whack on my left side and a flash of luminous yellow in my headlights.

I slammed on the brakes and came to a rapid halt.

'What the fuck…' I muttered to myself and quickly switched the car into reverse. I backed it up about forty yards when my reverse lights lit upon a tangled figure in the middle of the road. I grabbed the wheel brace from underneath my seat and jumped out for a quick look.

It was a jogger. He was lying on the tarmac moaning to himself and generally having a hard time of it. I knelt down beside him and saw that he was bad, though unfortunately for me, not bad enough. I couldn't risk a description of the car getting out before dawn and lying in the middle of the road, this one would be found a lot quicker than Mr Parnell. I lifted the wheel brace and gave him a quick whack on the top of the head to finish him off. A sickening crack told me I'd fractured his skull and all at once the jogger went limp.

I was just rolling him into a ditch at the side of the road when I heard an old lady's voice behind me asking if everything was all right. I looked up to the heavens, shaking my head and wondered how many more I was going to have to get through tonight before I was all finished.

'I say, is he all right? He took an awful knock. Does he need an ambulance? I've got a phone in the house.'

I turned around to see this white-haired old busybody stepping out of her secluded little cottage and scurrying across the road towards me.

'It's okay, I'm a doctor, I just need you to give me a hand with something. Is there anyone else in the house?'

'No, not since my George passed I'm afraid. Is he okay?'

'Yeah, fine, this way please, come on,' I said steering her to my back passenger door and bundling her in over a pile of bodies.

'Wait. What? Wait. What is this?' she started yakking before I gave her neck a good twist until I heard it snap.

'Christ almighty. Is there anyone else?' I said addressing the sky and shaking my head. I ran back to the old lady's house and pulled the door to, then jumped back in the car and was away. I covered Miss Marple up as best as I could with my free hand while driving along the long dark lane and almost ploughed head first into an oncoming BMW.

Both me and the BMW skidded sideways and screeched to a halt. The driver leaned out of the window and called me every name in the highway code book before revving his accelerator and speeding off.

Had he seen anything?

I doubted it. I couldn't make out his face in the dark so it was highly unlikely he could make out mine. All he'd seen was the car but by the way he was driving he'd be screaming at a lot of drivers before the night was out. Besides, he had a BMW and I had a hatchback full of dead bodies, I was in no position to chase after him even if I did have a machinegun close to hand and an eye witness running for the cops. I had no choice but to let him live to terrorise the roads another day.

I suddenly wished I'd left the jogger in the middle of the road around the bend for Mr BMW to plough through, thus wiping one off my slate, but you always think of these things after the event, don't you?

Once I'd put a couple of miles between myself and the old lady's cottage I found a quiet place to pull over and pack my passengers down properly so there would be no repeat of the unpleasantness with the late Mr Parnell. For a moment or two I pondered the notion of having Miss Marple up front in the seat next to me as she wasn't that blood-splattered and, with the seatbelt properly adjusted, she could look like she was just having a nap. I decided against it in the end as it all seemed a bit too creepy, even for me, and besides I didn't really like old ladies.

Once they were all patted down and completely covered, I journeyed on and finally reached the harbour at a little after 1 a.m. I gave the place a thorough going over for night fishermen and other such insomniacs before transferring the bodies from car to boat. It was hard work and it took me the best part of ten minutes to complete the task, which is a dangerous amount of exposure time, but miracle upon miracle, no one happened along and I cast off into the blackness.

As the boat chugged along on its own steam, I prepared the bodies for disposal. See, unfortunately, it's not just a case of going a few miles out and chucking them over the side, if that it was. No, you have to take several steps first to make sure they aren't found, and if they are found that they can't be identified – and this is where it all starts to get a bit unpleasant… well, a bit unpleasanter, if there is such a word.

There are two ways of identifying a body after death (three if you count DNA but we're still a few years away from a comprehensive database of the population just yet): fingerprints and dental records. The salt water, the fish and the crabs take care of the fingerprints, but the teeth were all mine.

I reached for my crowbar and went to work.

I didn't like doing this. I've gotten used to it over the last few years but it was still not one of my favourite chores, particularly when it comes to the ones at the back (what are they called? molars), they really have to be dug out and it's a grisly and smelly task. I had an idea for a little bomb to do the job for me. All it would need is a little bit of plastique, a battery and a timer. Stick it under the tongue, roll them in the drink and ten seconds later, there's a little pop and hey presto, no teeth, jaw or head left for anyone to ID. Quick and clean, no fuss, no mess. Even chuckled over the idea of patenting it. I could call it Bridges' Mouth Bomb or something. It was just a thought anyway.

Miss Marple endeared herself to me no end by having a full set of false choppers which I slid out and tossed over the side.

Once I'd taken care of the other three I had a quick look through their pockets and removed all of their belongings. After all, no point eradicating their dental history if you're going to leave their wallets in their pockets. When I looked through Janet's purse I saw that she had come out without a single penny on her which, in this day and age, is a bit presumptuous. Frank on the other hand had about £50 in cash so he ended up treating me and Janet to dinner, which I don't think Frank would've liked.

I got about a mile and a half out to sea and killed the engine. It doesn't do to go any further otherwise the Coast Guard looks at you on the radar and starts to wonder what you're up to. Frank was the first to taste the waters. I tied my weights around him with a good length of rope (I prefer plastic gym weights to the tradition- al breeze block as they're less likely to break if they hit something hard on the bottom and won't rot in the salt water), then I punctured his lungs and stomach to release any trapped air and heaved him over the side. Normally, if I've got more than one body to dispose of, I'll start the boat and drop the next one a little way off, but as I was a bit of a sentimentalist, I dropped Mand' in next to Frank, before moving on and chucking Miss Marple over another half a mile out.

The last into the water was Janet. As I plunged the sharpened screwdriver deep down into each of her lungs and belly I couldn't help feeling that our date hadn't been much of a success. This was typical of my luck with women. It was almost as if there was someone up there who didn't want me to meet a nice girl. Why me? Why couldn't things just work out for me once? Surely this wasn't a lot to ask for, was it? Other people met girls and settled down, in fact the majority of people did, so why was it so fucking impossible for me to do the same? I wasn't such a bad bloke, was I? A girl could do a lot worse than to want to be with me. A little company, that's all I wanted. I didn't want no pop star or supermodel or anything, just a nice ordinary girl to come home to at the end of the day. A girl to make me laugh and make me cry. I'd treat them like a fucking princess I would, I'd never lay a glove on them like some men do. Just a chance, just one chance, and I'd show them that I could be the most loyal and loving husband a girl would ever want.

I couldn't help but feel very depressed as I lifted Janet up on to the side and pushed her overboard.

'Oh well,' I muttered in an effort to cheer myself up. 'Plenty more fish in the sea.'

3. Mummy's little soldier

I finally got home about four in the morning, exhausted and downbeat, with the smell of blood and shit and death still fresh in my nose. I'd be stuck with it for days, it's always the same when you handle the dead, they stink so bad that they etch themselves into your sinuses so that you smell them on yourself long after you've scrubbed every inch of your body clean with a nail brush. It's probably just psychological, a memory of a smell rather than an actual smell. Either way, it's enough to put you off sausages for a while. The only other thing I could smell on myself was petrol from where I'd burned out the car and this smelled like eau de cologne compared to the other stuff. What my body cried out for was a long hot soak, a nice clean bed and a couple of sleeping pills to shut down my brain.

What it got was my fucking mum.

'Only me!' she called out letting herself in. It had begun. By 'only me', what she meant was: 'It's only me, no one important, I'm sorry if I'm a burden to you, just let me die where I fall, don't look at me while I cry.' She was a grandmaster at psychological warfare. Unbelievable, two words and she'd already gotten under my skin.

'Jesus, please. I'm tired, I'm achy, it's the middle of the night, I don't need this right now,' I snapped.

'Oh, I'll just go then shall I?' she whimpered pathetically. 'You don't want to see me then?'

'No, I don't. Not now, not ever!'

'Oh? If that's the way you feel about me. I'll just... I just wanted to see how you were, is that such a bad thing for a mother to want to do?'

'Yes, I don't need you in my head right now.'

'Ohh Ian,' she spluttered, her arms hanging limply by her side, her face the picture of human misery. She stood her ground and wobbled her lip for a bit, buying her assault a few more precious seconds before my defences collapsed. I hung my head, rubbed my eyes and let out a long strangled grunt of frustration.

'I can't handle you at the moment. I need some time for myself.'

'Well, look, I'm your mother, if there's anything I can help you with that's what I'm here for,' she said taking a giant step forward into my face.

'No. It's nothing,' I told her, but I knew that wouldn't be the end of it by a long way. If she had to tie me down and burn my nipples with hot pokers she would until I'd told her everything. Everything that had nothing to do with her in the first place. Everything that I wanted to keep to myself. Everything. Full stop.

'Please Ian, what's wrong love?'

'Nothing,' I repeated, trying to believe it. Trying to shut it down, but it was too late. She had her teeth in me and there was no shaking her off.

'You know, whenever I have a problem, I always find it's a great comfort offloading it on to someone else,' she said.

'I know, it was always fucking me,' I shouted at her. 'I never wanted your problems any more than you did but that never stopped you filling my head with it for hours.'

'Is it money?' she said taking the first of her guesses.

'No, I'm fine for money. I've got more money than I know what to do with. I don't need any money.'

'Because if it is, I'd like to help. I've got a little bit put aside for the odd luxury, but I don't mind going without. It's not much, but it's all I can afford. I'm not a rich woman, I'm sorry.'

'It's not money!' I repeated. She always used this one. She'd lie awake at night praying to Jesus and every angel in heaven that the day would come when I'd find myself on stony ground and have to go begging, cap in hand, to her. Oh yes, she'd love that; get her meat hooks into me good and proper so that I could've never gotten away. And it wouldn't've mattered if I'd got the necessary together to pay her back fifty times over because she would've never accepted it, a pound of my flesh was worth more than first prize on the Premium Bonds.

'Of course, I had to cash in my pension to give it to Ian,' she would've told people. 'Even though times were very hard. But, I try and make ends meet and don't let Ian know just how little I'm left with because that's just the sacrifice you have to make when you're a mother. Never mind, as long as he's happy, that's the main thing… Oh I'm sorry, please excuse my stomach grumbling, I had to send Ian over my dinner too because he likes to have two dinners sometimes, his and mine… Yes, I am hungry and a little weak but it's not important, the main thing is that he's my son and he has to have everything he wants. I can survive, I've done it before for him and no doubt I'll have to do it again. I don't mind, I really don't… What? What's that? No, I haven't heard from him in months, he doesn't come and visit me very much. I guess he's got more important things to do.

'I gave him life you know.'

Aaaaaaaaaaaarrrrrrrrrrrrrrggggggggggggggggghhhhhhhh-hhhhhhhh!!!!!!!!!!!!!!!

'IT'S NOT FUCKING MONEY!' I shouted at her as she started going through her purse.

'I only want to help,' she said holding out a crumpled fiver.

'You're not helping. You're driving me fucking bananas! Just leave it.'

'Is it work?' she said taking her second guess of the night (early hours of the morning).

'No. It's not work. It's nothing to do with work.'

'How are you getting on there? Is everything okay?'

'Yes mum, everything's just fucking peachy,' I told her.

'Is it your boss?' she probed.

'It's nothing to do with work. Why do I have to answer the

same question eight different fucking ways?'

'Well, what is it then? Is it a girl?' she asked, stumbling across my Achilles heel.

'No,' I said a bit too quick.

'Is it? Is it a girl? Who is she?' she said, rubbing her hands together and revelling in my embarrassment.

'Why don't you bring her home for tea?'

I realised there was no escape, she had me. My only chance was to talk the whole thing down and shake her off the scent... the smell... the death.

'Look, it's nothing okay. I had a date tonight, that's all.'

'With a girl?' she said all excitedly.

'No, with a fucking silverback gorilla! What do you think?'

'Who is she? When do I get to meet her?'

'She's no one,' I countered.

'Oh, no one. My son is courting no one is he?' she said playing to the galleries.

'She's not no one, she's just no one you know.'

'Oh and you know that do you? You know everyone I know?'

'She doesn't live anywhere near you, you don't know her.'

'Well, what's her name? I might do.'

'You don't.'

'I might. I know a lot more people than you think.'

'You fucking don't.'

'Who is it?'

'No one.'

'It's not Susan Potter is it?'

'You don't know her.'

'Oh, he's all shy about his new girlfriend he is! Ha ha ha.'

'She's not my girlfriend!'

'What, you're going out with someone but she's not your girlfriend?'

'I'm not going out with her.'

'You just said you were.'

'No, I just said I had, I didn't say I was.'

'What's the matter, did you split up? Is that why you're sad?'

'No, I'm sad because you're here and you won't fuck off. Why won't you fuck off?'

'Would you like me to talk to her?'

'I don't want you talking to her or *me*. I want you to die and have the decency to cease to exist.'

'It might help coming from me, you know, woman to woman. I could talk her round. Get her to take you back.'

'Take me back? Why do you automatically assume it was her that got rid of me?'

'Oh love, I didn't mean it like that, I just meant that if you want me to talk to her, I could maybe get her back for you.'

'That's exactly the same thing.'

'Who is she Ian? What's her name?'

'I don't know. I'm not telling you.'

'Oh Ian, why not? Please let me help.'

'Drop it! Drop it! Drop it!' I shouted smashing my fist repeatedly against the walls.

'Just tell me who she is. Please Ian, I need to know.'

'Christ, for the love of God, why must I have to tell you everything? She's got nothing to do with you. Why can't I be spared this just once? I'm tired, I want to sleep. I want to forget.'

'Look, it's important all right. I mean, I don't want my son going out with just any old girl, do I?' she said following me from room to room. 'I want to know what she's like. I want to know if she's suitable for you. I mean, what sort of a mother would I be if I just handed you over to anyone?'

Hand me over?

All I could hear was the shrill shriek of static and my hackles rising in unison. Every single hair, fibre and molecule in my body screamed at me to obliterate her but I couldn't. Events were too far beyond that now. This was now just a question of hanging on and trying to stay relatively sane. I had to try and collect my wits but my instinct wouldn't let me. Counter. Don't let her get away with that one!

'HAND ME OVER? You don't hand over. I'm a man you bastard, not a little boy. I can see who I want, date who I want, marry who I want and kill who I want. I don't need your permission or approval in any part of my life. Hand me over?' I laughed shaking my head.

'Oh, I see. It's like that is it? So what you're telling me is that I, your mother, have absolutely no say over my boy, that's what you're saying isn't it? That's what you mean.'

'YES!' I shouted. My God, she'd got it. Finally. 'You have no say whatsoever in anything I do – ever. My life is nothing to do with you any more. I want nothing to do with you any more. You're a leech that I can't pull off. Your body's gone but your head's still there, sucking away. No, you're worse than a leech. At least a leech is only after your blood, you want the whole fucking lot, soul and all.'

'Well, if that's how you feel, I will have to have serious thoughts about whether or not I let you marry this girl.'

There was silence for a very long moment while I stared around the room in breath-taking bewilderment. Was that too much? Would she really have said that? But she did, didn't she? I'd remembered it right, hadn't I?

Well, whatever. Even if she hadn't said it, it sounded like the sort of thing she definitely would've said.

I started screaming.

'Stop it! Stop it! Stop it!' I yelled, punching a big hole in the kitchen door and bloodying my hand.

'You're still my child, and you always will be and children have to obey their mothers. When you bring home a girl who I think is right for you, that's when I'll let you go and not before.'

'You don't have me. How can you let me go when you don't have me?' I wailed, trying to drill this into her but mum carried on having her own conversation regardless of whatever I said or thought.

'I'm sorry if you don't think it's very fair but I know best for you. I'm not going to apologise for being a bit protective of my little boy.'

'I'm not a little boy,' I yelled over and over again, smacking my hand against the floor, hurting it ever more.

The thing here was that I can't ever remember mum being protective of me when I actually was a little boy. I remember sitting on the steps outside pubs all night in the dark while she sat inside with my latest 'Uncle' and enjoyed herself. Most of the time I wasn't even noticed. I just followed her around and watched a succession of blokes quietly raid my piggy bank on the way out in the morning before mum had a chance to wake. Yeah, my piggy bank. That poor little fucker had more knives in its back than Julius Caesar.

Now, I don't mention this to try and milk a bit of sympathy from the bleeding heart brigade, what's done is done and good riddance to it with pink ribbons around its neck. No, I bring this up only to demonstrate just how much this 'I'm very protective of my little boy' crack really added insult to injury. Not that there was any point digging up the past and throwing it back in her face. Mum lived in complete denial. As far as she was concerned she was a model parent. Ma Walton and the Oxo mum rolled into one, just unappreciated by a cruel, unforgiving world for one mistake when she was but a girl. It was something I'd pay for with interest the whole of my life.

'Janet!' mum suddenly said. 'Is that her name, Janet? Oh, she sounds lovely.'

Where did she get that name from? I didn't say it, did I? Was I ranting and raving so much that I'd brought back Janet?

'When can I meet her, this Janet? When can I meet her?' she cooed.

'You can't,' I hissed. 'You're never going to meet her.'

'You can bring her round on Wednesday. I'll get in some cake and I'll dig out all your old baby pictures,' she frothed with joy. 'Tell her about all the times you used to mess yourself when you were a tot. About how I'd always know when you'd done a toilet in your pants because you'd go very quiet and stand behind the telly. Oh yes, I'll tell her exactly what sort of little boy she's getting involved with. See if she still wants to marry you then.'

Honestly, she used to say this all the time. Exactly where the incentive was for me to take a girl back I wasn't sure.

None of this mattered anyway because she was never going to meet Janet so there wasn't any point in letting myself get worked up about it. I almost found this comforting.

'You're never going to meet her,' I smiled.

'Don't talk nonsense, I'm bound to. If nowhere else I'll definitely see her at the wedding.'

'Never,' I just grinned.

'Oh what silly nonsense you talk sometimes.'

I just smiled again and repeated to myself: 'Never.'

Mum looked at me for a few moments then rolled her eyes with disgust.

'Oh Ian, you haven't killed her have you?'

'I blew her fucking head off. You should've seen it.'

'Oh dear, not again!' she sighed shaking her head sadly.

'What d'you mean "not again"? You make it sound like I do this all the time. That's only twice now.'

'Ian look, you have to stop this killing people. You'll never meet the right girl and settle down if you keep murdering them every time things don't go your way. Your father, he never killed anyone.'

'What are you talking about, he was in Korea, he killed loads of people.'

'Yes, but they were only Chinese, they don't count. I'm talking about real, proper people. It's not nice.'

'I don't remember dad meeting a nice girl either,' I said.

'I blame those people you work with. They're not a very

pleasant lot. Why don't you stop seeing them and get a normal job? You used to be so good with numbers. Why don't you be an accountant?'

'Oh please, don't start this one again.'

'Why don't you just give it a go?'

'Because I don't want to. I'm happy doing what I'm doing.'

'But, you don't even know what it'll be like unless you try, and I think if you really put your mind to it…'

'NO! No, I don't want to be an accountant. I like the job I've got. I don't want to try anything else.'

'See, I really hate people who are close-minded about things, who aren't even willing to listen to other people's ideas or points of views,' she said with absolutely no trace of self-irony whatsoever. 'Just give it a go,' she suggested.

'No.'

'But why not? You might try it and find you have a real talent for it.'

'No, I won't.'

'Well no of course you won't unless you actually give it a go.'

'Mum, I don't want to do it. I like doing what I'm doing.'

'You might like accountancy.'

I wasn't even arguing any more but that didn't matter.

'How do you know? How do you know? How do you know?' she rattled on. 'You remember Uncle Brian who stayed with us for a while' – rent free and constantly drunk – 'well he always wanted to open his own sandwich bar but never thought he could get a loan to start him up…'

'STOP!' Jesus Christ, couldn't I get through to her? No, evidently I couldn't because she proceeded to bang on and on and on about this fucking old ponce who managed to cadge together enough bread to buy this rat-infested crawl space under a railway arch to demonstrate just what a blinding success some people can make of their lives if only they put their minds to it (in case you're curious, the Tasty Snack sandwich bar was closed down by the

Health and Safety after Uncle Brian hospitalised half a dozen customers with his homemade chicken pies. He ended up doing a runner and drinking himself to alcoholism with what little money he managed to grab before the loan sharks got him – a regular entrepreneur was my late Uncle Brian).

'I only want what's best for you. I only want you to be happy,' she kept saying over and over again. 'I love you.'

'No,' I blubbed. 'No one loves me. No one even likes me.'

'I could've loved you,' said Janet suddenly joining in, water and blood spilling out over the carpet, her smell making me gag.

I closed my eyes and shook my head.

'But I didn't love you.'

'You didn't even know me,' Janet said.

'I could never've loved you.'

'Because I was fat.'

'No, not because you were fat. Nothing to do with that. It was other things entirely.'

'What's wrong with being fat,' said mum butting in. 'Hello, I'm his mother by the way.'

'Hello, I'm Janet,' Janet smiled shaking my mum's hand.

'I didn't say there was anything wrong with being fat. It was nothing to do with being fat.'

'Why couldn't you love me, Ian?'

'It just wasn't there.'

'What wasn't?'

'It wasn't. The spark, the thing. I didn't feel anything for you. I'm sorry.'

'Well I think she's a lovely girl,' said mum, spitting on the rubber stamp.

'I didn't love her,' I insisted.

'And that's your problem, you don't love anyone. You can't love anyone. You don't know how to.'

'I do.'

'No you don't. You don't even know the meaning of the word

"love". You're incapable of loving anyone but yourself. You're selfish.'

'That's not true, I'll show you it's not.'

'You didn't love me,' Janet chipped in.

'That doesn't mean a thing.'

'Doesn't it? You've never ever been loved, and you never ever will be. And you know why? Because you haven't got it in you. And it doesn't matter how many girls you take out, you'll spend the rest of your life alone.'

'No I won't. And I can love, you just see. Just you see. I don't care if I have to kill every girl in Britain, I will find my Mrs Right.'

4. The Aviary

There was that noise again, louder than before. Closer. I looked around for the source but it seemed to be coming from all directions. It was definitely in front of the trees but I couldn't see it no matter how hard I squinted. Logan kept on trying to talk to me but I couldn't concentrate on what he was saying. I walked away from the little huddle to try and find what was making the noise but they all followed me. It was actually quite frightening that I could hear it but nobody else could. Finally Prince Charles got really fucked off with me and said: 'Don't you ever answer your phone?'

I snapped awake to the awful, urgent clatter of a ringing telephone and knocked over several things on the bedside table before I was able to lift the receiver and stop the racket.

'Eh! Y'allo, it's me,' I gasped into the phone, falling back into the pillow.

'Don't you ever answer your fucking phone?' the voice on the other end demanded and, for a moment, I almost said: 'Prince Charles, is that you?'

'What? Who is this?'

'It's Eddie, where have you been? I've been trying to get hold of you for the last hour.'

Soon as he said the name I recognised the voice. Eddie, Eddie Sinton, or Handsome Eddie, as some of the lads called him. He was Logan's gofer and, with the exception of Logan himself, my main contact with the organisation. His calling meant they had a job for me to do.

'What time is it?' I asked him rubbing the sleep from my eyes. Sleeping pills always made me drowsy the next day and these hadn't had a chance to clear my system yet.

'Just coming up to lunch-time,' he said stunning me with his ceaseless quest for precision and accuracy. 'Logan wants to see you.'

'What time?' I asked him.

'Make it around five,' he told me.

'What, dinner-time?' I said.

'No, that's at six o'clock,' he corrected me, failing to note the sarcasm.

'Is that when you have your dinner then is it?'

'Yeah, why when do you have yours?'

'I don't know, about half seven,' I told him.

'That's not dinner, that's supper. Dinner's at six, supper's at about half seven or eight o'clock.' I couldn't help but get the feeling he'd had this beaten into him when he was very young and always late for meals and now had this timetable indelibly printed on his mind and his arse.

'All right then, I'll be there just after afternoon tea,' I told him and replaced the receiver.

I lay where I was for a bit, my head still wrapped in sleep's warm blanket and recapped the events of the night before. Was it really only twelve hours ago that I was lowering Janet into the water? It seemed like a lot longer. It occurred to me that Mr Parnell would've surely been found by now and that the headlines would be full of murder, madness and mayhem but when I switched on the lunch-time news all they talked about was the personal and rather trifling tragedies of pop stars, footballers and politicians. You know, it's sad living in such a superficial society.

Sad, but fucking convenient for me.

John Broad's club, The Aviary, was this big old flash affair just off Leicester Square. According to Eddie, he'd called it The Aviary because he wanted to give the impression that it was full of birds. Get it? Though from what I'd heard a better name for it might've been Yellowstone National Park because all you ever got in there were geezers. The Aviary was just one of Broad's many businesses. Besides this place, he owned bars, a couple of restaurants, some offices and a load of storage space down by the water. Most of his money (well, most of his legitimate money) was in amusement arcades though he had a couple of dozen scattered around the West End and elsewhere that absolutely coined it in for him.

For all that though, The Aviary was the centre of Broad's empire. It had been one of the first places he'd acquired back in the early seventies and was the place he felt most sentimental about, a notion I found quite bizarre. It was here, in the office upstairs, that Logan ran Broad's empire for him and it was here that I went to receive my instructions.

I knocked on the back door at five and Felix let me in and past with the usual scowl. Felix didn't like me. I don't know why, I'd never done anything to him, in fact I don't think we'd ever even exchanged more than a few words, but still he didn't like me. Not that this really bothered me; I didn't like him either so on the whole we got on fine. Eddie came galloping over the moment I stepped through the door and started doing his false, over-familiar bit with me while walking me to the bar.

'So how's it going? What you been up to? How's tricks? D'you watch *Blankety Blank* last night?' That sort of thing.

'How d'your date go? All right was it? Looking a bit fucked today my old son,' he said digging me in the ribs. I'd forgotten I'd mentioned Janet to him last week. It hadn't seemed important at the time, I mean, no reason not to. I didn't realise I was going to have to murder her did I? 'D'you give her one?' he persisted as I took a seat by the bar.

'Er, no, I didn't.'

'Why? What's up, you bent or something?' he said punching me in the arm and laughing. Before I had a chance to fuck him up he'd wandered off to tell Logan I was here.

The club was closed at the moment and for the most part

empty. There was Felix on the doors, Logan upstairs, Sam was probably in the back office with his nose to the mirror. There was Eddie of course, Phil would be up in the security booth, a couple of cleaners mopping and hoovering…

'How many millionaires tonight, hey squire?'

And then last, and by all means least, there was George the barman.

'Hey! Who'll be the one tonight, d'ya reckon?'

'I don't know George,' I told him.

'I wouldn't mind a bit of that for m'self, I wouldn't. Had four numbers last week, I did. Three different bloody lines though that was the problem. Oh, four numbers. You could get about £180 for that you could. My mate didn't though. He had four numbers only got £16. Bloody rip-off it is.'

A bloody rip-off. He was talking about the lottery. In fact, since it had started a few years back, that was all he ever talked about. It had gripped the poor old bastard like a madness and possessed his soul so much that now he no longer lived in the real world, he lived in Camelot. Mind you, to be fair, even before the lottery had taken off George hadn't really lived on the same planet as the rest of us, so there was no real harm done. He was simply a very single-minded individual, a boring bastard if you like, who could only see one colour of the rainbow or one star in the night's sky. Of course, like all boring bastards, he assumed everyone else was fascinated by the same thing as him. It was horse racing before the lottery came along. The football pools before that, or so I'd heard.

'There was a bloke come in here two weeks ago who'd won a bit over £2 million. He'd jacked in his job, jacked in the missus, bought a big flat in Chelsea and had a different tart back there every night. Thousands he was getting through. Thousands. What a waste!'

'What would you do with it then George?'

'Thousands. He must be bloody mad,' he pondered to himself not hearing me.

'George. What would you do with yours then?'

'Aye, had a string of lassies on his arm that night he did. One of them wearing this tiny little dress, barely covered her Bristols it did,' he told me making the universal big-tits hand gesture. 'He must've been off his rocker!'

'You wouldn't do that then George?'

'Me? Ho ho, no. Me, I'd stick it all in the bank I would. Wouldn't touch a penny,' he said, then went on polishing the taps.

'Mind you,' he started up again. 'I've got a mate of mine down in Mitcham…'

'George,' said Sam standing in the doorway of the back office. 'Make sure you have the mirror behind the bar polished before we open tonight. It was like a fucking dirty milk bottle last night.'

'Yes sir, right away,' clicked George reaching for the Window-lene.

Sam stood there a moment longer running his beady eyes over me.

'You going up to see Logan?' he asked.

'What?' I said, just to be awkward.

'Logan. You going up to see him?' he repeated.

'What?'

Sam clenched his jaw and screwed up his eyes, unsure of what to do, before opting for a bit of pointless bossing. He pointed at where I was sitting and told me to stay there until Logan sent for me. No sooner had he said it than I'd wandered off down the other end of the bar to talk to George some more and I only looked round again when I heard the door close behind me.

Sam Broad was the idiot son of John Broad and he had about as much skill for business as George had for conversation. To keep him out of trouble then and to keep the missus happy, daddy Broad had given him a job, a couple of blokes to boss about and made him downstairs bar manager, which was a bit of a joke really as, accord-ing to Logan, Sam couldn't even manage to tie his shoelaces until he was twelve. Apparently he just kept tying double reef knots so at the end of the day he could never get his shoes off.

George went about polishing for about another minute or so before he distracted himself talking about the lottery again. 'Four millionaires there were Saturday night. Wonder if they watched the numbers come out. Imagine that, hey, sitting there watching your numbers come out. I couldn't do that me, ho ho, no. I look 'em up in the paper next day. Couldn't sit there watching them come out, I'd have a heart attack I would!'

'George, who's that?' I asked discreetly pointing to one of the cleaning girls.

'A heart attack, that's what I'd've had!'

'George. Who's that? Is she a new girl?'

'Who?' he said, finally snapping out of it.

'Her with the foot. Is she new?'

'Who her? Aye, I haven't seen her before,' he told me, spitting into his cloth.

'What's her name?'

'Who? What, the new girl? I don't know. Hang on a minute I'll ask her.'

'No, wait!'

But before I could shut George up he'd shouted over at the top of his voice: 'Oi, you girl. What's your name? Gentleman here wants to know.'

'Fuck's sake George,' I told him. 'I didn't want you to say anything.'

'Oh, it's all right,' he shouted at her again. 'Don't worry about it. He's changed his mind.'

But I guess she did worry about it because she came hobbling over and stood by me all hangdog-like. 'It's Angela,' she told me. 'I just started today. I'm sorry, I know I'm not as quick as the others but I don't mind coming in earlier in future, I promise I'll do my share. I just need…'

'Hold it, slow down there, I wasn't going to bollock you or anything. I just wondered what your name was because I hadn't seen you before.'

'Oh, sorry,' she muttered, averting her eyes.

'And I don't know what you're talking about not being quick enough. I think you're doing fine,' I reassured her.

'Thank you,' she said and stood there in silence for a moment. 'Well, I'd better be getting on again. I'm really sorry…' she started to tell me again before I held up a hand and told her to forget it.

That was the first time I met Angela and God I was taken with her. In fact, I was so taken with her, I don't think I ever even noticed her club foot again after that. Or at least, I didn't mind it. No, not even didn't mind it, I actually liked it. It suited her. It was cute. It was adorable. It was part of her and so I adored it as much as I adored the rest of her, even more so perhaps. It got that I was so hooked up on her that for months after meeting her I couldn't even bring myself to look at any woman who could run for the bus without difficulties.

'She's lovely, isn't she George?'

'Who?' he said, spitting on a tray of clean glasses as he missed the cloth.

'Oh, never mind,' I said with a wave of the hand. At that moment Eddie reappeared and told me Logan was ready to see me. 'All right, come on then. Stay lucky George.'

'Lucky? If my numbers come in, I'll be lucky all right.'

We walked up the stairs and around the mezzanine to Logan's private office which was just next door to the DJ booth. As we approached Connolly came out and brushed past us as if on a mission from God. Connolly was Broad's accountant and a more bent number cruncher you couldn't wish to fill out your tax returns. Someone once told me that Connolly didn't use a calculator when he was going through the books, he used an oven. I forget who told me that now but I do know some of the lads sometimes called him Delia. He passed us without so much as a glance and hurried down the steps and away with percentages and numbered accounts no doubt running through his mind.

Eddie gave Logan's door a couple of light taps and pushed me on through, closing it behind me. Logan looked up and gave me a nod of acknowledgement before stuffing some papers away and chucking a file on the desk.

'Howdo, Ian. How you been keeping?' he said waving me into the chair opposite.

'Fine Danny. You know, all right,' I told him.

'How did that date of yours go last night?' Fucking Eddie that big-mouthed cunt!

'Erm… yeah. Okay. Could've been better I suppose, which reminds me Danny, I need a new car.'

'A new car? You've only had the other one a couple of months or so ain't ya? What d'you need a new car for?'

'Well, I had to burn the other one out last night. Spot of bother,' I explained.

'Burn it out? I thought you was only going out on a date last night.'

'Oh yeah, I was. I did. But, I had to end up burning the car out, you know?'

Logan looked at me in confusion for a few moments, scratched his head and clicked his teeth before dropping his head into his hand.

'Please don't tell me you rubbed her out again!' he said, shaking his head, unable to look at me.

'It wasn't my fault, I couldn't help it.'

'You couldn't help it? You took some bird out for dinner and you couldn't help murdering her. What's wrong with you, are you some sort of nutcase or something?'

'Look, I was compromised, I had no choice. Don't worry, everything's all right. There was no problem.'

'Is she going to be missed?'

'Not by anyone that matters. She's got no family to chase up, no real friends as such. She'll sit in a file for a few years with nothing happening and probably get wiped the next time the Old Bill upgrade their computers or try and train up some new staff.

No one's going to worry about her.'

Which was a bit sad when I put it like that.

'What about your connection?'

'Other than buying papers and the odd chocolate bar from her, there isn't one.' I told Logan about how I'd asked her out. About how I'd followed her home and asked her well away from the shop, the security cameras and anyone that knew her, and as I did so I couldn't help but wonder if I'd done that by accident or design. Design probably. Not with the intention of killing her, you understand, I probably just didn't want anyone seeing me asking a fat bird out. Or, more likely, I didn't want to risk the possibility of anyone seeing me getting blown out by a fat bird.

Not that it was because she was fat that I, oh whatever...

'All right then, we'll leave it at that,' Logan concluded. I didn't tell him about the five other murders I'd committed the previous night because that's the sort of thing that could get a man weighted down and wet himself. The organisation was much too important to risk letting anyone who knew as much as I did face a life sentence. One murder was one thing – not too difficult to shake off – but six? The exposure (i.e. risk of detection and apprehension) was massive. It was a risk I was willing to take, because I knew the alternative, but I doubted Logan would've shared my confidence if he'd known the truth.

I picked up the file and stared at a newspaper cutting of a middle-aged moustache wearer trying his damnedest to look serious for the camera.

'Alan Carpenter,' Logan told me. 'He's on the council down in Sutton, that's way down south. His address and details are in the folder. Can you do him by the end of the week?'

'What's the absolute deadline?'

'Sunday. Or, I guess, at a push, even Monday morning. The important thing is that he doesn't take his seat next Monday. What d'you reckon?'

'Hmm, looks pretty positive. Single, lives on his own,' I said, reading the dossier. 'Got a cat, which is excellent. Depends, how do you want it done really?'

'Natural causes,' Logan flinched apologetically.

'Oh no, not natural causes. I hate doing natural causes. Can't he have an accident?'

'Sorry Ian, it's got to be this way.'

'Why?' I asked stupidly.

'Come on, you know the rule,' Logan said.

The rule, ah yes, the rule. Never ask why. See, I didn't need to know. In fact, it was best all round if I didn't. My job was simply to kill. John Broad and Daniel Logan decided on the whys and wherefores, it was none of my business. I should've known better than to ask. The day I need to know why I'm killing is the day I'm no good to anyone. See, reasons don't ever make it easier to kill someone, they just make it harder. Reasons are very personal things. It doesn't necessarily tie that if John Broad thinks someone deserves to die that I'd think that too. And if I don't think someone deserves to die, that might be just enough to cost me my edge. Say for example John Broad's been enjoying raping women or murdering kids or something and someone's all set to expose him. Naturally Broad would want this person rubbed out and it would be my job to rub him out. But then, if John Broad was raping women or murdering kids it might be my opinion that he'd deserve to get exposed and therefore I might not carry out my task. That's just an example of course, to the best of my knowledge JB (as he was commonly known amongst the troops) hadn't raped or murdered anyone for a long time, but that's why the rule is there.

That's why there is no why.

I apologised to Logan again and memorised all the details I needed to from the file before handing it back. From what I'd read, I couldn't tell what Mr Carpenter had done to deserve his death sentence, but he'd upset JB somehow.

So now he had me to deal with.

5. Alan Carpenter's sticky end

The first thing you do when you get a job like this is watch them. You watch them at work, watch them at home, watch them wandering around the shops or in the pub or playing squash or standing around in a scout hut with a load of losers playing model trains. You get to know their routine, pin-point when they are at their most vulnerable and then plan your hit around that moment. The more you know about a person, the less you leave to chance. One time I followed this bloke around for three weeks before I bumped him off; got to know him so well it almost felt like I was killing a friend of mine. Not that I had that sort of luxury with Alan Carpenter. I only really had a couple of days' observation before I had to act, so I had to make sure the time we spent together was quality time. It was especially difficult seeing as it had to be natural causes because you need a certain window of opportunity to be able to pull it off. However, in Alan Carpenter's case, I had several things working in my favour. Firstly, he was a local councillor; secondly, he was gay; and thirdly, he had a cat. Now, you might not immediately see how these three things make him an easier target than the next man so let me explain.

Firstly, being a local councillor, he was probably a cunt! A real 'book-waving-starch-underpants-wearing-precedent - quoting-sub-section-paragraph-three-looking-up' sort of arsehole who lived his life by the numbers and reported his neighbours if they so much as tried to put up a bird-table without planning permission. A suspicion I had confirmed to me after only two days of following him around when I saw him ringing his neighbour's bell and asking him why he hadn't taken in his bin three days after collection.

'Just thought I'd check to see if everything was okay,' he said with mock concern.

'Why don't you give it a rest?' was the reply.

Secondly, as a gay man he was unlikely to have a house full of family. He might have a live-in lover or a string of male visitors banging on his front and back doors every night, but there'd be no kids. He'd have more freedom on his hands, be able to spend more time in his own company and the house wouldn't reverberate with the pitter-patter of tiny witnesses. As it was, Alan didn't seem to have any regular companions either, which was handy, though a little worrying as it threw up the element of spontaneity. The last thing you need when you're all set to kill someone is them bringing back a load of blokes off the local common for a pants party. I borrowed a van off Logan just in case.

Lastly, there was his cat. This beautiful little creature, who purred away by my feet and followed me around the house while I got things ready for Alan, needed feeding every evening. Councillor Carpenter had to come home.

I love cats, they're great; intelligent, affectionate, lovable, and this one was particularly nice, so picking it up and giving it a few slaps and a bit of a rough time was galling, even though it was unfortunately necessary. See, if you're hiding in someone's spare bedroom waiting for them to turn in for the night, the last thing you need is a cat meowing at the door trying to get in to see you because you've been stroking it all day. A bit of a shake and a growl in the cat's face and that's all that's usually needed for it to give the spare room and the horrible bastard inside a wide berth for the rest of the night.

And that's where I was one Friday afternoon. Less than a week after learning of Alan Carpenter's existence on the planet, I was camped out in his spare bedroom, waiting for him to come home from work so that I could bring it to an end. I'd made all the preparations. It was a natural causes fatality so I'd had to break in an hour or two before Councillor Carpenter clocked off so that I could check the lie of the land and make sure I was able to take him out without any fuss or nonsense; one mark on his chubby little face or one scream in the night and the theories surrounding the passing of the neighbourhood's favourite civil servant would touch upon more than a dodgy ticker.

So, how to do it? Well, there are several ways you can take someone out cleanly, but my own personal favourite is the simplest – sleeping pills in the kettle.

As I've said, I'd watched Alan for several days and one of the first things he did when he got home from work was stick on a brew and have a nice cup of tea in front of the news. So, four or five extra-strong sleeping pills in the 'stinging nettle', as Logan liked to call it, would see him drift off blissfully in his favourite armchair, ripe and ready for an easy killing.

And so that was how it happened. The last images of this rich and colourful world Alan saw was a report on NHS staffing levels and the expansion of the private sector's effect on recruitment, so I imagine he died a happy man. I snuck down an hour or so after he stopped moving and found him dead to the world – if you'll pardon the pun. This first thing I did was give his cup a good rinse and wash out the kettle; the last thing I needed was the GP to trundle downstairs after signing the medical certificate and find Alan's neighbour and a couple of coppers out for the count around the kitchen table. That would've really set alarm bells ringing.

Once I'd done that, I set about manhandling Councillor Carpenter upstairs to the bedroom. He was a big fellow and no mistake and it took all my co-ordination and precision to avoid staving his head in on the banisters on the way up. About the only way I could do it was to grab his arms, roll him forward on to me and carry him up on my back like a bag of coal. By the time I got him up and dumped him on the bed I was fucked. Still, time was on my side so I had a bit of a sit-down and got my breath back before I got on with the job.

The cat popped its head round the door and had a quick look at what I was up to, so I gave it a conciliatory stroke and a tickle under the chin and we were mates once again. 'Sorry about that,'

I told it and made a mental note to open up a tin of Whiskers for it before I left.

Alan began snoring like a buzzsaw now that he was on his back and I set about taking off his clothes, folding them up nicely and putting them on the chair at the end of his bed. The cat came over to join in the fun and helped out by taking a swipe at Alan's grey flannel trousers as they passed by his head.

Alan was soon down to his altogether and looking pretty fucking horrendous with it. 'These gays have got no standards, have they?' I muttered to the cat. 'I mean, look at him and look at me and I bet he still gets it more than me.' The cat didn't really have an opinion on the matter although I did catch him looking at me for a moment as if to say: 'Well go on then, now's your chance.'

I fetched the syringe out of my little bag and removed the protective plastic cover. Insulin. That was what was contained in the syringe, insulin. It occurs in all of us naturally and we need it to live, but too much of it and you're in all sorts of trouble. Diabetics can't produce insulin and therefore have to give themselves daily injections of the stuff to help them maintain their blood sugar. For a diabetic, a syringe full of insulin means life, for a non-diabetic, it means death. Weird, isn't it? Mother Nature has a real ironic sense of humour doesn't she?

Of course, if you're thinking of trying this at home, you should be well warned that excessive insulin levels will show up at any post-mortem. The days of mysterious eastern poisons, blow darts and Agatha Christie are long gone, if they ever even existed. With science what it is today, it is virtually impossible to kill someone in a way that is undetectable to others, which is why you have to stage the death in such a way so as to discount the need for any such nosiness.

Hence, he has no marks or bruises or cuts or abrasions about him. His clothes are folded up neatly. He's found in his pyjamas in bed (which, believe it or not is where most of us will check out), the cat's been fed and he's a big fat fucker. It doesn't take a genius to figure out that he died of a heart attack in his sleep: too bad, very sad, sign here please doctor and you can get back to your golf. It was a Friday as well, and so it was fairly safe to assume what with being single and having no immediate family, it was unlikely Alan would be seriously missed by anyone until Monday, by which time he would've had a chance to cool down to room temperature and throw a big question mark over his exact time of death.

I rolled Alan over and readied myself to give him his injection.

If you're wondering why natural causes jobs are so unpalatable to me, this is the reason. There is only one place on the human body where a needle mark from a hypodermic won't show up. Can you guess where that place is? Yes that's right, it's inside the arsehole. Every other square inch of your skin and that needle mark could be found, and once a needle mark is found, in a case of sudden death, the police aren't far behind. Logan did tell me about this idea he had about removing the eyeball from the socket and injecting a clotting agent directly into the brain to bring about a stroke, but to be honest that sounded even more unpleasant than sticking a needle in someone's arse so I decided to stick with the tried and trusted.

I parted Alan's sweaty buttocks with my fingers and held them apart with one hand while carefully guiding the syringe in deep. This was a thankless task, I thought to myself as I pricked the skin and slowly sunk the plunger. It would've been so much easier to drug him and chuck him down the stairs a few times, but Logan had ruled that out and what Logan wanted, Logan got. I felt particularly uncomfortable with the fact that Alan was a homosexual as well. I know it sounds a strange thing to say, like as if doing this qualified as some sort of gay sex and made me a homosexual like him. I don't know. It was just a stupid knee-jerk response to the situation. I think I'm probably a bigot, though I've never given it much thought before. Whatever the case, I doubted very much whether Alan would've got any sort of cheap thrill from his murder if he'd been awake. At least, I hoped not.

The cat gave a quiet meow as I withdrew the syringe and Alan joined in on the debate with a long, drawn-out fart straight into my face. All that was left to do was stick him in his pyjamas and tuck him in. As I rolled him on to his back and buttoned him up, Alan started to sweat and gasp for breath. I pulled the covers over him, felt his forehead and sat with him for the next couple of hours while he went into a coma and died. It was a slow but painless death for Alan, and despite him opening his eyes towards the end and thrashing about a little, I don't think he ever regained consciousness.

Not the worst way in the world to go, which was something I suppose.

Alan lay there, silent and still, while the cat and I went downstairs and got something to eat. I returned about an hour later when the sun had set and closed the bedroom curtains. I placed a glass of water on the bedside table, had one last check around his person for false teeth still in his mouth or contact lenses still in his eyes, that sort of thing, then said my goodbyes. Downstairs I saw that the street was empty, left a GP's appointment card on the table in the hallway where it would be easily found and slipped out as quietly as I'd entered.

You know, this might sound a bit creepy, but in my line of work there are times when you can't help but feel like the Grim Reaper.

Alan missed his meeting on Monday, which I imagine pleased John Broad no end, and after several unanswered phone calls, a car was sent for him. I watched the drama unfold from the back of my van across the street. This fella turned up at about 11 a.m. and rang the bell a few times. He looked a bit lost, peered through the front windows, called through the letterbox, then, for reasons best known to himself, he looked up and down the street, as if searching for inspiration. After a minute or so he rang the bell again, looked through the letterbox then got into his car and drove off.

Half an hour later the same guy returned and rang the doorbell again, though he didn't look too confident about it being answered as he never stopped sipping from his McDonald's coffee. He was only a young bloke and I could see from my position that Alan's disappearance had turned into a right result for him. After another ten minutes of sitting in the car staring down the street, he made a quick call, looked at his watch and strolled off to the pub at the end of the road.

Half an hour later the Old Bill turned up, assessed the situation, dragged this young lad out of the boozer and forced an entry. Plod stepped back out talking into his radio and reading the card I'd left on the table in the hallway. Matey interrupted him to ask if he could go up and have a look, but was turned down flat.

'I think you should get back to the office,' Plod advised. 'He doesn't look like he'll be wanting to go anywhere today.'

'No, not yet. It's lunch-time,' he replied looking at his watch and sloped off back down the pub.

It took another thirty minutes for the doctor to arrive and rubberstamp Alan's medical certificate, then when everyone was happy, some elderly woman (probably his mum) was chauffeured up, given a few hankies and left to it. That was all I needed to see, the signature on the medical certificate and the Old Bill driving off. That ended my relationship with Alan Carpenter.

The doctor came out of the house, told the old lady how sorry he was, then got into his car and drove away. I watched a couple more minutes for the police to do the same before climbing into the driver's seat and leaving Mrs Carpenter to her grief.

As it was a Monday afternoon the supermarket car park was not even half full. I circled until I spotted where the doctor had parked, pulled in next to him and waited. He returned to the car after about ten minutes carrying a small bag of groceries and put them down as he fumbled with his keys.

'Hey doc!' I said cracking open the door and stepping out.

'What's for dinner?'

'Fish,' he merely replied, eyeing me nervously and looking around the car park.

'Mmm, very nice. You know I like fish and it's not too difficult to cook but I never know what to have with it; rice, new potatoes, it all just seems a bit bland. What are you having with yours?'

'Chips,' he told me.

This was Alan's doctor. Someone in the organisation had already got to him and now I was just dropping off the rest of the money. Dr Ranjani would've been taken aside and told in no uncertain terms, 'A patient of yours is going to die in his sleep in the next week. You'll be called to the scene by the police. You'll sign the medical certificate and tell the Old Bill there's no need for an autopsy. Do this and you get ten thousand in cash and never see us again. Fuck about or go to the police and it becomes personal.' At which point pictures of his wife and kids (and any other relative they could photograph) would be produced to underline our seriousness.

'If you're worried about it, let me just enlighten you,' they would've gone on. 'The man who's going to die is a kiddie fiddler. It's all about to hit the papers and our employer, who knows him and only just found this out, is frightened of being tarred with the same brush by association. So, he's doing something about it to make sure justice is done and his own reputation is protected. Are you the sort of bloke who'll put his life and the life of his family at risk for the sake of a kiddie fiddler?'

Of course not. Not that any of it was true, but Dr Ranjani wasn't to know this was he?

So Ranjani played ball. He went round Carpenter's when he got the call, shook his head, said something along the lines of: 'I warned him something like this would happen but he wouldn't listen,' certified him dead and advised the police that no post-mortem was needed. See, it's like I was saying, insulin would definitely show up in a PM, as indeed most drugs would, but if you've got a genuine GP in your pocket to recommend otherwise then you're laughing. What flat-foot's going to argue with the family practitioner? All I have to do is make sure the police find his appointment cards and let them do the rest. And they will always call. That's the beauty. In the case of sudden non-suspicious death, the police are advised to call out the deceased's own doctor as he or she will have knowledge of the patient that may shed light on why they've turned their toes up. It's standard procedure and it works almost every time.

Almost every time.

Once in a while, however, it won't work. The police don't find the cards or they've got a bit of a saucy-looking pathologist on call or something, in which case it's in the lap of the Gods. As long as the victim looks like he's passed away peacefully and there's no obvious motive or reason for suspicion then the saucy pathologist will just sign it off too. Well, not everyone can have a detailed autopsy. There are 60 million of us in Britain alone and it is reckoned there are thousands of deaths every day. I don't know exactly how many but I remember reading it somewhere and thinking it was a lot. All the pathologists in the land working double overtime couldn't possibly hope to keep up with demand so what's the point of chopping up some fatso who you know died from a heart attack? And so that's how you do it. That's how you get away with murder. You stage the death so that nobody suspects foul play.

Recruiting the doctor is really just the icing on the cake, but you can never – and I mean never – take too many precautions when you're committing murder. You can't afford to, the risks are just too great. But like I say, that's how we get away with it – dotting the 'I's and crossing the 'T's.

How many people do you suppose there are in the ground who were victims of murders that nobody knows about?

Of course, there are no guarantees, so it's not a bad idea to own a boat and have a big chunk of running money and several passports in case things go tits up.

Anyway, I digress.

'How shall we do this?' Ranjani asked, wiping his brow.

'Just open the passenger door and move aside, I'll sling it in. We're pretty shielded here so I don't suppose we need to bother with any secret handshake stuff.' He did as I said and I threw the remaining £5,000 we owed him on to the leather upholstery as he attempted to look as suspicious as possible.

'Any problems?' I asked.

'No, nothing. He looked like a heart attack waiting to happen anyway and by the time I coloured in his medical history the only thing they couldn't figure out was why it hadn't happened sooner.'

'Okay, don't go sticking it all in the bank or buying anything enormous with it otherwise you might go attracting yourself some unwanted attention.'

'Okay,' Ranjani nodded stiffly.

'And don't worry, it's a good thing you've done today.'

'I hope so,' he said, looking down at the bag on his seat. 'What now?'

'Now, you forget all about Carpenter and you forget all about me. Oh, and one last thing, don't go moving house for a few years.'

'What? Why not?'

'Why? Dr Ranjani, we trust you, but we don't trust you that much. We want to know where to find you if you go shooting your mouth off so you're to stay in your current house for at least another five years. And I don't care if you win the lottery or have 68 more children, you stay where you are until we're sure Carpenter's old news.' And with one wag of the finger I drove off leaving JB's newest recruit sweating all over his fish.

6. Lift conversation

I went back to The Aviary and told Logan it had all gone smoothly. I didn't really need to do this, a telephone call or a text message would've done, but I wanted to see Angela again. It wouldn't have done to let the memory of that first meeting fade, I had to underline my existence with a second conversation while I was still fresh in her mind. I saw her as I left Logan's office, hoovering the carpet near the bar. She was as beautiful as I remembered. No, more so. I'd thought about her a lot in the course of the last week and suddenly seeing her standing not twenty yards away made her seem very real indeed. In fact, she was the most real person I'd ever laid eyes on. I felt my throat dry and my heart start to pound as I made my way around the gallery, to the stairs and towards Angela.

What was I going to say? That was the question that only occurred to me when I was about two feet behind her.

'Hi,' I shouted at her as I passed, but my feet didn't bother hanging about for any sort of reply. They were another ten feet past her and halfway to the door before she finally located the source behind the speeding greeting and returned it with a 'Hi' and a smile of her own. But then what did I do? I was in no-man's-land. I couldn't very well do a quick U-turn and wander over and talk to her like normal because the moment had gone. What I was trying to stage as a chance encounter would suddenly look like it had a purpose. She would wonder what I was up to and I'd have to get to the point and I didn't know what the point was, I hadn't worked it out yet. But then, I didn't want to keep walking because that would take me to the exit and my opportunity to try and get to know her a little bit would be gone and I'd end up regretting it all week. What should I do?

Before I knew it I found myself wobbling around in the middle of the dance floor with one leg heading in one direction and the other wondering whether it shouldn't just have a quick think about this a moment. Angela stared at me while I danced around and agonised for a few very long seconds before I realised I had to speak. There was a very real danger of me looking an idiot if I didn't hurry up and say something.

'Mopping the floor then?' I asked brightly.

Angela stared at her mop and then back at me. 'Yes,' she informed me.

I headed for the car.

I tried to decide what I should've said rather than 'Mopping the floor then!' and concluded just about anything. 'I like your pinny.' 'We must stop meeting like this.' 'Look out your hair's on fire!' Anything. What a cunt! I sat up the rest of the night making sure I wouldn't be caught out like that again and worked out my patter until I had the whole of the next passing encounter carefully scripted and choreographed right down to the gentle cradling of her elbow as she laughed at my ad-lib jokes.

'How are you today? Working hard?'

'Fuck off slimebag!'

'I know I am, but what are you?' was, of course, the nightmare scenario and all the elbow-cradling in the world wouldn't turn that one around. But I was pretty confident it wouldn't come to that. All she had to do was give me a chance. See that I was a nice guy, that I wasn't as bad as all the rest and things should go to plan.

All that remained was the when.

The only time I ever went over to the club was to see Logan and that really wasn't all that often. It could be months before I saw her again and someone else might've seen her by then. I had to think of some reason to be there.

Unfortunately, nothing came to mind. I couldn't go back the next day, not twice in a row, it would've started to look too suspicious. And it didn't pay in my business to start making people suspicious as they invariably came to all sorts of dangerous conclusions. I was desperate to see Angela however, so I decided to take a chance, parked across the street from the club and waited for her to knock off work. I knew exactly what I would say.

'Hi, how are you? Can I offer you a lift?'

Angela would see me, her face would light up and she'd climb into the car expressing her gratitude.

'Just finished work?' I'd ask and she'd say yes and tell me all about her day and the things she'd cleaned.

'Where are you off to now? Perhaps you'd like to get a drink before you go home? On me, of course.'

She'd tell me she could slaughter a drink and I'd suggest… where could I suggest? Somewhere local. Somewhere quiet. But where? I didn't know anywhere around here. To be honest, I didn't know anywhere up my way either, so where could I take her? Perhaps I should go and check out a few places before she came out so I'd be ready for it. Perhaps we should skip the drink altogether and go for a meal, after all a nice restaurant was easier to find than a nice bar. Perhaps I could even take her back to my place and cook her a meal. Hang on, shit, I didn't have anything in. Perhaps I should go to the shops. What should I cook her? Perhaps we should get a take-away. Perhaps…

… my mobile was ringing.

I looked at the number. It was coming from the club.

'Hello?'

'Bridges, where are you?' It was Logan.

'Er, why?'

'All right, let me rephrase that. What are you doing over there in your motor?'

I turned round and looked at the club. I couldn't see anything because of the smoky black windows but I knew Logan was standing there looking at me.

'Yes, I can see you. We can all see you. What are you doing?'

'Nothing,' I told him, though this was a dangerous line. I had to come clean. 'I was just waiting for Angela, the cleaning girl. I was going to give her a lift home.'

There was a slight pause while Logan put his hand over the telephone and shared this information with someone else then he came back on.

'Look Bridges, we've had this chat before about hanging round the club unnecessarily and that goes for outside opening hours an'all. Now, we've got a lot of the boys here who want to get on and go and do things, but no one wants to leave the club while you're sitting out there, 'cos they all think they've been marked. Now be a good lad and piss off will yah. I've got a business to run.'

And that was that. I'd been rumbled.

Not only that, I'd placed my life in serious risk chasing after a woman. I drove off completely defeated. That was my last chance with Angela. I couldn't possibly go back anywhere near the club again, not for a good few months at least. I'd blown it.

The man upstairs had won.

That big, son of a bitch bastard who watched over me and made sure I never found anyone to be with had won.

I hated thinking this way. I wasn't really a religious man but sometimes that's how it felt. Like I was part of some great cosmic conspiracy to deprive me of the normal happiness that everyone else took for granted. My needs weren't that much different from anyone else's were they? Why was it that I had to be alone? Why did I have to be different?

You know what, sometimes, I swear to God, it really did feel like there was someone out there who was trying to ruin my life.

It's funny, in that respect, I think I almost knew how Alan Carpenter felt.

I tried to put Angela out of my mind and remain single-minded. I have quite a monastic life when I'm not working and I've tried all sorts to fill my days: yoga, judo, meditation, painting toy soldiers, anything you can name – the trouble is they're all so boring. That's what hobbies are like. Boring. I've never felt overwhelmed to make a model of the Cutty Sark out of matchsticks or fly a model aeroplane around in circles on the Common. I've done both of these things before but I never enjoyed them. I just did them because I didn't know what else to do. God, all I've ever wanted was a little company. Just someone to lay next to at night, hold when you're feeling lonely or laugh with when you're feeling happy. Is that too much to ask?

I didn't know, all I did know was painting pictures of my fruit bowl or sitting on the floor surrounded by a load of smelly candles humming to myself weren't much of a substitute.

I was having no luck at all putting Angela out of my mind and feeling very depressed about my limited opportunities and what I could do about them. I was driving along, mulling over all this to myself, making myself feel nicely miserable when all of a sudden I slammed on the brakes and almost caused a dozen cars to concertina up my arse.

There she was.

Standing on her own, across the road, waiting for a bus. I pulled out into the traffic, cut across two lanes and screeched to a halt a few feet away from Angela, causing her to knock over her shopping bags and almost topple over at the suddenness of my appearance.

'Hi! Hi! Hello!' I shouted at her swinging open the door. 'It's me!'

Angela stared blankly for a few nervous moments before recognising me. 'Oh, hello,' she muttered.

'Need a ride?' I asked.

'No, I'm fine,' she replied. 'I'm getting the bus,' then pointed to the double-decker motoring down the high street towards us.

My hopeful smile cracked as I saw another opportunity slipping away.

'Are you sure?' I urged. 'It's no trouble.'

'It's okay, really. I'm only going three stops.'

'I don't mind,' I whined.

'Thanks all the same,' she declined.

I pondered to myself whether 'please' would sound too creepy when the bus tooted at me to move on.

'Bye,' Angela said, picking up her shopping.

'Wait!' I shouted after her. 'Wait! You don't want to ride home with all the dregs. Get in, I'll take you.' It was only after I'd said this that I realised that, as Angela probably took the bus regularly, strictly speaking she was one of the dregs.

She flashed a smile in my direction by way of a farewell and walked around the back of my car to the bus in the middle of the road. I jumped out of the driver's seat and gave it one last go.

'Angela please, let me drive you home, I really want to talk to you about something.'

Angela turned and eyed me suspiciously. 'Talk to me? What about?'

'It's nothing bad, I promise.'

The bus driver and several passengers scowled at us through the windows as Angela dilly-dallied over whether or not to accept my offer before the closing of the bus doors made up her mind for her.

'Okay,' she said, climbing into my car and sitting the bags on her lap.

I took a second to thank the man upstairs and wonder what the hell I was going to say to her before climbing in next to her and pulling on my seat-belt.

'Where to?' I asked.

'Home,' she told me. 'It's this way, I'll show you where.'

I pulled out in front of the bus, hanging my arm out of the window to stick two fingers up at the driver for tooting at me and smiled across at Angela. Angela failed to return my smile and shifted uncomfortably beneath her groceries.

'You said you wanted to talk to me about something?' she reminded me.

'Er, no,' I said, then quickly corrected myself. 'I mean yes.' I checked the mirrors and changed gear a few times to buy me some time to think something up before asking: 'Er, how are you?'

'Fine,' she told me.

'How are you finding the job?' I tried again.

'Fine,' she repeated.

'Good,' I nodded sincerely. 'Good.'

Er!

'Good,' I nodded again.

Er!

'My name's Ian,' I suddenly thought to tell her. 'Ian Bridges.'

'Yes I know,' she said.

She knew? She knew my name. That was great. She must've thought something of me if she'd bothered finding out my name. I wondered who she'd asked and how she'd phrased it. Had she been subtle? A little coy? Or had she just come out with it and demanded to know who I was and what I was called? My curiosity ended up getting the better of me.

'How do you know my name? Who told you?'

'You did, the other week.'

'Did I? Oh!' Bollocks.

I racked my brains for a moment or two to try and remember my patter, but for some reason all I could come up with was a dozen questions about her mop.

'Have you... er, have you just finished work?' I asked.

'No, shopping,' she told me lowering her eyes to her shopping bags.

'Oh, right. Yeah. Hmmm. Er...'

Why was this so difficult? Why was Angela making it so difficult? Surely it was obvious I was interested in her. Couldn't she have at least made a little effort to respond? I mean, she couldn't have had that many offers with her foot being the way it was, so you'd have thought she would've shown a bit more enthusiasm or... I don't know, even gratitude, for the fact that I was prepared to make such an allowance. How many men would've shown her the same consideration? Didn't she see, I was ready to love, and not even despite her foot, but because of it. I'd show her genuine love, blind love, love that overlooked any obstacle. Didn't she understand what I was offering? The chance to be loved like a normal person. Wasn't that worth something to her? A few words back? A little civility? A smile, for crying-out-loud?

I wondered to myself if I'd misread her circumstances. I looked down at her hands. No wedding band. It had been the first thing I'd checked. It was the first thing I always checked. All right, she hadn't been married but maybe she had a boyfriend. Not according to Eddie. I'd asked him the last time I'd popped in to see Logan and he'd assured me that she was unattached. Maybe he'd been wrong too.

I really wanted to check through her shopping bags and see what sort of groceries she was buying, multi-packs or your individual portions – like the ones I bought. I couldn't see anything peeking over every now and again and I think Angela started to suspect I was looking at her foot, so I stopped.

Angela told me to turn left and then right and then left again, then pointed to where she wanted me to stop and I could feel yet another opportunity slipping through my fingers. I pulled up outside her house and she shifted about in the passenger seat to get at the door handle and I knew it was now or never. I had to ask her. My heart gave a sickening thud when I realised this as I knew I'd be going in blind. No words of encouragement, no green light, no guaranteed answer. I just had to come straight out with it and hope she didn't screw her face up in disgust.

'Thanks for the lift,' she said stepping out on to the pavement. 'Bye.'

'Wait,' I yelled at her clambering from the car. 'Erm, do you drink?'

'Sorry?'

'I mean, you know, what do you fancy doing?'

Angela stared at me as I wrestled with my tongue.

'Doing?'

'Yes. With me. Would you like to have a drink with me?'

'I'm sorry, I've got to put the dinner on now.'

'Well look, come with me and I'll buy you dinner. Don't worry about it.'

'No, it's not for me,' she said looking back at the house and I felt my heart sag. 'It's for my mum.'

'What?' Had I heard right? 'Your mum?'

'Yes, I live with my mum. She's not very well. I look after her.'

This was fantastic news. Living with her mum. Definitely no fellas on the go then. I was still in with a chance. And what's more, she'd love me for not only putting up with her, but with her mum too. Well, by that I mean we could visit her sometimes, I wouldn't mind that. And I'd always be polite, so her old lady would like me and see that her daughter was well looked after. Things might be a little tricky in the short term for Angela, we wouldn't be able to go for a drink tonight, but I could pay for some home help, get her mum all taken care of so that she could spend her time with me.

In the light of this information I refound my optimism and asked her again.

'Well, how about tomorrow night, we could go out then if you like?'

'I can't.'

'The day after that?'

'Sorry.'

'What about during the day?'

'I'm working.'

'Don't worry about that…' I started to say, then wondered just how I was going to phrase it so that my reassurances about her financial situation didn't sound too much like bribery – or prostitution. 'What I mean is, you could take a day's holiday.'

'I can't, I don't get holiday.'

'Well, what about after dinner-time, in the evening?'

'That's when mum needs me the most.'

'Surely she can manage one night on her own!' I said, giving a voice to my thoughts.

'Sorry.'

We stood facing each other for a few desperate moments before I broke off my gaze and let Angela go. I couldn't hide my emotion as I suddenly felt nothing but crushing disappointment churning up my insides. I caught her eye again and cleared my throat to say goodbye, but nothing but a croak came out.

'See you,' she said.

'Yeah. Take care,' I conceded unhappily.

I climbed into the car and closed the door so softly that I had to reopen it and slam it shut. I slotted the car into gear and I was just about to pull away when Angela knocked on the passenger window. I wound it down.

'We could go out Thursday if you want. It's my day off.'

'Thursday?'

'Yes, in the afternoon. Mum's used to me being at work in the afternoon so it won't be a problem for her. If you still want to, of course?'

'Yes, yes,' I enthused. 'That would be brilliant!'

Steady on Ian, don't overdo it or nothing.

'I could come by and pick you up. What time?'

'One o'clock.'

'Okay, I'll see you next Thursday at one o'clock. I'll call by here.'

'Okay, see you then,' she smiled and hobbled up the garden path to her front door. I was so excited I didn't want to drive off until she'd disappeared inside.

I had a date.

I had a date with Angela. God, I could barely contain myself. I knew I could do it. A little persistence, I'd been right all along.

I had a date.

Angela.

Shit! What could we do?

7. Labour of love

I had what I thought was a stroke of genius and took Angela to the London Aquarium that first afternoon. It was the perfect non-pressure date. No sitting across a restaurant table staring at each other and wondering what to say. We could stroll around at our leisure, check out all the tanks and make fish small-talk if the conversation dried up. It was divine inspiration. See dates, particularly first dates, were always a minefield for me. I mean, what did you do? A meal? The pictures? The pub? What did couples do to get to know each other? Surely they couldn't spend their whole lives stuffing their faces, watching films and drinking their lights out, but really, what else was there?

Now, I knew the Aquarium wasn't any sort of long-term solution, I'd still have to come up with something good to do the next week (and it would have to be as good, if not better, than the Aquarium), but it was a good start. She'd see that I was thoughtful, intelligent, sensitive, not your average run-of-the-mill get 'em drunk and get 'em off brainless moron. I was someone serious. Someone to know, someone to trust, which was all well and good, but of course, the true beauty of it was that if she liked the Aquarium I could take her to London Zoo, the National Gallery, Hampton Court, the London Dungeons, Madame Tussauds until she knew and trusted me well enough to go to bed with me.

I picked her up at one o'clock and we drove to the Aquarium in near silence. Angela showed neither excitement nor disappointment at the prospect of seeing so many fish in one place so I put it down to first date nerves. I had to remind myself that for Angela it was a first date too and she was probably just as nervous as me.

The Aquarium itself was everything I had expected; colourful, interesting, beautiful, but still Angela seemed unmoved. We walked around for about half an hour with nothing more meaningful than 'quick look, there's a red one' passing between us before Angela complained that her foot ached and she needed to sit down. It hadn't even occurred to me that with her foot the way it was a day walking around was doing her no favours. No wonder she'd been quiet. Bang went London Zoo and Hampton Court. Mind you, at the same time so did any danger of her dragging me off to a disco, so it wasn't all bad news. The fact remained though that suddenly our choice of dates had become somewhat limited. But then again, this was all Angela's fault, I was completely blameless. Surely it followed then that Angela would be forced to make more of an effort to compensate for imposing these restrictions on me.

How wrong I was.

We found the cafeteria, bought a couple of coffees and suddenly the day turned into every date I'd ever been on.

The conversation disappeared faster than the drinks and soon I found myself staring at Angela trying to work out if I'd done something to upset her.

'It's an interesting place though, isn't it?' I said.

'Yes,' she replied softly.

'How's your coffee?'

'Fine.'

'Is it?… Mine's fine too,' I said, taking a sip. 'Do you want a cake?'

'No thank you.'

'Are you sure, there's chocolate ones and everything.'

'I'm fine thanks.'

'Well, if you change your mind just say something and I'll get us both one.'

'Okay.'

'What, okay you want one?'

'No I'm fine.'

'Right, I get you.' I looked around for a bit before starting a new line of enquiry. 'How long have you been a cleaner?'

'About six years.'

'Oh right, where did you work before?'

'At a school in Dulwich.'

'Really! Hmmm. Did you like that?'

'Yes, it was fine.'

'So why did you get a job at The Aviary?'

'Better money.'

'Are you short of money then because I…' Angela dropped her gaze awkwardly and I suddenly realised I'd stepped on the first mine and lost both ankles. We both went quiet for a few moments before I tried to make amends. 'Did you always want to be a cleaner?'

'No,' Angela replied. 'Not really.'

'What did you want to do?' I asked.

'I don't know,' she shrugged.

'I thought all little girls wanted to be princesses or veterinary assistants or something.'

Angela just pushed out her lip to indicate she didn't have an opinion on the matter.

'Really?' I said nodding my head. The thirty seconds passed without comment.

What was the matter with her?

If she didn't want to be with me, why had she asked me out? I mean, what was her problem? I'd met shy girls in my time but Angela took the fucking biscuit barrel. Was she on word rations or something? It played on my mind that in all the time I'd known her, the ignorant cow hadn't asked me so much as one single solitary question. Nothing. Was she really that incurious about me?

I could feel it burning me up and squeezing my jaws together as I watched her fiddle with her plastic stirrer.

Our second date would be easier, I told myself, once we'd got the awkwardness of the first date out of the way. In fact, it would even give us something to talk about. Then again, maybe not.

'So what did you want to be?' I tried again, a little more sharply this time.

'What do you mean?' she replied, and at least I had my first question.

'When you were a little girl, what was it you wanted to be?'

Angela sat in silence for a good long time and I thought she had taken to ignoring me altogether before she finally replied: 'Happy.'

I studied her face as she returned her attentions to her splintered plastic stirrer and saw for myself the great unhappiness in her heart.

'Does that mean you're not happy now?' I asked.

'Not much, no.' Her demeanour sagged even further and right then and there I so wanted to be the one to make her happy. She was like me in so many ways, all she needed was a little love. I could give her that love. She could return it in kind. We'd found each other for a reason.

'What would it take to make you happy?' I asked her hopefully.

Angela looked up with confusion etched across her face.

'It's just a question. I'd like to know,' I reassured her.

'I wish my mum was all better,' she told me.

I nodded with empathy in the hope that this would hide my disappointment.

Mum? All better? What?

This wasn't the answer I'd been looking for. I mean, I knew she wasn't just going to come straight out with it and say: 'It's you Ian, take me away from all of this,' but I thought it might at least be something I could get involved with. A holiday. An operation for her foot. A man in her bed. Security. Some bloke who needs sorting out. Anything.

But her fucking mum?

Who could give a shit about her? And that wasn't being harsh or anything, but come on, how old was Angela anyway? Twenty-eight? Thirty? It was time to move on, think about herself.

'Of course that's how you'd think,' I could hear my own mum saying. 'You've never thought about anyone but yourself your whole life, have you?'

I blocked her out before she grew too loud and attempted to get to the heart of Angela's problem. Maybe she just needed a few words of advice or a nudge in the right direction from someone who'd been through the same sort of thing.

Not that I had, but she wasn't to know that.

'What's wrong with your mum?' I asked. Angela looked embarrassed as she answered, which was a positive sign.

'Alzheimer's,' she told me, holding my gaze. 'She's not too bad at the moment, some days she can almost cope, but other days...' Angela trailed off thinking about those other days. 'Other days it's hard. Very hard.'

I reached a hand across the table and laid it on top of hers to demonstrate my concern. Angela left her hand there to be held and only pulled it away when I said:

'You know, it sounds to me like she should be in a hospital.'

'My mum doesn't need to be in a hospital, she just needs me.'

'I'm sorry, I didn't mean it like that, I was just thinking of you. It must be a terrible strain on you, what with the job and... everything else,' everything else being the code phrase for 'your big foot'.

Angela snapped back. She didn't see it that way and it wasn't a strain and she could cope and her mum didn't need anyone else but her and all the rest of it, so that all I could do was back-pedal until she'd accepted that I meant no harm by my remarks.

At least I'd found a little chink in her armour.

'When was she diagnosed with it?' I asked softly.

'Six years ago,' Angela replied, staring through the table.

'Six years.' I shook my head with sympathy and told her how sorry I was, while I wondered how long that gave the old girl to go. How long did Alzheimer's last? Six take-away from what? I decided not to ask. There was just no sympathetic way of wording it.

'Do you have any brothers or sisters?' I asked. She didn't.

'What about a dad?' Long dead. 'So you're all alone then?' I said, pouring it on.

'No, I've got mum!' she told me stopping me in my tracks. I had to be careful, I'd dealt her out already simply because she didn't have total control over her loaf, but to Angela she was still a person. In fact, she was the only person. It would be hard getting her to see otherwise.

We sat and talked for the next half an hour about Alzheimer's, mother-daughter responsibilities and mashed foods before Angela panicked about how late it was getting and asked if we could go. I dropped her off at her door and she almost didn't even look back as she got out of the car until I asked her if she wanted to go out next Thursday too.

'Well, er. I don't know. I'll have to see how mum is,' she said shifting awkwardly.

'I had a really nice time,' I told her. 'I'd really like to see you again.'

Angela tried to Umm and Ahh herself a little slack, though when she saw there was none forthcoming she conceded to see me again.

I hated seeing her squirm, but I was doing it for her.

The following week we went for a meal and by and large we got on okay. Most of the conversation was taken up by her mum and all that old stuff, which was a bit of a chore at times, particularly when she was telling me about all the things her mum had suddenly remembered on Monday only for her to forget again on Tuesday, but at least we were talking.

The week after that we went to the pictures, and after that it was another meal, then it was a go on the London Eye and a pizza and so forth until one day I stopped and realised that we'd been seeing each other for more than two months. Every Thursday for three hours in the afternoon we'd gone out and talked and laughed (yes, even laughed) and grown closer, but when I jotted it up in my head we'd still shared little more than a day and a bit together. That couldn't be right, could it? Other couples saw more of each other over the course of one weekend than I'd seen of Angela ever.

It wasn't fair. How the hell were we ever going to get to know and love each other at this rate? I worked it out in my head that by the time we'd put in enough hours together to say that we truly knew one another, I'd have fucking Alzheimer's myself. It wasn't fair.

That Thursday I pestered Angela into taking a Saturday night off to be with me but pushed so hard that she ended up in tears. 'I'm sorry,' I pleaded with her. 'I'm sorry, please forgive me, I can't help but want to be with you.'

'I thought you understood,' she said, her voice full of frustration. 'That's not going to happen.'

We drove home in silence.

I feared for the following Thursday. I'd grown so fond of our little dates that I planned my whole weeks around them. It was no wonder the months had flown by. Logan had had nothing for me in all that time so all I did any given week was exercise, map out the next date in my head and read up about Alzheimer's on the web. I didn't know what I'd do if she told me she didn't want to see me again. My fears were allayed when she leaned over to the driver's seat, gave me my kiss and told me she'd see me next week.

The next date passed without any real incident and I was just beginning to relax and think we were all back to normal when she cancelled the following week. Her mum had had a fall while she was out with me one Thursday and bruised up her hip. Angela was beside herself. She jacked in her job at The Aviary, curled back into the tightly-knit ball she'd been when we'd first started dating and put the block on anything that got her out of the house for more than half an hour.

I was heartbroken.

She'd come to mean so much to me that when our Thursdays went for a burton a lump of me went with them. I couldn't even see her to reason with her, she had to make a clean break of it, she told me 'And I'm sorry, it's not you, I love you, I just can't see you… it was just never meant to be… and I wish I hadn't started this… and there's nothing we can do. Goodbye.'

She loved me!

She said it. She loved me…

… but there's nothing we can do?

That was too cruel. Not only was it too cruel, it was also not true.

There was definitely something I could do.

8. A kindness

Angela's mum struggled in my grasp as I dragged her towards the stairs. She was stronger than I'd expected and more slippery than a bag of eels but she wasn't getting out of this one. Angela might've treated her with kid gloves, but mine were plain black and leather and putting up with no nonsense. We struggled at the top of the stairs for a few moments while I tried to get a decent hold on her.

'Oh-h-h-h, Angela,' she kept pleading. 'Help me!'

'Be quiet. Be quiet!' I whispered, trying to reassure her, then leaned back on one leg to counterbalance myself and threw Angela's mum headlong down the stairs. I'd launched her in such a way as to ensure that her head bore the full brunt of her landing and heard a loud crack as it met the stairs six steps from the bottom. She came to rest pretty quickly in the hallway just a few short feet from the front door and turned the surrounding carpet scarlet in no time at all.

I felt her pulse.

There was still a very faint beating. I couldn't very well drag her up the stairs and send her on her way again, what with all the blood everywhere, so I put my hand over her mouth and nose until all signs of life disappeared.

I looked at my watch. Angela had left for the local shop ten minutes ago. If it was just a loaf of bread or a tin of soup she was picking up she could be back in less than another five, and if there was one thing guaranteed to put the permanent mockers on our relationship it was catching me curing her mum of Alzheimer's. Now that would've been ironic. The one thing standing between us before was her mum. I solve that little problem for her and someone else gets to enjoy the benefits.

Well, that wouldn't happen. I checked that the coast was all clear and left via the back garden.

I didn't want to leave it too long in case I was pipped at the post, so I phoned a few days later to see how she was.

Out of the blue.

'There, there, there, let it all out,' I said, stroking her hair. My sleeve was almost soaked through with all the tears she'd shed but I didn't move it. I let her stay where she was and bawl and blub and cry for all she was worth because she was in the best place for it – my arms. 'Shhhh, shhhh, shhhh.'

'It's all my fault,' she sobbed over and over again. 'It's all my fault.'

'Come on now, don't talk nonsense, it's not like you pushed her down the stairs yourself, is it! It was an accident.' Angela's head was on my chest so she couldn't see my face as I looked away and remembered. 'Something like this was bound to happen, you couldn't watch over her twenty-four hours a day. It was just a tragic accident.'

But Angela was having none of it. She blamed herself for everything: for not being there when she'd fallen; for not putting her in a care home like everyone had urged her to do; for only telling her mum she loved her a hundred times a day instead of two hundred – for being in hospital with her foot when her father had died, which was where I figured it had all begun. She tore herself out of my arms and ran upstairs to her mum's room, where she locked the door and stayed there until I'd gone. She refused to even see me the next day and told me to 'fuck off' the day after that (language I'd never heard her use before), and it wasn't another two days before she'd calmed down a little and agreed to cry in my arms again.

Angela spent the best part of the next week, up to the funeral and beyond it, mourning and torturing herself and trying to push me away and I was just about to give the whole thing up as a lost cause when I heard her laughing.

I'd been in the kitchen making us a cup of tea and I heard her in the living room laughing away to herself like a schoolgirl. I rushed through to see what she was laughing at and saw it was *Only Fools and Horses*. The telly had been on in the background. I hadn't even been paying it any attention as I'd been focused on Angela, but Angela had been lost in it and was now crying with laughter as Del and Rodney walked around this smashed-up chandelier. At the end of the episode she retreated into her shell again, no doubt to chide herself for daring to laugh less than three weeks after her mum had exhibited her brains on the hallway carpet, but the steam valve had definitely turned. Just a little, for just a few seconds, but it had turned.

The next day I bought her every episode of *Only Fools and Horses* ever released on DVD.

And then I bought her a DVD.

'You've been so very good to me, I don't know what I would've done without you,' Angela said satisfyingly.

'There, there, that's all right, I was glad I could be there for you. I care about you so very much, I couldn't bear to see you unhappy.' I gave her my sincerest smile and watched as it was mirrored on Angela's face. 'Here,' I said and topped up her glass again. Angela took a couple of big sips and held my gaze affectionately.

'Are you not having any more yourself?' she asked when I left my glass empty.

'No, one's enough for me. I very rarely drink. I don't really like it,' I told her, thinking that I'd told her the same thing at least twice before. Well, she'd been pretty single-minded in those days, it was excusable that she'd forgotten.

'Me neither. But I hope you don't mind if I push the boat out tonight. I think I could probably do with it.'

'No, no, not at all. Anchors away,' I urged her. Angela took another sip and let out a deep sigh. The transformation had taken less than a week. Only the previous Saturday she'd been smashing cups in the kitchen and deliberately injuring her hand on the draining board, but now she had the calmness of acceptance. She'd come to terms with her loss and, for the first time in months, was aware she had a future, and not just a past. Obviously, it had taken more than *Only Fools and Horses* to get over her despair, but not that much more. A sympathetic shoulder and time, that's all. The simple fact was that no mind, no matter how devoted, could grieve indefinitely. It had just been Angela's time to move on.

And now it was my time too.

I'd done everything right by her. I'd stood by her when she was distraught, I'd listened to her ramblings, I quashed her self-rebukes and I'd put up with her outbursts. I doubt there was a man in the world who could've been a better friend to her than I had been through those difficult months. She was my leukaemia girl and I'd proved myself to her beyond question.

So now it was my turn to take, her turn to give. And I didn't mean sex or anything as gratuitous as that. I simply meant love. Love, support, understanding, companionship. Nothing every other person on the planet didn't have a right to expect, so why should I be any different? Why should it be so criminal that I should want to find someone to spend my life with?

And now I had.

'You're the kindest man I've ever known. I don't deserve you,' Angela said.

'You do, I promise, you do,' I reassured her as I didn't want her convincing herself that she wasn't good enough for me. 'I love you, Angela. I adore you and just want to be with you.'

'Why would you want to be with me? I'm nothing. You're so kind and wonderful you could have any woman you wanted.'

Point of order: I hated it when women said this to me because it showed a fundamental lack of understanding on their part. I'd tried, believe me, I'd tried. If it were true and I could have any woman I wanted then I'd probably be off having them all wouldn't

I, not sat here talking to just one. 'You're so kind. Kind and wonderful. Kind guys can have any woman!' Oh really, is that right is it? I'd been kind my whole life and never got anywhere. What was I supposed to do, walk up to women on the street and tell them how kind and wonderful I was? If they're not interested, then they're not interested, so they're hardly going to give you a month's trial to see just how kind and wonderful you are, are they? Christ, did Angela even remember how she treated me those first few weeks? Awful. Like utter crap. I'd had to murder her mum before she saw how kind and wonderful I was.

'I don't want any other woman,' I told her. 'I want you.'

'I want you too but...' she started to say, then let it trail away.

'But what? What's the problem now?' I demanded and immediately regretted including 'now' in the sentence.

'Nothing. I don't know. I'm sorry, I can't think straight, my mind's all over the place.'

'Angela, I love you,' I told her again, this time really emphasising it, as if that was the problem.

'Please, don't keep saying that,' she said screwing her face up as if my words had just struck her in the guts.

'I don't understand. What? What is it?'

Angela looked at me for a very long time and slowly un-wrinkled her face. 'It's not you,' she said. 'It's me.'

'What is? Angela, what's wrong? What have I said?'

'You haven't said anything, I promise. I'm sorry, I don't mean anything by it. I just get really frightened and confused sometimes. I mean, my mum only passed away a few weeks ago.'

'I know,' I replied.

'Oh, let's forget all this, it's just the drink talking, that's all,' she laughed, suddenly brightening. 'Don't pay any attention to me.' Angela fixed me hard in the eye and went all serious again. 'I do care about you a great deal. You know that, don't you?'

'Yes, I know that. And I want you to know that I care for you too. That I'll do all I can to make you happy. I'll always be here for you, and I'll never hurt you.'

'I know that,' she said and a tear appeared at the corner of her eye. She turned away to wipe the tear up with her napkin, then turned back and said something that made my heart leap in my chest.

'Do you want to go to bed?'

'Yes. Yes, I do,' I said, my mind in a swoon at the reality of it all. And then up we went.

Was this really it? Had I really found the woman of my dreams at last? I thought I had.

But then, the path of true love never runs straight, does it?

9. Arrangements for Angela

'We need you to kill her!'

Logan handed me a picture of Angela as if I'd never seen her before.

'What?'

'Sorry, lad, but it can't be helped. Orders from The Man,' Logan shrugged his shoulders apologetically.

'Danny, I'm seeing her. She's my girlfriend. My fiancée even,' I pleaded with him.

'I know you are, that's why you've got to do it, it can't be anyone else.'

'It wouldn't be right,' Eddie said behind me nervously. 'Any of us taking out your bird. Wouldn't be proper.' Logan had clearly anticipated a potential violent reaction, which was why Eddie was standing behind me with his .38 not very well concealed in his jacket pocket.

'But I love her,' I told Logan. 'Please Danny.'

'What, you think I haven't had to kill people I've loved before? I know how you're feeling, but it's just an emotion, that's all. A weakness. Put it out of your mind and think of it as just another job. It's important. You know I wouldn't ask otherwise, we don't kill people for the fun of it. It has to be done.'

'She's just a cleaner…' I started to say but Logan cut me off.

'She's not just a cleaner, Ian, she's a police informer. She's been in the Old Bill's pocket since the day she started here. Christ only knows what she's told them.'

'No, that's not true,' I said staring at her photograph.

'It is true,' Eddie told me. 'Our man in CID has it on the up and up. Blue Circle concrete.'

'But, it doesn't make any sense. She had a sick mother,' I said, then thought better about going down that road.

'Yes, and she needed the money to take care of her. Desperate people do desperate things,' Logan said eyeing me very carefully. I wondered if he thought I was a desperate person. What desperate things had he imagined I might do? This was a very dangerous situation and I suddenly became aware that I had to be extremely careful in what I said. In Logan's world, you were either in or out. And you didn't want to be out.

I tried to reason with him one last time.

'But, surely, she doesn't work here any more. Problem solved.'

'I wish it was as easy as that,' Logan said sadly. 'I truly do, but it's not. See, she's gotten involved with one of my most trusted and able men, and that compromises the whole organisation.'

I thought about this in silence for a moment while Logan stared straight into my eyes.

'Oh my God, it's me,' I suddenly realised. 'I've killed her.'

'It's not your fault, son, you weren't to know.'

'But, I have though, haven't I, I've killed her?'

It's a terrible thing to know that you and you alone are responsible for the death of someone you love. It's more guilt than any one man should have to deal with. A pit the size of the Grand Canyon opened up inside my stomach and I felt like I was going to throw up. I'd killed her. I'd loved her, now I'd killed her. I wondered if this was how Angela had felt when she'd got back from the shops and found her sick and elderly charge had charged headfirst down the stairs.

'I'll stop seeing her,' I told Logan, but I couldn't lie to myself. I'd already dismissed that idea as unworkable before I'd even said it on the lines of 'if I can't have her, nobody can'.

'Sorry, Ian, it's gone too far for that.' Logan sat opposite me with his fingers entwined and said nothing more until I'd found my composure.

'Do I have to, Danny?'

He looked away, unable to hold my gaze.

'I'm afraid so, whether it's you or whether it's someone else, Angela Hawthorne has to be taken out. It's best if it's you who did it, we can't have any personal vendettas inside the organisation, you have to see that.'

Danny and I sat in silence for a good long time. I held the black and white photograph of Angela a few inches from my face and watched as two tears fell on to her head as if I'd aimed them. At that moment, there in that photograph, Angela looked more beautiful and precious than she'd ever looked before. This was the woman I loved. This was my lady, my partner; the woman who, only last night, had lain naked in my arms, kissed me lovingly and told me that she wanted to spend the rest of her life with me.

Did Logan seriously believe I would kill her for him?

'I'll do it,' I told him.

I closed my hand over Angela's mouth so that she wouldn't scream and woke her up. She immediately started struggling beneath the weight of my body but she wasn't strong enough to budge me. Her eyes finally penetrated the darkness and recognised my face.

'Shhh, shhh, be quiet, you're in terrible danger,' I whispered to her. 'I'm here to help.' Angela stopped her struggling and lay quiet. I removed my hand from her mouth and held a finger to my lips.

'What's wrong?' she whispered back.

'Someone's coming to kill you,' I told her. 'We haven't much time.'

'Kill me? What, I don't understand, why would anyone want to kill me?'

'They think you're a police informer,' I said and pulled her suitcase down off the top of the wardrobe. 'Come on, get dressed.'

'A police informer? That's ridiculous, I mean what have I got to inform about?' Angela protested swinging her legs over the bed and rubbing her eyes. 'I don't even know any policemen.'

'It doesn't matter if it's true or not, all that matters is that they believe it.'

'Who are they? And how do you know all this?'

'They are your former employers at The Aviary. It's run by gangsters, didn't you know? They've convinced themselves that you've been eavesdropping at keyholes and phoning the Old Bill.' I stopped piling her clothes into the suitcase and stood and faced her. It was the moment I'd been dreading. The moment of truth.

Or at least, a sort of truth.

'As for me, well I work for them. It's where I met you, remember? The silly bastards didn't realise we were, you know... seeing each other.'

How do you tell someone that it's you who's been dispatched to kill them? That in order to get out of that office with your life intact, you'd had to agree to end theirs? Whether or not you ever intended to go through with it becomes irrelevant. Mortal mistrust suddenly enters the equation. Put it like this; if someone told you that they'd been ordered to murder you, but had decided not to go through with it, and you were halfway down a cliff, and they lowered down a rope, would you let go of your safe handholds and grab hold of the rope?

I wouldn't.

'You're a gangster?' Angela said with surprise.

'No, not really, I'm just an adviser, really. I help them buy property and stuff,' I said through my teeth.

'You're a gangster's estate agent?' she responded, almost sounding disappointed.

'Erm, yeah, if you like,' I told her. 'Whatever.'

'Why would they tell an estate agent?' she said, suddenly suspicious.

'Well I'm not actually an estate agent, I'm more of an executive.'

'An executive gangster?'

'Look, shall we get going or wait until we're riddled with bullets?' I snapped.

'Sorry,' she replied. 'I'm frightened and babbling.' I walked over to her and gave her a hug and could feel her trembling like a leaf against my stomach.

'Shhh,' I whispered in her ear as I kissed her hair. 'It'll be okay. I promise you, I won't let you get hurt. Trust me, trust me.'

We finished packing what essentials we could carry and got Angela dressed up in warm clothes and left via the back door. It was almost three o'clock and a cold moonless night. A stiff breeze stirred the trees and kicked about the litter in the back alleyway, making it near impossible to detect any premeditated movement lurking in the shadows.

It was a night for murder if ever I'd seen one.

'Stay close,' I whispered to Angela as I checked to see that the alleyway was all clear. I stepped out into the near blackness and waited for my eyes to adjust before I continued. If Logan had planned something for us it would happen now, when we were exposed and vulnerable. Anywhere there could be an assassin waiting: up in a neighbour's window; behind the bins; at the end of the alleyway; in one of the parked cars. I covered them all with my silenced Glock and almost whacked three cats on the way to my car, before we were safely seat-belted in and moving.

'Where are we going?' Angela asked.

'France.'

'Wait, I haven't got a passport,' she suddenly flipped. Women are such petty animals, aren't they? 'Your life's in danger. There are men all over the place who want to kill you. France is safety.' 'Hold on, I haven't got the proper documentation – and a library book that needs taking back. I'll have to stay here and get killed.'

'Don't worry about that, I can get you one over there, I've got a few contacts.'

'Over there, but how are we going to get there if I haven't got a passport?'

'I've got a boat down in Kent. We'll sail across.'

'A boat? What if it capsizes? I can't swim.'

'It's not a pedallo Angela, it's a boat. It ain't going to capsize.

Look, just stop worrying, we're in the clear now. We'll be in France before lunch-time, then we can go anywhere you like. I've got plenty of money, so we'll live it up for a bit and see the world. What do you say?'

'Can we go to Egypt? I've always wanted to go to Egypt,' she said all excitedly.

'Then we'll go to Egypt,' I told her and we drove on into the night.

That was fairly typical, I thought to myself. Trust her to want to go to a country full of horrible mummies.

We got to the boat some time after half-four and quickly got stowed aboard. All the time I kept a careful vigil over the surrounding harbour just in case Logan had anticipated this move. Everything was quiet. The only sounds were the roar of the sea and the breaking of the waves on the harbour defences. It was going to be a choppy trip.

The boat rolled about as we clambered in and Angela, hardly nimble on her feet as it was, was very unsettled.

'Wait, are you sure about this?' she asked.

'Don't worry, I've done it a dozen times,' I replied.

'What about your car?'

'What about it?'

'What if someone finds it there? They'll know we're in France,' she pointed out.

'What do you want me to do with it, bring it with us? Shoot my gun in the air and chase it away? Forget it, it's not important. Just get down out of sight at the back of the boat and stay there.'

Angela's lip wobbled as she laid down on her side behind the engine. She was clearly worried about the crossing and doing all she could to delay the inevitable. I cast us on our way and ruffled her hair to lend some reassurance, but it didn't really do the trick. Hair ruffling very rarely does.

The engine struggled as we fought our way out to sea, through the harbour defences and past several buoys before we'd made it into open waters. The boat rocked and crashed about through the chop, causing Angela to vomit all over the deck – nausea and fear, a colourful combination. I looked aft and saw her bent double and groaning over a sliding pile of puke, the picture of complete misery, and wondered if this was her first time outside of England.

I put this and all other thoughts out of my mind and concentrated on the sea.

At three miles out I stopped the engine and went back to check on Angela. Her hair was splattered with sick and her face was white and puffy.

'I'm sorry,' she looked up and said. 'I couldn't help it. I don't feel well.' Angela screwed up her face and started bawling. It had all been too much for her. Only a few hours ago she'd been tucked up in bed, safe and sound, dreaming of the happier times ahead, then suddenly she was on a boat, running for her life and leaving everything she knew behind her. Her alarm wasn't even due to go off for another three hours. She must've wondered a few times if it was all just a horrible dream.

I cupped a hand around her chin and wiped the tears away with my thumb.

'That's okay sweetheart. Here, lean over the back of the boat, you'll feel better for it.'

'No, please, I'll fall in.' I laughed at that.

'You won't fall in, you're in the boat. Just poke your head over the tailboard if you're feeling sick. I'll go and make us a nice cup of coffee to warm us up.'

Angela did as I told her and turned around slowly and peered over the side, all the time keeping a good firm grip on the wooden rail. 'It's so cold,' she croaked.

'I know it is, my darling,' I replied and put two bullets into the back of her head.

She wouldn't have known or felt a thing. I'd kept my promise to her. I grabbed her torso to stop her falling back inside the boat and splashing the deck and my clothes with blood and tied her in place until the worst of the seepage had stopped. Twenty minutes later I was rolling her into the same waters she'd been so terrified of.

'Goodbye Angela,' I told her wiping a tear from my eye. 'I'm sorry about this, I really am.'

I stared at her face one last time as she sank beneath the black surface; so beautiful, so captivating. My heart felt like lead at the thought of never seeing her again.

So why had I done it?

I've asked myself that same question a thousand times since and the only real answer I've ever come up with is: I'm a hitman, it's what I do.

It sounds a little bit pathetic I know, but at the end of the day that's what it boiled down to. There were simply too many reasons to kill Angela, and not enough to keep her alive. And in circumstances like those, I had to obey my primary instincts. I didn't have to like it, I just had to do it. But then, that was something I was well used to by this time.

Besides, she was a police informant. How long would it have been before she'd betrayed me to the cops? She'd been using me all along, just like Logan had said. She'd never loved me, it was all too clear now. I'd had to protect myself. And not just myself, I'd had to protect the organisation. In fact, the truth of the matter was I'd had to protect myself from Angela and the organisation. It was a minor miracle JB hadn't decided to simply do away with the pair of us together, just in case I'd been gotten to through Angela. Cut out the cancer clean, so to speak. No risks. There was still a good chance of that happening, in fact. I had to be on my guard.

All these things and still it didn't make it any easier.

I lowered Angela into the water and watched as she slipped into the blackness and disappeared. My eyes welled up and I wiped more tears away with my salty fingers, making them sting and water all the more.

Had I done the right thing?

Of course I had. She was a liability and had to be silenced, Logan had made it plain.

But had I?

How would I ever know? Should I have taken the risk? But I couldn't, what right did I have to make that decision? It had been JB's call as it always was and he must've had good cause to order such action taken.

'We don't kill for the fun of it,' Logan had said and he was right. We didn't. So, JB must've had it on good authority that Angela presented a very real risk. And that was good enough for me. The proof was in the pudding, there simply was no other reason to have her killed. But still…

Had I?

I couldn't help but think over the fact that I'd killed an entire family. An elderly sick mother, a kindly caring daughter. A whole household of history, life and loves – and I'd wiped it out. What was wrong with me?

It was yet another thing to push to the back of my mind and try to forget about.

I started up the engine and headed back into shore. It was just starting to get light and the wind was dropping a tad, levelling out the seas. I hadn't gone more than a few yards when an enormous underwater explosion followed by a great torrent threatened to tip the boat over and me into the water. I held on to the wheel while the boat righted itself and wiped some of the splash from my face.

The mouth bomb worked, but I think I used a little bit too much Semtex.

10. Night of the demons

I've said before that I don't drink. Well that's true, but sometimes I drank. There's a difference, which might not be clear at first, so I'll explain. As a rule, I don't touch alcohol as I don't really like it or its effect on me and I like to stay fit – I need to stay fit. Occasionally though, when things get too unbearable and it hurts to stay lucid, I have a drink. For one night and one night only, I buy a bottle of whatever label catches my eye (usually scotch) and get my unhappiness roaring drunk. It's not something I do very often, maybe once or twice a year, but it's very therapeutic.

You have to touch rock bottom before you can start to pick yourself up again.

So, when I got home from the harbour, I locked all my weapons away in the safe, stuck the key in a padded envelope and posted it to myself and went and bought a bottle of Bell's, a bottle of Smirnoff and a bottle of Gordon's. The thing with the guns and the safe, that's for my own safety. I can't allow myself access to a weapon when I'm in my drunken state otherwise I'd top myself, I know I would.

'Having a party?' the Indian behind the counter asked me.

'Yes, if you like,' I told him.

Though only me, my self-pity and everyone I'd ever killed was invited.

I secured the house, locked all the doors and windows, drew the curtains and poured myself a drink. I hated the taste of scotch. That horrible, malty, nasal aftertaste lingered in my sinuses and coated my tongue and made me want to retch. It always took a few to reacquire the taste, though the burn felt good on the back of my throat and I drained the contents of the glass in two more gulps.

'It's so cold,' Angela suddenly said again and I quickly refilled the glass. 'It's so, so cold.'

I saw her face beneath the water, lifeless and pale. I couldn't get the image out of my head. I tried to think of her happy and laughing, though when I finally managed that, it was even worse. I'd never see her smiling again, not that I'd seen her smile much in the past, she was always a bit of a misery-guts – but no more than me.

'You're the kindest man I've ever known,' she told me over and over again as I drank my scotch and tried not to think about what might've been.

Bizarre thoughts occurred to me as I drank: I imagined Angela and Janet and Rose slipping their bonds underwater and drifting about until they bumped into each other on the sea floor to talk about me.

'Oh yes, he's a bastard that one, look what he did to me,' Rose tells them. 'He strangled me with a rope, at least you got off lightly with a head shot.'

'Lightly?' Janet says. 'I curse the day he came into my shop. He made himself out to be such a mister nice guy, buying me dinner, giving me his pudding, when all along he never gave a shit about me. He doesn't give a shit about anyone, that one.'

'You're right there,' Angela says drifting up. 'Do anything for me? Take care of me? Love me? The only person he loves is himself.'

'Every man I've ever been out with was better than Ian.'

'It takes more than giving up your pudding to make you a man.'

'Ian only killed me because of my foot. If I'd had a normal foot, there's no way he would've killed me. All the times he said he didn't care about my foot and then he goes and kills me. He's just the same as every other man I've ever met.'

'He's worse.'

'A good man wouldn't have strangled me, a good man would've taken care of me.'

'A good man would've thought nothing about giving me his pudding, not made such a big deal about it.'

'A good man wouldn't even have noticed my foot. I'm a woman. I need a man. A good man. He's not even a man.'

'He's just a loser.'

'An evil pathetic little nobody.'

I knocked the half-empty bottle on to the floor as I fell off my chair and landed heavily in the glass pieces. I tried to clamber to my feet but my body weighed a ton and every time I hauled myself off the floor, I lost my balance and fell back into the glass.

I rolled over on to my side, picked several shards out of my arm and watched with fascination as the blood poured out of the cuts and ran in small rivers down to my elbow.

'That's not a cut,' Rose told me. 'That's not even a scratch, that's nothing.'

'You want to see a cut,' Janet said. 'Have a look at my head. Until you've got one of these you don't even know what a cut is.'

'He couldn't handle that,' Angela goaded me. 'We can handle that but he couldn't. He can dish it out, but he can't take it himself. He's a fucking coward.'

'I'm not going to shoot myself,' I told them all. 'Not now, not never.'

'No, we know you're not. You're not man enough to,' they all shouted at once.

'You can't even tempt me.'

'No, because you're selfish. You've always been selfish, ever since you were a baby.'

'I'm not selfish.'

'You are, look at this,' Angela said, pulling her hair back to reveal two golfball-sized bullet holes in the back of her head. 'This is not the work of a selfish man?'

'I need a drink.'

'If you hadn't have locked it in the safe you could've drunk that cyanide. It would've been very quick, you wouldn't have felt a thing.'

'I'm not going to kill myself!'

'Why not? Nobody loves you, you're all alone in the world, no one would care, and you'd be saving a lot of people a lot of unhappiness. How many more women will you end up killing if you don't do the only decent thing you can do?'

'No! I'm not going to do it, I don't want to do it. Please!'

'In your shitty, worthless, insignificant life, it is the one and only thing you can do to redeem yourself. It's too late for us, but you can save others.'

'People would finally respect you.'

'Yes, in a way, you'd be a hero. And you've always wanted to be a hero, haven't you?'

'A live hero, not a dead one. What's the point in being a hero if you're not around to enjoy it?'

'But all the best heroes are dead.'

'And good luck to them.'

'Is it because you're scared?'

'No, I'm not scared.'

'There's nothing to it. It doesn't hurt.'

'Go on, shoot yourself and see.'

'No.'

'Give it a go.'

'No.'

'We'll be waiting for you.'

'I can't, all the guns are locked away.'

'Get the key.'

'It's in the post.'

'No, it's only in the box. The collection doesn't come for another hour, you could get it if you really wanted to, you've got time.'

'Get the key.'

'Just get it, you don't have to do anything once you've got it. Just go and get it.'

I cracked open the Smirnoff and took a big gulp. I could just go and get it I supposed, just to have it, just to shut them up. I'd put it upstairs and keep well away from it, but at least I'd have it. I looked at my watch. Fifty minutes. Time was on my side. But if I had it, might I then shoot myself?

No, I wouldn't do that.

Would I?

I didn't want to, that I firmly believed. But what if they had a point? How many more lives was I going to ruin? How much was enough? What reasons did I have for going on? I couldn't think of any offhand. My only reason for being, it seemed, was to kill for Logan. I had no family, no friends, no chance of ever finding someone to share my life. Why prolong the agony?

Why couldn't I just find someone to be with?

Oh God, I'd loved Angela. If only she'd known. I'd loved every inch of her body. And I didn't care about her foot, I'd loved her foot. She was so beautiful, so sexy. That first time we'd made love, I'd never known feelings that powerful. I'd been so nervous, so excited. Her skin was so perfect, I'd touched her all over. Her breasts. Her legs. Her thighs. The way she'd held me. Taken charge. Indulged herself fully.

I'd do anything to have her here with me now. Anything...

An enormous sense of shame and self-loathing swept over me as I wiped up the sticky result of my trip down Memory Lane. How low could I get? Masturbating over the remnants of a lost affair. Was this all Angela had meant to me? The life, the love, the trust she gave to me and I honour her with a wank? At that moment I hated myself.

They were right, I was no man. I was a loser. A useless, pathetic, nasty, little nothing. Maybe I should get it over with, do myself in, blow my brains out, do the world a favour. Angela was right, they were all right. Now for the first time in my life I could see things clearly. There was no point in hanging around. I was miserable and I was making everyone else miserable. It would never change, it would always be the same. I was scum, I was vermin, I was nothing. I'd killed plenty of people in my time, so why couldn't I kill myself?

How hard could it be?

I had forty minutes left. I could get to the postbox no problem. Unlock the safe, stick a gun in my mouth and bang, that's it.

It would be so easy. Why hadn't I done it before?

I'd do it, I'd get the key. Definitely. I'd thought about it so many times in the past, well this time there would be no bottling out. I'd do it. I'd eat a bullet. In fact, I could hardly wait.

This was it. This was definitely it.

At that moment I made a promise to myself that I was going to do it. One hundred per cent. Abso-fucking-lutely. And this time, I meant it.

Let's get that key and in less than an hour I can be dead. Hooray to that! Let's go.

And you know what, if I hadn't have passed out where I lay, I honestly believe I would've kept my promise.

I don't know what time it was when I came to but it was dark and I immediately wished I was still unconscious. My head felt like it had a metal spike driven through it and my legs and crotch were sore where I'd wet myself in the night. A stench of alcohol and urine filled the room and I gagged a couple of times but nothing came up but burning bile. My head swam as I hauled myself up and staggered into the kitchen in search of water. I brought the first glass back up straight away but managed to hold down the second and third and fourth and fifth until my belly was so bloated and tight after the last glass that I brought a good half a gallon back up and had to start again. I sent three painkillers down with glass number four MkII and sought out the sofa before I fell down.

It was still dark when I next came to, though it felt a lot later. The pain in my brain had eased up a little but my legs and crotch were sorer than ever and I quickly realised that I'd wet myself again –

twice in one night, a somewhat unwelcome record that I'm pleased to say I have yet to break. I threw my clothes in the rubbish and stood under a steaming hot shower until I was wrinkled and red and wondered why I had done it to myself.

That's when it all came back to me; Angela, the boat trip, the choppy Channel, the mouth bomb, the betrayal, the killing. Another killing.

The emptiness I suddenly felt inside me almost knocked me off my feet and I craved another drink to numb the pain.

I stepped from the shower and made a beeline for the bottle of vodka in the living room.

It wasn't morning yet, it was still my night, my one night.

I could do that.

It doesn't matter how private you make your parties you'll always get gatecrashers and, sure enough, just before dawn my mum turned up.

'Only me, I saw your lights were on, thought you could do with a lecture on where your life is going wrong.'

'Brilliant. Just what I need,' I told her drunkenly. 'That's exactly what I need right now. A big long lecture and argument on everything I've ever done wrong ever. Fucking super!'

'Drinking again?' she began. 'I thought you'd given all that up?'

'Nope, I have never said that in my life,' I told her, taking a big mouthful of foul-tasting vodka.

'Oh, you did, I distinctly remember you telling me you didn't drink and look at you, you're drinking.'

'Nope, I'll say this again in case you didn't quite understand it the first time round, I have never said that in all of my life.'

'Oh, you have, I know you have. You said it to me loads of times. Your memory can be very convenient when you want it to be.'

At this I just laughed, it was too ridiculous to even argue over.

'Okay mum, I'll tell you what, if that's the way you want to play it, then that's the way we'll play it. I hereby declare that after this drink I will never drink again,' I said, then finished what was left of my glass and poured myself another, not forgetting to give her a smile and two fingers.

'Oh Ian, I do worry about you, you can't go on like this, you know. I have an idea what we can do to get you out of this.'

'I like the sound of it already.'

'Go to the police and tell them what you've done. I promise, they'll listen to you.'

'I fucking bet they will!' I roared with laughter.

'No, no, just hear me out. Tell them about the people you work with and what they make you do and I guarantee you, they'll help you.'

'Are you joking? They'll lock me up and throw away the key.'

'Oh, must you exaggerate everything? Can't we have one sensible conversation without you twisting everything out of proportion.'

'I'll get life, life plus life for what I've done.'

'Ah, yes, see, that's why you've got to tell them that it wasn't you who did these things, that it was your so-called friends, they're the real villains. Tell them that you didn't know what you were doing, you were just a bit easily led and you'll be okay.'

'I won't be okay, I'll go to fucking prison for the rest of my life.'

'No, no, you won't, they'll understand.'

They'll understand? Was she serious? Of course she was serious, no one's eyesight is duller than that of a desperate mother. Sure I was a bad'un and yes, I'd killed more people than I could remember but that was just because some big lads made me do it. None of it was my fault really.

'Look, I'm not saying that you won't get into trouble, but that's something you just have to face. I'll go in with you and speak to them if you want. They'll listen to me.'

'Oh really, and why's that?'

'Because I'm your mother.'

'And they'd give a shit about that because…'

'Oh Ian, please, let's not start all this nonsense up again. Just get your coat and we can talk about it down at the station.'

'Fuck off! Why can't you hear me? I'm not going.'

'You have to, you have to.'

'I'm not throwing away my life.'

'You won't, I've already explained everything to you, it's the others who'll take the blame, not you.'

'I am as much responsible as Logan or Broad, I pulled the trigger. I will get done just as much as they will.'

'You won't, I'll see to it you won't.'

'Mum, I'm a gangster. Nothing you say will make any difference.'

'Ha! I've never heard anything so ridiculous in all my life. A gangster. You're nothing of the sort.'

See what I was up against. Nothing could get through to her; no reason, no reality, no logic or sense. This was how life was and if you didn't agree then she'd nag and nag and nag and nag and nag and nag until you did. Mind you, even then she'd nag some more.

'A gangster, I ask you!'

'I am as much a gangster as Logan, Broad, Eddie or Felix.'

'I know you probably like to think you are, and the others have probably told you you are but, believe me, you're not. My son is not a gangster.'

'I am.'

'You're not.'

'I am!'

'No, no you're not.'

'Oh, this is pointless, can't you just go away and leave me alone?'

'No I can't, I'm your mother and it's my job to take care of you.'

'And you think seeing me go down for life would be taking care of me?'

'Oh for goodness' sake, will you stop with this life rubbish, it's getting old.'

Something inside me almost wanted me to turn myself in and get a hefty life sentence just to fucking show her.

'What is it, have they got some sort of hold over you or something? Is that why you don't want to go to the police?'

'Who? Logan and Broad?'

'Yes, have they been threatening you because if they have all the more reason to tell the police everything.'

'They haven't said anything.'

'Well they must have. I mean what other reasons could you have for protecting them like this?'

'I'm not protecting them.'

'You always were easily influenced, I'd hoped you would've grown out of it by now. You don't owe them anything you know.'

'I know that.'

'Then prove it, go to the police.'

'Mum, I can't. Why can't you see that there is no them and me. We're all in it together.'

'For the last time, you're not. You only do these things because they make you do them.'

'No I don't! For fuck's sake, I make my own decisions. I am my own mind. I don't do anything I don't want to do.'

'Is that right?' asked Angela. 'You don't do anything you don't want to?'

11. Killing cousins

What can I say about Craig Fisher that hasn't been said before? He's thoughtful, serious-minded, a good student and a joy to be around. Yes, I think it's fairly safe to say that none of these things have ever been said about Craig Fisher before.

The cocky offspring of some relative of John Broad's, Craig had spent the best part of his life moving in some very unsavoury circles and living off his uncle's reputation. When Craig finally did get himself into bother JB, rather unsportingly, stepped in and bailed him out. I'm not too clear on the full story, all I know is what Logan told me.

'He says it was a fight, but that's bullshit, he was waiting for him in there. He did him in cold blood.'

Craig, apparently, didn't have much patience when it came to being owed money, especially when it was being specifically withheld to undermine his reputation. Suddenly, people were saying things like, 'Can't even get his five grand out of Laidlaw,' and, 'Where's JB when he needs him?'

The cracks were starting to appear. Reputation was everything as far as Craig was concerned so he had to act. He simply had no choice. Laidlaw finished his pint and went to the toilet. Craig was there waiting for him with a revolver. Craig shot him twice, once in the back and once in the head, which was admirably professional. However, running through a crowded pub, splattered in blood and piss, holding the murder weapon after two loud bangs had got everyone's attention, wasn't.

Therein lay the problem.

What should JB do about his relative? He could've just left him to face the music and go down for life. Craig knew nothing about the workings of JB's organisation so he could've let him rot in the

Scrubs, but that wasn't really an option. He was young, he was family and he'd made a mistake, so what? What are you going to do, punish him for the rest of his life for making a mistake? Of course not, so what should he do?

'How about killing him?' Logan had suggested, but what was the point in silencing someone who knew nothing.

So, I found myself standing in Logan's office the morning after laying Angela to rest. I didn't know why I was there. I thought Logan was getting ready to do me in too, so that there was absolutely no connection between JB and a police grass. I was standing there, armed to the teeth, taut as a spring and one sudden movement away from taking down everyone within twenty feet of me while I listened to Logan outline what JB had proposed.

'You're not serious?'

'Afraid so, sunshine. You're learning him and if you don't like it, well that's just hard lines ain't it?'

'But I don't know anything about training killers.'

'You don't need to teach him to kill, he can do that already. We just want you to teach him how to get away with it. He ain't quite mastered that part yet.' Logan stared at me. 'Why don't you sit down for fuck's sake? You're giving me neckache.'

'That's okay, I'm fine standing.'

'What part of that sentence made you to think I was worried about you being comfortable? Get your fucking arse in that chair. I ain't talking to you up there.'

I looked behind me at Eddie and trusted my instincts enough to allow that Logan wouldn't have given my assassination to a plank like him, not when Logan knew for a fact all that I needed was half a second to turn the office into a war zone.

I sat in the chair.

'Now look,' Logan began, 'you don't have to use a blackboard or a sandpit or nothing, just teach him what you know.'

'I'm not sure what I know,' I told Logan. 'I don't really think about it.'

'Well now's your chance. Come on, Bridges, for fuck's sake, you were trained yourself. Just tell Craig everything Barry told you when you first got out of the nick and all the stuff you've learned since then.'

'Is that all? Danny, that'll take months.'

'Yes, I know and I'm sorry if this interrupts your hectic social life but luckily you ain't got one. You know I personally think it'll do you some good to have someone around you for a change. You've become very maudlin just lately. You bring me down every time I fucking see you.'

'Oh, I feel better about myself already.'

'Nothing personal, but you are a miserable cunt, Ian. And I think it would be quite therapeutic for you to have someone to talk to, tell stuff to.'

'And what makes you think I haven't got anyone to talk to already?'

'Ian, please, I know you. You bent my ear'ole for five long years while we were in the shovel, all about the cunts you went to school with or the cunts you worked with or your fucking mum and all the rest of it, so pardon me if I don't go believing your life's one long round of dinner parties and canasta evenings. Once a loner, always a loner, as they say.'

'I'm not…'

'Ian, I'm not saying this like it's some sort of bad thing or nothing. In fact, for the job you do it's perfect. Why d'you think I took you on in the first place? And quite frankly it's probably best all round if you ain't out dancing the night away laughing and joking and telling everyone about fucking wa'sisname's arsehole or whatever. But you know, there is a world of difference between shooting your mouth off to outsiders and sharing what you know with one of your own. You've been bottling it up for too long. I'm telling you, it'd do you a lot of good having someone like Craig about.'

'Yeah, well why can't you make him a woman then?'

'That's not a problem Ian, you've got your choice of any of Crystal's birds any time you want. You used to use them all the time, I don't know why you stopped.'

'I don't want prostitutes,' I told him.

'Oh right, you want the Queen of England or something, I suppose.'

'No, just something in-between, if that's not too much trouble.'

'What, like the Pope?' Eddie mused, in an effort to make Logan look like Einstein.

'All I'm saying is…' I started, but Logan cut me off.

'Yeah, I know this is all very sad but if you don't mind let's just get back to what we were talking about in the first place: Craig. Oh,' he said severely, waving a finger in my face, 'and don't go thinking you can blow his brains out and make out he was scratching his head with his gun, I know how your mind works. Craig will not be killed. It is your job not only to train him, but to protect him too. Even if that means from himself.'

'Can't Barry do it? He taught me, why can't he teach this arsehole?'

'Barry's out of it all. And I'm not sending Fisher all the way down to Buenos Aires to disturb his retirement just because you're not a mixer. You're doing it, end of discussion.'

And that was that. Suddenly I had an apprentice to train. But why? Aside from the fact that JB wanted Craig to disappear out of reach of the long arm of the law, what other reasons could there be for palming me off with the fugitive?

JB wanted Craig to replace me? That police grass incident had undermined their confidence in me. Logan didn't trust me any more. Craig would be their new boy. Once I'd taught him everything, the first job they'd give him would be me. He was my replacement. I was to teach my own killer.

No, I wasn't buying that.

JB wanted me to teach Craig. He wanted another fixer to do jobs for him. And if he wanted another hitman, that must mean he didn't want me. No, maybe he wanted two. Four even if you counted Felix and Phil. He was gearing up for something. What?

Jesus! All those years of not concerning myself with the whys and now I couldn't think of any. Except that I was being replaced and that this was a trap, but then again, I thought everything was a trap. Maybe everything was. Just traps that hadn't been sprung yet.

Why had Logan called me a miserable cunt? I hardly ever saw him, how would he know if I was miserable or not? Obviously just baiting me into agreeing to take on Craig. And what's he talking about prison for? That was years ago, people change don't they? If I remember rightly everyone was miserable in the nick, not just me.

And another thing…

'Are you meditating or something?' Logan asked. 'Only I have got a business to run so if you don't mind fucking off out of it, I'd be awfully grateful.'

I got to my feet.

'Okay Danny, when does he start?'

'You can start today if you like. Eddie'll take you over to the flat. It's in your neck of the woods anyway, so it'll be nice and handy for you. You need any money or anything else, give me a call. Other than that, I don't want to know, he's your responsibility. I don't even like him so don't go bringing him round here and don't go phoning me up to tell me what a cunt he is 'cos I already know. All right now, mind how you go. And for fuck's sake remember, he's still wanted by the Old Bill so don't go night-clubbing or going back to his old manor to settle any old scores. If he wants a bird, take him down to Crystal's and chalk it up on the slate, and if he wants a drink, buy him a bottle from the off-licence, I don't care, just for fuck's sake lay off it yourself. You stink like a fucking distillery. Now fuck off. Goodbye.'

I stood my ground for a moment waiting to see if there was any more but that was obviously my lot so I followed Eddie out of the office, down through the club and out to the car.

I looked about briefly as I walked through the disco. George was topping up some of the optics from the tap and all about cleaners were getting the place ready for the evening crush. One of the girls caught my eye.

She had to be new. She had curly shoulder-length auburn hair, freckles and deep blue eyes. She looked so beautiful in her blue and white pinny I thought I'd trip over my feet. At that moment she looked up and caught me staring at her.

She smiled and as she did so her eyes twinkled in a way I thought they only did in cartoons.

I held her gaze for about two seconds then tore my eyes away. 'No,' I heard myself mutter. 'Don't fall for it again.'

We drove over to the flat in my car, Eddie jabbering on every inch of the way. I was able to blank most of it out, but every now and again I'd hear a phrase like 'It doesn't 'alf sting when you get it in their eyes apparently' and my defences would crumble.

The flat was in a shabby old part of Stockwell over a small parade of shops. There were garages round the back along with rusty old iron stairs that led up to a couple of front doors. Very discreet all in all. Eddie knocked on the door and let himself in with the key without waiting for a response.

'Craig, it's me. I've got someone I want you to say hello to.'

I kept a firm grip on my Glock in my pocket. It was now if it was ever. Craig appeared at the entrance to the living room yawning and scratching himself as he ambled into the hall in his boxer shorts. Two hands on view, nowhere to hide a weapon. I reasoned this one was safe. I checked the rooms either side of the front door and then the bathroom and the living room before relaxing my grip on the handle. Eddie and Craig had watched me as I'd zipped about the place and it was Craig who spoke up first.

'If you count to twenty I'll go and hide if you like.'

I fixed my gaze on him and he flashed me back a toothy grin and waved. 'You're Craig,' I said to him.

'I know, it says it in my shorts,' he replied.

'Do you know who I am?' I asked him. 'Or why I'm here?'

'No, but if you come in and have a cup of tea, we'll sit down and try and remember together.'

Eddie was shaking his head at Craig and frowning.

'Go and put some clothes on Craig, you've got some business here with the man and I wouldn't fuck about if I was you. Go on, get going.'

Craig disappeared into the bedroom. Eddie wandered into the kitchen and ran the kettle under the tap. 'Want a cup of tea, Ian?'

'No,' I told him, but he went ahead and made himself and Craig one.

'You should be getting back, I can take it from here.'

'I'll just have my tea then I'll fuck off. Don't worry, I won't go cramping your style, crack on. Be my guest.' I was just about to start talking when Eddie interrupted almost immediately. 'This is Ian, by the way. He's the geezer I was telling you about,' then whispered very quietly so that only Craig, me and himself, everyone inside the flat in fact, could hear, 'the hitman.'

I stared at Eddie as he nodded and winked at Craig a bit more then suggested he finished his tea on the tube back to London. Two minutes and a bit more nodding and winking later, he was gone.

Craig stared at me blankly, waiting for me to talk. When I didn't say something immediately he jumped in and commented, 'Turned out nice again, hasn't it?'

I shook my head and wondered where to begin.

'A few serious questions. A few serious answers. You know why I'm here?' I said sitting down opposite him.

'A job. Something about a job. You're going to be showing me the ropes and I'm meant to do whatever you tell me to do,' he said, tagging on the end, 'as long as it isn't anything gay. No offence, you're a handsome man and everything, it's just not really my thing.'

'Mine neither,' I told him quickly.

'Oh no, don't get me wrong. I didn't say it was. I was just saying, you know, I wasn't into that sort of thing. Just so we both knew. Just so there was no misunderstanding.'

'There won't be any misunderstandings!' I exclaimed. 'I'm not gay.'

'I know you're not, you keep telling me for some reason,' he said all innocently. 'You can't be too careful though,' he went on. 'You don't know who's batting for what football team these days.'

'When you're ready,' I said, folding my arms.

'Sorry,' Craig replied. 'Better to know where we both stand from the off, don't you think?'

'I hear you killed someone,' I said and watched him nod. 'You want to know how many people I've killed?' I asked him.

'Yeah, how many?' he said, his curiosity suddenly pricked.

'Thirty-four,' I told him and waited for him to look suitably impressed before I continued.

'Funny, I thought it would've been more,' he said glumly.

I leaned forward and looked him square in the eye. 'It might well be before this afternoon's out.'

Was he stupid or something? I was a killer. I had a gun. What was he doing? Did he really think JB's name and reputation cut any mustard with me? Well, actually he probably did seeing as I worked with him, but still, you don't fuck about and tease someone who kills people for a living, not unless you're a fucking idiot? Jesus!

I decided to try a different approach.

'You've killed one person, I've killed thirty-four. We're both murderers, okay big deal. Doesn't mean a thing. The biggest difference between us is that you're up to your neck in it after only one job whereas I'm free as a bird after thirty-four. So go ahead, fuck about all you want, I just thought you might like to learn how to stand on your own two feet. But if you'd rather spend the rest of your life sitting in this flat trying to wind up an empty armchair, that's great, go ahead, because I'm off in two minutes. And the next time I knock at your door, it'll probably be because JB wants one less problem to worry about.'

This got his attention.

'I'm sorry. Ian, is it? I'm sorry Ian, I'll be serious. I promise, no more fucking about, cross my heart and… well, all that other stuff. Go on, you were saying? I'm sorry.'

I fixed him firmly in the eye and gave him my steeliest stare and watched him shrink.

This was the first day of the rest of my life.

And it looked like it was going to fucking suck from here on in.

12. Getting away with murder

Of course, I couldn't really have harmed a hair on Craig's head even if I'd have wanted to but he didn't know this so it gave me a bit of authority over him, which helped us both while we tried to get used to each other.

I left him after an hour or so and told him to be ready at nine the next morning when his apprenticeship would begin.

What should I tell him? I wondered. Where should I begin? I had to try and tutor someone else in something I seemed to have a natural talent for. How did I do that? When faced with a chestnut like this you can't help but become a little introspective. What was it I did that made me better at killing than other people?

Lack of guilt, probably.

I know that sounds stupid, especially seeing as I am guilty but I don't feel particularly guilty about the things I've done, I never have. So what if I have to kill you? I don't know you (well, not usually anyway). So what's there for me to get all tearful about? I can't imagine you standing over my grave and weeping uncontrollably when I snuff it so what's there to talk about?

Guilt. That was it.

Guilt is your mind's way of tricking you into doing thirty years for no real reason. Most killers do their thing in the heat of the moment and feel so bad about it that they usually betray themselves somewhere down the line by involving a third party in some pointless search for absolution. It's like they're longing for the other person to turn around and say, 'You did the right thing strangling him with his own belt. I would've done the same in your shoes. We all would. Don't sweat it.'

Like I say, guilt, it's your mind's natural defence against self-preservation and it's imposed upon us by society as a whole. It's drummed into us from an early age and we're all brainwashed with this fucking *Waltons* set of family values to stop the world we know crumbling down about our ears and rape, pillage, murder and anarchy taking over.

Morality, religion and football, according to Logan. The three failsafes which keep a 'civilised' society in check. Remove any one of these and God help the rest of us.

The thing is though, if you've never felt like a part of society in the first place then you're hardly likely to buy into its rules. You see, you obey the rules and you get a reward, and your reward is to make friends and money, live a productive life, find love and pursue happiness. This is the pay-off and it's what everyone accepts. But if you've got no friends, you can't find happiness, love or acceptance, then where's your vested interest in keeping the status quo?

Hence, when I kill someone, I don't feel bad about it, therefore I'm probably much more likely to get away with it.

How the fuck did I explain this to Craig though?

I thought about my first murder. Well, not actually the first one as the first three I killed were all in prison and you're dealing with a completely different set of rules in there. See, when someone gets killed in prison, everyone usually knows who's done it, but no one says anything, as that's how the social order works. On the outside though, the murderer's identity is not commonly known by the general population until he's caught, therefore feelings of guilt and recrimination come into play more because the validation of his actions by his peers is missing. I don't want to get too heavy with this shit but basically it all boils down to the fact that people want to be forgiven for what they do and/or be seen as the big man in the process.

At least, that's what I reckon.

I do know what I'm talking about because I got a flavour of this state of mind after doing my first job on the outside. Ben James was his name and I shot him in the chest five times. It would've been six but I remembered at the last minute to put one in his head, like Barry had told me. That's the professional way – apparently. Body shots to take down a target, head shots to close the deal.

Anyway, I remember standing over him, watching his brains leaking out all over his carpet and thinking to myself, 'Oh my God, you've done it now, Ian. You're going back inside and this time it's life and no sympathy from the judge.' A split second of totally unreasoned panic set in and a million irrational thoughts sped through my brain. Was it too late to save him? What if I told the jury what he'd done to me in prison? Oh my God, what if they found out about the others I'd done inside. Fuck.

Shit.

It seemed like an age before I pulled myself together enough to move but when I did I slipped out of the house and into the street to find the neighbourhood quiet. On the way home I felt like the guiltiest man ever to set foot on the Underground (and that's saying something) though much as I stared at all the faces around me out of the corner of my eyes, no one pointed, screamed or nodded their head towards me knowingly. For days I walked around convinced that every person I passed in the street knew what I'd done (How could they not? It was so obvious!) until I was almost bursting at the seams to cry, 'All right, all right, I did it. There are you happy?' just because I couldn't bear the awful anticipation any longer. I guess it must be the same for most murderers. You can put yourself through hell and back waiting for that knock on the door, so much so that you end up turning yourself in just to put yourself out of your own self-made misery.

I don't know whether I would've taken that course of action myself, but then at the end of the day I didn't need to because I had the one thing most murderers didn't – a confidant.

Logan not only knew that I'd done the deed, but by supplying the gun, the silencer and the address he'd helped me do it. I talked to him about it a couple of days later and you know what, that was that, a huge weight was lifted off my shoulders. Well, some of it anyway. He shook my hand, told me what a good job I'd done and congratulated me on my first official hit. Barry gave me a paternal wink and told Logan he thought I was a natural and Eddie brought us all a drink.

It had been the same in prison. Logan would want someone done. I'd do them. I'd tell Logan about it. He'd say what a good chap I was. I'd earn a bit more respect from the other prisoners and a bit more fear from the guards, who'd suspect but be unable to prove, and I'd feel better about myself.

I'd also get away with it every time.

So, how did I get all this across to Craig?

Admittedly, on first inspection, Craig hadn't seemed racked with remorse about what he'd done, which was a good thing (unless he was in the dock, of course) and he hadn't hesitated when called upon to act.

Okay, so he could do the job. There was potential there. He was an uncut stone and I was the jeweller. No, he was the circus monkey and I was the man with the whip. No... oh bollocks, it didn't matter what parallel I drew it all boiled down to the same conclusion, the basic theory was already in place, which was probably why JB had set him journeying down this path rather than sleeping under another, so I would concentrate on teaching him the practical side of things and leave his conscience to work the rest out for itself.

So, what did this entail?

There are dozens of ways to kill someone: part of the secret to getting away with a murder is knowing which is the right one for a particular job. Shoot them, stab them, poison them, blow them up, strangle them, run them over, push them off somewhere high, drown them, suffocate them, feed them to nasty (not very common), fix their car/bike/plane/ boat/submarine/ horse, electrocute them, slice them open and let them bleed, cut their heads off, burn them, bury them, drop something on them, drop them on something (something pointed), gas them, break their neck, mince them or lock them in somewhere and leave them there for a very long time. And if all that lot doesn't work then you can just plain bash them over the head.

Most of these methods are fairly self-explanatory but there's more to killing a man than just piling in there and hoping for the best.

Take stabbing, for example. Killing someone with a knife is a very specialised skill. Sure you get burglars and wannabe hardnuts topping people with blades all the time but these people are just plain unlucky. Ask any of them in the cold light of day if they had meant to kill the other person and most will tell you that they didn't. Plenty of people get stabbed a dozen times and live to see the next day. Why do you think so many of these poor women who're abducted and murdered are found with multiple stab wounds? I personally doubt their killer's done it in a fit of blood-lust fever. Going by experience I'd say it's because he's found that no matter how many times he stabs her she simply refuses to die. Multiple stab wounds are the mark of an inexperienced killer.

The heart, the throat and the brain. These are the three places to aim for if you want to drop someone quick, but it's difficult. The heart and the brain are protected by bones and I'd give you long odds on hitting the bullseye first time. The throat, on the other hand, is soft and exposed and more accessible if you're approaching from behind. At the same time though, it can be very messy and very noisy. The amount of forensic you end up splashing about the place and all over yourself will keep SOCOs (Scene of Crime Officers) in overtime for a week. And it's just not a pleasant way of doing it, especially when you've got access to guns, so why go to all the trouble?

Guns are the cleanest, quickest and most efficient way of killing an individual. That's why the army gives them to the soldiers and why your average loopy bastard off the street isn't allowed to buy them over the counter (except in America). The trouble is though, they make a lot of noise and they leave a mark on a bullet as individual as a fingerprint. So, if you're going to use a gun, you have to either make sure the bullet, the body or the gun is never ever found if you want to get away with it. That means you'd better have access to a lot of guns, a lot of untraceable guns. I have. JB has contacts all over Eastern Europe and since the Cold War finished, that place has just become awash with weapons. The organisation can get me pretty much anything from machine guns, pistols and high-velocity rifles to grenades, plastique and anti-personnel mines – whatever the job requires. I use it, give it back, then it changes hands several times and usually ends up in Ireland where the Paddies hand it in whenever there's an amnesty.

Poisoning? Well, we've been over that one with Mr Carpenter. Hit and run? Not sure enough first time round unless you want to back over them a couple of times, but then what's the point? Presumably you're running over your target to make it look like an accident. Well, all that goes out of the window as soon as you put the stick in reverse. Blowing them up? Like I say, I can get all the explosives I want the same as the guns and even if I couldn't, all I'd have to do is look up the ingredients on the internet.

If I had to choose my own personal favourite I would have to say strangling. Simple, effective, clean, anyone can do it. Piece of rope or a tie, wrap it around someone's neck and don't let go until they become a bit heavy on you. Mind you, even then, keep it tight for another minute, some people like to play dead. All you have to bear in mind is that you're going to leave fibres behind. However, as long as you haven't used your old school tie or a rare length of maritime rope sold in only two shops in the country you should get away with it. Just get rid of the murder weapon and get rid of any clothes it may have come in contact with. And by that, I don't mean leave them out for the bin men. Burn them.

Right, once you've got your method sorted out, there are a hundred other things you need to know to get away with murder. Transport, witnesses, surveillance equipment, whether or not it

13. In the line of fire

'Squeeze, don't pull,' I repeated for the fuck knows how manyth time. It was week four of killing by numbers and the deadliest thing I'd allowed Craig to hold up until this point was a pencil. I'd concentrated mainly on background research and the importance of getting to know your target. I'd put together a few mock dossiers on local businessmen and had Craig knock them off on paper a few dozen times before his restless expression became too unbearable to sit across from any more so I decided it was time he fired a few guns.

Bang! (Well actually, with the silencer it was more like a Phhut!)

'You're off again. I can't see where the round's going but from watching your recoil my guess is six inches to the right.'

'But I'm aiming at the fucking thing. I'm right on the middle of it. Who lined these sights up, Mr fucking Magoo?'

'The sights are right, it's your shooting that's off.' I snatched the rifle out of his hand and put three rounds into the dummy's chest from a kneeling position. Well, it was only 100 yards.

'I know what you're doing, you're aiming to the left to make it look like I can't shoot properly. Give me it, I'll show you.' Three missed rounds later Craig still wasn't convinced. 'Maybe just a bit further to the left.'

'Why the hell would I do that? I'm trying to teach you to shoot.'

'I don't know. For a laugh?' he ventured.

'Craig, I'm shooting plum. It's your technique that's letting you down. You're jerking the trigger rather than squeezing. You're anticipating the rifle's kick so much that you're whipping your shot off into those bushes every time you fire. Now look, relax, take a few deep breaths, clamp the rifle tightly to your shoulder and don't pull on it when you fire.'

Phhut! Another blade of grass died somewhere out in the meadow.

'Okay, try this. Don't aim. Don't even look through the scope. Just clamp the rifle to your shoulder and slowly squeeze down on the trigger until the rifle fires.'

'You don't want me to aim?'

'No, just fire. I don't even want you to look. Close your eyes and just feel the action of the rifle. Don't worry about the bullet.' Craig stared at me stupefied.

'What's the fucking point in that?'

'The point is that I should've taught you how to fire a weapon before I try and teach you how to aim.'

'I know how to fire a gun, I have done it before you know,' he objected.

'Yes I know, and how far away from your target were you?'

Craig thought for a moment. 'About an inch,' he answered.

'The idea behind a rifle is that you don't have to walk up behind your target in the bog and shoot him at point-blank range,' I told him, reloading the weapon and handing it back to him. 'Just do as I say before we run out of ammo.'

Craig resumed his position on the ground and shouldered the rifle. He closed his eyes like I'd told him to and gently squeezed until the rifle fired then looked up at me.

'Better. Feel the difference? You're not anticipating the shot, you're just squeezing. Now do it again.'

Craig finished up the clip, rolled on to his side and handed the rifle back to me. I reloaded the weapon and jotted down how many shots that was before handing it back to him. 'Now you're ready to aim. Just do as you were doing then but aim for the target. Believe me, from this range, you should've had more than that one by now.' I raised the spare scope to my eye and smiled as I saw the dummy's midriff jerk three times. Craig opened his closed eye and smiled, searching for approval, which he got, before putting one in the dummy's head. Naturally, he then went and spoiled it by not getting any of his next four on target, but he'd learned the basic principles, so now it was just a matter of practice.

An hour later and 234 bullets less to threaten the world with, I decided it was time to pack up and call it a day.

'The thing is, right, although you should be proficient with a rifle, the truth of the matter is that you'll probably hardly ever have to use it. A rifle's only used to take out people you can't get close to. Protected people, important people, and they're not usually the types of people JB wants done.'

'Oh yeah, who's that then?' Craig asked.

'Small-time villains, people who rip him off, people who don't pay the protection, the odd resident he wants to evict, that sort of person.'

'Grasses?' Craig asked, forcing me to think of Angela. I hesitated a moment then nodded in agreement.

'Yes, grasses too,' I said turning away for a moment. 'Okay, look, I'm going to get the dummy, you pick up the shell casings. There should and had better be 234 of them. Don't miss any, use the metal detector if you have to, that's what it's there for. I'll go and get the dummy.'

I slung the rifle over my back and started to walk towards the dummy before Craig said something. 'You can leave the rifle here if you want, I'll pack it away.'

I stopped in my tracks and turned to face him. Did he think I was stupid? I wasn't about to hand him a rifle and walk out and become a target myself. He'd have to be a bit more cunning than that if he wanted to rub out old Bridges. 'I don't think so,' I told him with a smile and carried on walking.

'Hang on, wait a minute,' he shouted after me. 'If you're only collecting the dummy, what do you need to take the rifle with you for?' he said running after me.

I spun around again and backed off as he approached but Craig stopped just short of me. 'Go and pick up the cartridges, go on,' I waved him back.

'No way man, I ain't falling for that one,' he said, suddenly ill at ease with his isolated surroundings.

'What one? I ain't doing one on you.'

'Yeah! Prove it then and leave the rifle with me.'

'Fuck off!' I said. 'What, so I can go out there and be your target! I don't care what kind of shit shot you are you ain't practising on me.'

'I won't! Why would I?'

'Well why would I want to shoot you then?' I asked him in return.

'I don't know. Maybe you're a nutcase or something.'

'I'm not going to shoot you,' I told him.

'Then why do you need to take the rifle with you?' he asked again.

'To stop you from shooting me.'

'I won't!' he protested.

'Bollocks,' I protested back. 'Look, if I was going to rub you out I've had hundreds of opportunities before now haven't I?' This made him stop and think for a moment.

'No,' he disagreed. 'No, you ain't, because this is the first time we've come away together somewhere quiet. You already told me about carrying bodies through the woods and all that stuff and how it's best if you can get them to walk out to the hole themselves.'

He was right, I had. Actually it was quite rewarding to see that some of this stuff was sticking, though at the same time it was a little unnerving how competent and cunning he was becoming.

'Okay, good point. But you're still not thinking properly are you? What about this then, I've stood over you a dozen times today holding a loaded rifle, I could've plugged you any time,' I said jabbing my finger in his direction to underline my point.

'Ah but you wouldn't would you?' he retorted. 'Too easy. Not sporting enough.'

'Wrong,' I laughed. 'The first rule is always kill when it's easiest. I'm not a sportsman, I'm a professional and it's my job to kill at the moment the target is most vulnerable and I am least at risk.' I shook my head in disapproval. 'This is basic stuff. Sporting! That's what the baddies do in James Bond, throw him back his gun or give him a head start or something and James Bond always gets away and comes back and kills the baddies, everyone knows that.'

Craig nodded in agreement and thought for a little while longer then continued his argument. 'All right, okay, I've got it. You already told me that rifles aren't used to kill from three inches away so there you go. Maybe you thought if you were too close I might just be able to stick out a hand and defend myself. That's why you need to get some distance between us and catch me unawares. Yeah. Yeah,' he smiled, all pleased with himself.

'I'm not going to kill you,' I repeated again.

'And I'm not going to kill you either,' he agreed.

'Good, then that's settled. Now go and pick up the cartridges.'

'Up yours,' he snorted. 'I'm coming with you.'

'Look, we can't leave all our gear unprotected,' I told him.

'Fine,' he agreed. 'I'll go and get the dummy then.'

'Go on then.'

'Okay. Give me the rifle then.'

We stared at each other for longer than heterosexual men are meant to before a compromise finally occurred to me.

'I'll tell you what, we'll break the rifle down. You take the stock, the barrel and the scope and I'll take the rest. Agreed?'

'Can the bit you've got still fire?' he asked.

'Not from 100 yards out, Jesus, Craig, if I can hit you from there with what I'm left with then I think even you'd have to admit that that would be a pretty good shot.'

'Give me the clip too and any round chambered and you've got a deal.'

I did as he said and we broke the rifle down and walked off in separate directions. It occurred to me that Craig must've distrusted me as much as I distrusted him, but why? What would I have to gain by rubbing him out? I ran through a few ideas but nothing stuck. I wondered if someone had said something, Eddie maybe? It didn't matter, whatever the excuse was, this distrust between us was a dangerous thing. Supposing it got so bad that one of us decided to do something about it rather than run a further risk. This was a potentially dangerous situation.

I reached the dummy, pulled out the spare scope and had a quick look back towards Craig and almost ducked when I saw him standing there with the scope to his eye watching me back. He gave me a wave which I returned and pocketed the scope again. I pulled the spike out of the ground which held my old hessian dummy in place and started back.

Yep, Craig was coming along nicely. The question was though, could two hitmen really ever trust each other fully? Well, that and why would I bother using a rifle on Craig when I had two pistols, a knife and a length of very, very, very common garden rope on me?

Training ticked along at a snail's pace after that. The mistrust that was slowly festering between us began to hamper lessons and neither of us wanted to be around the other when there were weapons in the room, so I began showing him a few martial arts moves. I'm not all that good at it to be honest but I have just about enough bastardised moves from Judo, Tai-Kwon-Do and Karate to take a knife off an attacker or kick two people in the bollocks at once. I'm just not disciplined enough to make any more than that stick, I've always been far too reliant on weapons.

Come the seventh week and a phone call from Logan and I had to go away and do a job on a suspected informant, so Craig enjoyed a week's holiday... on his own in a flat in Stockwell. I left him six pistols, four revolvers, two automatics (no ammo, of course), to study, strip down, oil and reassemble over and over again so that he got to know what function every moving part performed. I also left him my copy of *Day of the Jackal*, which I thought he might enjoy. Craig explained that he hadn't read a book since school ('I've coloured a few in though') and that it might take him a bit longer than a week to get through, so I took the book back and got him the video instead (the Edward Fox version, not the stupid Bruce Willis remake).

When I returned the following week he asked me, 'So, have you ever done it with a bloke then?'

'No! Of course I haven't!' I exclaimed. 'What the fuck makes you ask that?'

'That film you got me. Matey turns out to be a poof in it. I just thought you were getting at something, that's all,' and with that, suddenly he'd found another reason why not to turn his back on me.

I don't know what would've happened if the situation between us hadn't been resolved but I suspect one of us would've ended up dead and I suspect it wouldn't have been me. The turning point came a couple of weeks later when we were out in the woods again, this time with handguns. Craig had just successfully blown holes on my patched-up dummy with my Smith & Wesson when I reached inside my jacket and handed him my Glock.

'Give this one a go, see what you think,' I told him and Craig put three in the chest, one in the shoulder, two in the head and two wide until the clip was empty. He handed it over and I slipped in another clip for him and stared at the target for a moment. 'I don't know,' I said, 'maybe it's too close.' I handed him back the gun, walked out to the dummy and moved it back ten yards. I turned around and was just about to start back when I saw Craig holding my freshly loaded weapon by his side and stopped in my tracks. I stared at him for a few agonising moments before a look of realisation spread across his face. Craig looked at the Glock and then at me and fought to suppress the grin that was breaking out across his face.

'Not too clever,' he gloated with shameless glee. 'And there was me beginning to think you were infallible.'

'Don't do it,' I implored him. 'You don't have to.'

Craig raised his free hand and gestured for me to be quiet. He looked like he was struggling to think of something to say before he held up the gun so that it swung underneath his finger and slowly put it on the ground by his feet. 'Fuck me Bridges, you really don't trust me, do you?'

I relaxed a little, walked forward and picked up the Glock from by his feet.

'I told you, I haven't got it in for you man, but Jesus, you really thought I did, didn't you?'

'Yes, I did, so I had to be sure,' I told him.

'What do you mean?'

'I mean, that was deliberate. I'm sorry but I had to put you to the test to see where I stood with you.'

'That was? What do you mean? You mean you gave me a gun and walked out in front of me unarmed just to see if I'd shoot you?'

'Cleared the air a little hasn't it?'

'Fuck me, you are a nutter. You risked your life just to clear the air?'

'Don't be ridiculous, I risked your life. These are blanks,' I said and fired the Glock around his feet. 'Probably a good job you didn't choose to wind me up,' I continued pulling a small Pocket 9 from my sock. 'Out of the two of us, I was the only one with live ammo,' and fired three demonstration shots into the hessian dummy. Craig stared at me with open-mouthed outrage.

'You motherfucker!' he gasped. 'You... you... you fucking mother!' he choked, cleverly rearranging his last two words to make a completely new insult.

'It's how I'm still alive,' I told him. 'You can't afford to trust anyone in this line of work. Here,' I said handing him the Pocket 9, 'give it a go if you like.'

'You were going to shoot me?'

'Only if you shot at me first,' I explained. Craig seemed too dumbfounded to think of anything meaningful to say further on the subject so he settled for calling me a wanker and mumbling the word 'fucking…' without it actually leading to anywhere before taking the pistol from me.

'All right then Einstein,' he started. 'What if I were to shoot you now?'

'Why would you? If you weren't going to shoot me five seconds ago why would you want to shoot me now?'

'I don't know, maybe I'm a nutcase or something. Anyway, my point is, you've just given me a loaded gun while you really are unarmed this time.'

'So?'

'So, what's to stop me shooting you now?'

I thought about this for a moment and wondered where Craig was going with it.

'Well, nothing I suppose, except the fact that you've shown that you have no good reason to do so.'

'What if I'd just been tricking you into giving me this gun knowing all along that the other one was full of blanks?'

'If you had been then you must have to be some kind of living genius or something.'

'That's me,' Craig declared.

'So, are you going to shoot me?'

'No.'

'Then take it from me, you're no genius.'

'And what would you know about it, mastermind? You just handed a loaded weapon to someone you thought five seconds ago was aiming to kill you. So, out of the two of us, who's more of the genius, me or you?'

I thought about this carefully before concluding it was definitely me. By a fair few miles.

'All right then, what are you going to do about it?' I asked him.

'When?'

'Look, this is pretty simple stuff. You have no reason to kill me,

I have no reason to kill you. Now we've both layed our cards on the table and we can relax a little around each other. Agreed?'

'Agreed. Unless we're both nutcases, of course.'

'Yes,' I sighed. 'There are only three reasons you should have to kill when you're a hitman: orders, self-preservation and practice. And none of those things are applicable between us.'

'I could still kill you now though,' he said.

'No you couldn't,' I argued back.

'I'm not saying I will, I'm just saying I could.'

'You couldn't.'

'No, you're missing what I'm saying,' he repeated. 'Yeah okay, I agreed with you when you said I'm not going to kill you because I ain't got a reason, but I could if I wanted to.'

I sighed and shook my head. I had the feeling this conversation could've gone on until it got dark and then light again.

'All right, all right, I know what you're trying to say but you're wrong, you couldn't kill me even if you wanted to.'

'Oh, and why not?' Craig asked indignantly.

I snatched the Pocket 9 out of his hand, losing patience with him a little. 'Because these are blanks too,' I told him and fired them into the ground to demonstrate.

'You suspicious cunt!' he gawped.

'Yes, you're right,' I told him. 'I always like to be doubly sure.'

'Are you ever going to give me a gun with real bullets in it again?'

'Not if I can help it.'

14. The third reason

The next day I took Craig out on the boat and showed him the ropes. Then I showed him how to tie them around people and dump them overboard. Finally I showed him something I'd never shown anyone else before – the approaching harbour from the deck of my boat.

I'd come to the conclusion that Craig had no real interest in doing a job on me for himself (other than being a nutcase perhaps) so I figured the only reason he'd take me down would be if he'd been ordered to do so by JB or Logan. Therefore I decided to isolate him from the organisation so that he had contact with no one but me from now on. Up until this point I'd never taken him back to my house, preferring instead to work from his flat in Stockwell, but this was no longer secure enough for my liking, so we packed up his gear and he came home with me. He didn't have much stuff. A few clothes, an alarm clock, some toiletries and 'that gay video I'd given him' as he insisted on calling it.

Back at mine I got him stashed away in the back bedroom and showed him around the place, telling him what he could and could not touch. Most of my things fell under the latter.

'Oooh, nice computer,' he cooed. 'Does it work?'

'Of course it works, what would be the point of having it if it didn't?'

'I don't know,' he said. 'You could sell it I suppose.'

'I use this a lot,' I told him. 'I don't know how computer literate you are but this'll be the next thing I start you on.'

I approached the computer and shook the mouse, waking the machine up.

'This will be one of your most important weapons,' I said

double-clicking on the net connection icon. 'Information is the key to a successful hit and there's all the information in the world in here at the touch of a button. Street maps, building plans, transport timetables, business addresses, personnel details, even the home addresses and telephone numbers of politicians and celebrities, if you know where to look. You've got all this plus weapons information, plans for bomb-making, medicines and poisons, security company details, banking details and all the rest of it. There are a thousand and one, no make that a million and one, unregistered sites that post up stuff you wouldn't believe and until the world-wide governments manage to rein it all in and somehow police the web it's all there for whoever knows where to look.'

Craig listened carefully staring intently at my machine.

'Got any games?' he asked.

'Games? No.'

'Oh, all right then,' he said and wandered off towards the TV.

Against considerable odds, we managed to continue with Craig's training and live under the same roof together in relative peace. I hadn't got much sleep the first few nights, it felt so strange having someone this side of my impregnable security precautions. It was sheer fatigue that finally won me over on the third night and after that I was able to sleep normally again, albeit with the bedroom door locked and barricaded.

About the only real serious argument came when I insisted Craig crop his hair close like mine.

'It's important,' I told him. 'If you're going to do this job you've got to take every precaution to safeguard against leaving any forensics. Loose hairs left at the scene are like Christmas presents to SOCOs.' I went on to explain how I shaved, waxed, pumiced and manicured myself from head to foot a few days before a job to minimise the risk of leaving hair, skin or nails behind (eyebrows and eyelashes excepted, but even these were groomed carefully for loose hairs) but all Craig could do was object.

'Oh, fucking hell man, two geezers with short hair living together. Why don't we just get tight T-shirts and a pink Citroën and be done with it?'

It took the best part of a morning to convince Craig to part with his thick black locks but he finally agreed when I reiterated the fact that I only ever shaved a day or two before a job.

'We doing a job then?' his attention suddenly pricked.

'Not a sanctioned job, but it's time to put into practice what you've learned and take out someone for real.'

'Who?' he asked excitedly.

'I've found you someone.'

Claire – could I find anyone sweeter? Even her name sounded like the child born of clean and air. She could've been a princess, if it wasn't for the fact that she was a stripper. Still, she was perfect.

Poor Claire.

Women are much harder to kill than men. That's not a fact, that's just my opinion. They have a fuller armoury than men. Men can only really defend themselves on one level – physically, but women have so much more to their game – pity; distress; sexuality; these are the big guns they can pull out when they're threatened and sometimes they can be just as effective as a fist in the face. Of course, I'm only talking about young women here, old ladies I could kill for fun all week long and not feel the least bit bad about it. But young women…

I've thought about this before, why it's harder to kill a woman than a man (if you happen to be a man that is) and I've come to the conclusion that it probably goes back to instincts and all that. As far as Mother Nature is concerned, us chaps are meant to take care of women, look after them, protect them against danger, not shout 'Oi, catch!' and throw them electric fires when they're in the shower. And of course, the more beautiful the women, the more we want to take care of them. And this is where things start to get a bit tricky when it comes to killing them. It's quite astonishing just how many thoughts can flash through your mind in the blink of an eye, especially when you've got a beautiful woman on her knees begging you for her life. I don't want to dwell on this too much because it's not nice – but it is true. If you pause, even for a second, to listen to all the voices in your head, spelling out the possibilities, even the most resolute of professionals can get sidetracked into not doing what they're supposed to do.

I know what I'm talking about here.

We all make one mistake…

Therefore, I decided if I was going to give Craig a test I might as well make it a real test; better he fucked up under laboratory conditions than the first time he went out on his own. So, I set out to find him a woman. A beautiful woman.

There are plenty of beautiful women working in the bars, offices and hospitals of London, but finding a truly sexy, available and accessible target among the normal population could've taken weeks. What I needed was a concentration of sexy girls to choose from and a guaranteed time and place to start my observations from.

Lap dancing clubs.

There are a glut of them in and around central London and the West End. And they are perfect hunting grounds for killers. I'd spent two weeks getting to know a dozen different lap, table, pole and exotic dancing clubs and a dozen different girls. I paid for dances, I tucked £10 notes between sweaty breasts, I bought £6 bottles of lager that had 'Duty Free' written on them and followed the cabs home at night until I finally settled on Claire.

She was perfect. Cute as a button and as sexy as a whore. She had the long leggy body of a dancer and the outgoing friendly demeanour of an airline stewardess and I would've happily married and settled down with her, if it wasn't for the fact I was fixing to kill her. In fact, the first time I saw her I thought to myself, 'I can't do this one, she's too nice' – that was how perfect she was. I followed her around for another week or so, compiling a basic dossier on her, then turned the lot over to Craig.

Well, he did it. He didn't like it, and we had a couple of days of heated arguments about my choice of target but in the end, he finally did it. And in the end, that's all that matters. I'm not going to dwell on the details on this one because there's no need and I'd rather not. Some things I don't even like talking about. Suffice to say, Craig completed the assignment I'd set him and staged the scene of the crime to make it look like it had been committed by the regulation stalker fruitcase. All that remained was for us to quietly slip away and for the courts to throw the first simple-minded road sweep the police pick up into prison for the next twenty years.

'You're a hangman, not a judge, remember that. The sentence has already been passed down, all you're doing is carrying it out.'

I had a bottle of scotch waiting for Craig at home and poured him a very big drink. Then I poured him another one. And then another. He gulped the stuff down like it was some kind of antidote for what he'd just done but there was no escaping it that easy.

'Look, that's about as horrible as it gets,' I tried to reassure him. 'Short of cutting people up and carrying them around in small briefcases, I guess.'

At that point Craig puked up all over his jeans and my floor though if truth be told, there wasn't much left after the van-ride home.

'You should try to eat something,' I told him. 'Replace what you've lost.'

'Ohhh, why don't you leave me alone?' he groaned wiping the back of his hand across his mouth. He sat breathing heavily for a moment or two then heaved again but nothing came out except 'Fuck…' so, he picked himself up and staggered off in the direction of the bathroom. I watched him go then fitted the silencer to my Glock. This was a dangerous time for Craig, whether he knew it or not. His life depended on how he reacted to seeing the true horrors of my profession. It's all well and good fancying yourself as some designer hitman who kills the corrupt politician with a sniper rifle from five hundred yards and escapes on a rocket-powered jetbike, but that's the movies. I kill people for a living. It's what I do and it's not heroic and it's not glamorous.

And that's the way it should be.

Craig was sitting his hitman finals and he didn't even realise it. All he had to do was keep it together enough not to renounce the whole thing and he'd live. You see, if Craig stumbled back from the bog declaring 'never again, never again' then that would tell me he obviously had a problem with it. And if he had a problem with himself doing it, then it would follow that he'd probably have a problem with me doing it. Before we know it he's skidding down that slippery moral slope that comes out down the bottom by a police station. Not that we'd ever let it get that far. If he so much as ever hinted at doing anything that could vaguely be construed as 'the right thing' I'd put a pillow over his face as he slept and pull the trigger. I'd have to get permission from Logan first, of course, but believe me I'd get it.

Craig wandered back wearing new socks and trousers and propped himself up against the doorway as I mopped the last of his sick up.

'Tell me you were the same after your first one.'

'Why?'

'I don't know. Whatever.'

'Whatever back. It's different for everyone.'

Craig pushed himself off the wall and managed to prolong his fall until there was a chair underneath him. He rubbed his face, reached for the scotch, then thought better of it and went back to rubbing his face.

'Just tell me this is normal. That it gets easier than this. That this is just first-day jitters, like breaking the photocopier or burning down half the factory. You want the old hand who's been doing the job for years to come up and say, "Yeah, same thing happened to me when I first started."'

'If you like,' I said, taking the mop and bucket outside to the kitchen then rejoining him in the living room.

Craig stared at me in a way that suggested he had been expecting a bit more.

'You want to know if I felt like you do now after I killed my first person?' I asked.

'Yeah. Did you?'

'No. But I have since. See the thing here with you and me is different because the first three or four people I done I done out of either self-preservation or outright aggression, a bit like you and that whatsisname in the pub toilet.'

'Laidlaw.'

'That's right. You weren't chucking your guts up all over the carpet or trying to drink yourself silly after popping him, were you? No, that's because your blood was up and he had it coming. It was personal between you and him and you showed him good and proper.'

'I'd do it again tomorrow if I could,' Craig agreed.

'I don't doubt it. But the thing with you and the stripper was that there was no you and the stripper. You didn't know her from Eve but you still went and done her anyway and when you done her there was no aggression, no outrage, no anger, no revenge or anything like that, she was just a job, that's all. She'd never done anything to hurt you but you killed her all the same. Why?'

Craig looked at me a little accusingly.

'Because you told me to!'

'No, because I ordered you to.' Craig looked like he was about to heave again but his stomach had given up just about all it was going to by now so he reached for the scotch to give it a little more ammunition. 'You did what you had to do, so put it out of your mind and know that you did well. Not many people could've done what you did today, so think about that if you like. You're all fucked up and full of guilt because it feels wrong, but that's the real skill to this job. You could have all the guns, bombs and black belts in the world if you wanted but if you can't put them to use on who you're supposed to do, then you might as well have nothing.'

Craig nodded but continued to sit shivering in his seat. I didn't doubt his head was in a spin. I mean, it's one thing to commit a brutal horrible murder, it's quite another to then have your tutor come in and mark you on it.

'So, your first kill, who was he then?' he said, taking a sizeable swig which must've stung his red-raw gullet by the way his eyes filled up with tears.

'First ordered kill?'

'No…' he choked, bringing scotch back up through his nose, which must've been nice. He held out a hand to show that he'd like to pause the conversation, then ran off in the direction of the kitchen. He returned a few moments later with a glass of water looking bloodshot, gaunt and a little green around the gills, then flopped back down in the chair again.

'I hate scotch.'

'So do I,' I told him.

'Well why d'you fucking buy it then?'

'It's a good drink to drink when you're not too happy about yourself.'

'Thanks. Very thoughtful. Just what I needed I'm sure.'

'Worked, didn't it?'

'Well that depends, if the idea was me honking up all over your floor, then yes, it worked a treat. Nice one.'

'Give it time and enough jobs and you'll come to… respect scotch,' I told him, then trailed off and came back with a name I'd hardly thought about in, what was it, ten, twelve, fourteen years, something like that. 'Breen.'

'Who was he?'

'He was muscle to the No.1 on my landing, a bloke called Ben James. They used to come along, take my stuff and give me a good old-fashioned hard time about things – well, everyone did in those days. One day I just got fed up with being the world's favourite victim so the next time he came calling on me I opened his throat up for him with a shank I'd made out of a razor blade and my toothbrush. Caught him just right as well, nice and deep, right across the jugular. Bled all the way down the landing and died hardly believing it himself, I should imagine.'

'Didn't you get done for that?'

'Of course I got done for it. Murder's still illegal in prison. It's the only one I've ever been convicted of. My lawyers were competent enough to get the charge reduced to manslaughter but not quite competent enough to stop me from getting life for it all the same.'

'Bummer.'

'Yes, I remember thinking it was all a bit shit myself at the time. But then, at the end of the day life for manslaughter doesn't take quite as long as life for murder, particularly when you've got a sympathetic parole board.'

'Sympathetic?'

'Yeah, you know, bribed.'

'Logan?'

'In a roundabout way, yes. See, when I was convicted for Breen I was moved on to the Scrubs where associates of Ben James were waiting for me. I was a dead man and I knew it so I figured about my only chance was to go psycho nuts the first time anyone said boo to me and not stop for anything. People will always give you a wide berth, no matter what your size, if they think you're loopy enough. So, when three bruisers paid me a visit one recreation time I launched myself at the biggest one, got my teeth around his neck and didn't let go for nothing.'

'You did that?' Craig said, wearing the same look of surprise Breen and… what was his name, Jacobs or Jacobson or something, had worn when I'd jumped them all those years ago.

'Well, he was a mountain of a bloke so there was no other way I was going to take him on. Besides, I'd made up my mind what I was going to do for days before it all came down to it and spent the whole time psyching myself up so that when it happened I was prepared for it. I must've looked a fucking sight with blood all over my face and everywhere else because the other two legged it and it wasn't until the screws knocked me out that they were able to prise us apart.'

'Did he die? Matey you bit?'

'No, but he never sang in the prison choir again.' I smiled, all pleased with myself that after so many years I'd finally gotten around to using that line.

'Did he sing in the choir then?' Craig asked.

'Hmm? No, no it's just a… you know… euphemism,' I explained.

'Well, that's probably the last thing he was worried about then wasn't it?' he said retrospectively.

'Whatever,' I sighed.

'So where did Logan come into all this?'

'Logan? Well, Logan was one of the top dogs in the Scrubs. He wasn't the No.1 but he shared the same bowl, if you like. He became quite interested in me after the incident with Jacobson and one day came knocking on my door. "Keep your muzzle on son, I'm only here for a chat," he says. I didn't believe it for a second. Every chat I'd had since I'd been in the nick had either ended up with me getting a black eye or losing all my toiletries. I was ready to take his nose off in one bite and spit it back in his face if he so much as looked at me funny but Logan was nice and casual. "Super place you've got here," he says. "Bought it or are you renting?" You know his brand of jokes.'

'Not really. I don't know him that much, to tell the truth.'

'No, I shouldn't imagine many people do. Anyway, he tells me he's heard I've been getting a bit of a hard time from the other lags and he can do something about it if I want. "I'll get 'em all off your back, cock. No one'll fucking so much as sneeze in your direction if I give the word."'

'Oh yeah, what was he after then?' Craig asked.

'Exactly. I thought he was a poof at first, although don't tell Danny I said that. So I asked him what he wanted from me and he just gives me a wink and says, "The odd little favour now and again."'

'Watch your bum time.'

'How little and how odd?' I ask. '"I heard you done in one of Ben James's lads. Handy piece of work by all accounts. Could've just been a fluke I suppose but then you go and do Jacobson" — or whatever his fucking name was — "the minute you step in this place and it's got me thinking that maybe the boy can handle himself. You wouldn't think it to look at you, I mean you look like a streak of piss but then so do half the Category A nutters in here. I could find uses for you son."'

'Uses?' asked Craig. 'Topping people?'

'A "specialist", that was what he called it. "To be called upon in times of trouble as a last resort. Someone who can do a job for me without a second's thought. If that's you then your stay here'll become sweet. Oh and don't worry about being at my beck and call all the time, jobs like the ones I'll have for you come round once in a blue moon – but when they do, there's no fucking about, you do 'em," he tells us. Well, I mean, what am I going to say? Up yours, I'll look after myself? Of course not, so I told Logan I'd do it, if for no other reason than simply not to make any more enemies and here I am all these years later, still working for him.'

'Who did he get you to knock off inside then?'

I told Craig all about them. Harry Gardner and Mr Ashton; a direct rival and a screw. I saw them for what they were the moment he told me about them, suicide missions, both of them. No one else would've touched them with a bargepole, but Logan needed them doing and rather than land one of his own lads in it, I was called upon to make good for several years of fear-free living. I was like his own personal kamikaze pilot. Logan was probably more surprised than anyone when I actually got away with them – well, I say I got away with them, no one gave a fuck when I did Gardner but a year later when I did Mr Ashton, I found myself at the angry end of every screw's size elevens. It didn't matter that I was never convicted of either crime, they all knew I'd done it so it was open season on poor old Bridges. Luckily, Danny got out that year and had JB use his influence to extract me too. It took another year or so (and a few quid and several brown paper bags) but eventually they swung it and I was out.

'And Logan set you up here and got you a job on the firm?'

'That's the long and the short of it.'

Craig thought about this for a while. The colour had started returning to his face and he was now able to swallow without sitting up suddenly each time as he did so. It was not a story I'd told to anyone before, probably because I'd never had anyone to tell it to. I'd like to think that had I still been with Angela I could've shared it with her. I wonder what she would've made of it.

A case for the prosecution probably.

Logan was right, I would've betrayed him and myself to her had we not found out about her, though that didn't make things any easier. I still felt an empty pang in my chest every time I thought about her, but I found I was thinking about her less and less. It was still all there, still in my memory, but like the boxes I had up in the loft, I was caring less and less about their contents as time rolled by.

Logan had also been right about Craig He'd been a welcome distraction and I'd got quite used to having him around. I even found myself enjoying passing on my knowledge to someone else and I'd got to feel quite the sage, which was the first time I think I could ever say that. Even when I was with Angela, all we ever talked about was telly or food or tropical fish or something and as my knowledge of these things hardly exceeded hers, I couldn't really blow her away with anything profound or insightful. My specialised chosen subject for the last dozen years had been getting away with murder, and seeing as one of the key elements to this is not telling anyone, well that was the main string to my bow gone.

Craig was sitting quietly thinking things out for himself when I suddenly realised what I'd forgotten. I didn't know where my mind was, I suppose I'd being working for Logan so long I'd just come to take it for granted. I jumped up out of my seat and headed upstairs to my bedroom.

Craig was still sitting quietly when I returned and flinched when I chucked him what I'd brought him. The elastic band must've broke or slipped because the bundle exploded in his lap showering him with £50 notes. A hundred and forty nine of them altogether.

'It slipped my mind but that's yours. It's a little bit light but that's all the cash I've got in the house at the moment. I'll make it up to you.'

'What's all this for?' Craig asked gathering up the notes into one great thick wad. When I saw the puzzlement in his face I could tell that after everything else he'd had to get to grips with today he'd overlooked this one rather important little detail the same as I had.

'You did a job this afternoon. You do a job, you get paid for it.'

15. Silencing witnesses

'Yeah, yeah, yeah, but all that bullshit aside, can he do it?'

I hated it when Logan referred to my carefully considered answers as 'bullshit' 'guff' or 'fucking twaddle'. He'd asked me a question. I had answered it. Sometimes there's more to an answer than just 'yes' or 'no'. Try telling Logan this though and he'd just say 'No there isn't' except probably without the 'there isn't'.

'It's a simple question!' he said, screwing up his face at my inability to catch on.

'It's not a simple question Danny, it's a fucking complicated question,' I tried to tell him in return.

'What: "Can he do it?" That's about as simple as it gets. Either he can or he can't. You've had him for fuck knows how long now so if anyone should know it should be you.'

'There's more to it than that. Yeah, sure he can do it but I don't know if he's ready yet or...'

'Fine, that's all I wanted to know.'

'But Danny...'

'That's all I wanted to know,' he told me in such a way that I could actually hear the full stop in his voice. Logan held the silence for a minute for effect then continued. 'I've got a little job that needs doing.'

'Then send me,' I told him. 'He's still got the stabilisers on his guns.'

'I am sending you,' Logan told me. 'What do you think I've got you here for? Brighten the place up? Hardly. I'm sending the both of you, so try not to go twisting your fucking knickers about in knots until you know the full score.'

'Okay Danny.'

'Okay Danny. That's right. Okay. Now listen, we're investing time and money into young Craig for a reason – the same as we did with you – and one of these days we're going to want to put him to good use, but we can't hardly do that with him cooped up in your drum for the rest of his fucking puff now can we? No, so JB wants – if he's a good horse that is – JB wants to invest a bit more money and get his problems sorted out for him. You with me so far?'

'I think so.'

'Lovely. Because there's seven little cunts out there pointing seven little fingers. JB wants those fingers broken off.'

'Topped?'

'Nothing so naughty. We just want them to stop pointing.'

I mulled this over in my head for a moment or two and Logan let me. He could see my brain ticking away and he didn't interrupt.

The seven little fingers belonged to the seven little witnesses in Craig's case. Actually there had been more than seven witnesses, there'd been a whole pubful, but the clever majority were concentrating intently on the dart board when Craig had emerged from the bog, all guns blazing. As you would. But seven drinkers had been silly enough to fancy a bit of attention, so they'd come forward, signed statements and told their friends they'd give them a sneaky wave from the stand. These people were the basis of the case against Craig, and as solid as that case looked, it was only as solid as these seven separate resolves. Everything else was circumstantial, as legal types have a tendency to say.

'Has JB got something in mind already?' I asked.

'No, he says leave it up to you, just as long as you get those traps shut without starting World War Three then it's whatever you want. You got some ideas or what?'

'I'll need to know more obviously but I think I know how we should go about it. I might need a bit more help besides Craig though.'

'Ask and you shall receive,' Danny said with a regal wave of the hand.

'We've got home and work addresses on all seven?'

'That's what we pay our taxes for,' Logan smiled, in a way that told me some policeman's kids would have a very nice Christmas this year.

'Okay. Let me have everything you've got and I'll check out a few things first, then I'll get back to you with the plan.'

To tell the truth, I had been wondering about this myself for some time. Just how was Craig meant to operate freely when he was being sought in connection with a murder charge? London is a big place, eight or nine million people at last count, but it's still not that big. It's certainly not big enough to hide a murderer in.

'Not big enough to hide a murderer in? Eight or nine million people? What are you talking about? It's like hiding a needle in a haystack,' you might say, and I'd agree. But try to imagine hiding your needle after all the little bits of hay in the stack had been asked to keep their eyes open for it, see how far the little prick gets then.

'He could stay out of sight, stay under the floorboards or something,' you could again argue, but then JB didn't get to where he was today by employing people who lived under floorboards. No, if he wanted Craig to start coming good for him, then he'd have to see to it that his problems were dealt with accordingly.

The way I saw it, we had to hit all seven at once, or at least in the space of an hour of each other, while they were relatively vulnerable. Try hitting one or two at a time and the police might come down on JB's organisation like a ton of bricks (which they undoubtedly would) before we had a chance to make all of their witnesses' acquaintances. Logan agreed with me and gave me Felix and Phil from The Aviary, 'Handsome' Eddie, Brian Faulkner, one of JB's blokes from the docks, and a couple of guys he knew, Ray and Dominic. So many jabbering mouths made me nervous, but seeing as the plan depended upon them and everyone knew what would happen if they fucked over JB, I figured there was nothing I could do about that other than my bit.

If someone's going to be silly, then they'll be silly. You can't let that sort of worry affect your every plan otherwise you'd never do anything. Not the sort of thinking that got us to the moon. Mind you, for all the good that did us, I don't know why we bothered.

I sorted us into four teams. Felix and Phil I knew and trusted the most so I put each of them with Ray and Dominic, who I knew and trusted the least. Brian went with Eddie which left me and Craig looking like a matching pair.

The plan was simple: each team (masked and looking scary) would knock on a target's door, clobber them, then tie them and their family up and put them through hell and back (or at least as much hell and back as they could fit into five minutes). They'd scare them with guns, reel off a list of relative's names and addresses and threaten their wives, husbands, partners, kids, pets and pot plants until they wet themselves (the witnesses that is, not the teams), then they'd get the hell out of there and three of the teams (me and Craig, Felix and Ray and Phil and Dominic) would race to a second assigned target and give them the same treatment. It all boiled down to timing and speed. The police might get called to one disturbance, but by the time they'd assessed what was occurring every other witness on the list would've been hit.

And, just to underline the seriousness of our intent to our silly seven, Craig and I would martyr the last name on the list.

Paul Jeffrey was the ideal sacrificial lamb. No children, no wife (or at least, not any more), no future (again, at least, not any more), an office manager and a virtual alcoholic. He was every hitman's dream target. A regular routine, a physical wreck and no close family to get in the way or demand justice.

Bless him.

All the other witnesses had either children, brothers, sisters, mothers or husbands who would nag on to the police for the rest of their lives if we rubbed out one of theirs, but Paul had no one. Just a flat, a job and a pub. Yeah, he had a wife up in Derbyshire somewhere, but she had a new man these days and much as I'm sure she wouldn't wish anything bad to happen to her ex-husband, I couldn't see her doing much more than buying a nice black number for the funeral.

'Now everyone knows exactly what they're doing do they?' Danny said as he saw us off. Everyone said they did. 'You're all fucking sure?' he repeated. 'Because I don't want any of you stupid cunts killing anyone else except matey boy otherwise we'll be here till fucking Doomsday rubbing out witnesses. All right. See you all back here at ten. And don't none of you get nicked otherwise I'll be throwing a bit more work Bridges' way.'

I pressed the gun into Mr Harper's face and cocked the trigger. Craig had a length of fishing line around his fiancée's neck and was jerking her back violently while talking her through what he was going to do to her after she was dead. Mr Harper would've liked to have screamed or begged or something at this point but the thick electrical tape across his and his pretty fiancée's mouths meant that neither had a chance to interject until me and Craig had shared our thoughts on his decision to take the witness stand.

I moved around behind the chair and yanked his head back by the hair so that the gun was pressed hard against the back of his neck. Mr Harper and Emily (I've always liked that name) were now facing each other and after four minutes of mental and physical assault they must've thought their time had finally come. Blood dribbled from Emily's neck as Craig began strangling her again and I could feel Mr Harper squirming with frustration beneath me. I let him watch for a few more terror-inducing seconds before delivering the coup de grâce.

'Rape her,' I told Craig. 'Do it now.'

Craig pulled her chair back and she fell on to the floor. I did the same with Mr Harper's so that he immediately lost sight of what was happening with Emily. Imagination is sometimes so much more powerful than image. I thrust the gun into his eye socket and bore down on him so that my cold-blooded eyes were just inches from his and finally showed him the only doorway out of this nightmare. 'Retract your statement,' I told him.

Until this moment it had all been about the terror. We'd made no mention of a deal or a demand or anything of that nature. We'd simply used the time to instil as much pants-pissing fear into them as possible to make a deal seem all the more attractive when it finally was put on the table.

Mr Harper nodded so hard against my pistol that he almost made me knock the trigger. I withdrew it slightly in the interests of safety but kept my face where it was.

'I fucking mean it,' I growled. Mr Harper nodded again, keen to get across that he understood. 'Don't make us come back. They can't protect you,' I told him and quickly stood up.

I pulled his chair into an upright position and cut the ropes that bound his wrists; well we didn't want anyone else having to free them now did we? All we wanted was the statements to disappear, not another seven crimes investigated. Mr Harper looked across at Emily and saw her untouched except for the mark around her neck. Of course we wouldn't have really raped her but when you're going for maximum fear, minimum time, you have to wheel out the big guns. It's not a nice thing to have to do, but then, it's not meant to be.

I pushed Mr Harper back down as he tried to stand and drilled into him one last time the seriousness of our intent. 'Don't phone the police, don't go to the hospital and don't say nothing to nobody. One week from now you and your solicitor are going to go and see this Inspector Leonard and withdraw your statement. I don't care what he says, what he offers you or what he threatens you with, if that statement isn't withdrawn a week from now you and her are dead.'

I let this hang in the air for a moment so that when he heard about Jeffrey tomorrow he'd have one of those 'there but for the grace of God goes I' insights, which was exactly the plan.

We left the Harpers to a sleepless night and were halfway to

Jeffrey's a few short minutes later. I phoned Logan to make sure everyone had checked in after their first assignment and was on their way to the next. The other teams were synchronised to hit their targets exactly five minutes before me and Craig hit ours because, as the team responsible for the only killing of the evening, it was important to make sure everything else had gone like clockwork and no one had been bagged, before we turned it into a murder inquiry. It had. To a man they'd done their jobs and no one had gone overboard. I almost couldn't believe it. I'd been convinced Eddie was going to fuck something up before the night was out; shooting himself, Brian or an aeroplane down or something but even he'd done his part and no more.

Now there were just three targets left and Eddie and Brian had finished for the night. Things were going well, but never so well that they can't all suddenly blow up in your face.

'Try it again,' I told Craig, standing behind him in the shadows.

'I've rung it three times already, he's not there,' he replied, blinking behind his ski mask.

'Just try it again.'

Craig rang the front doorbell a fourth time and backed off away from the door. We readied ourselves to jump like coiled springs the moment he opened the door but he never did. No one did.

'The bastard's gone out,' Craig said, straightening up after a time. 'What are we going to do? We can't hang around here all night, someone might see us and phone the Old Bill.'

'Oh you reckon do you?'

'Oh yeah, definitely,' he said without a trace of irony.

I stared at him for a bit before turning and heading back to the car. I climbed in behind the wheel, pulled my mask up and let Craig ask me what we were going to do several more times before I started the engine. 'Maybe six will be enough,' Craig said hopefully. 'Maybe they'll chuck the case out if they've only got one pair of eyes left.'

'Maybe,' I said. 'But the trouble with maybe is that it's only maybe. Maybe some of the others'll develop a bad case of the stiff upper lips. Maybe they won't take us seriously without making an example of one of them. Or maybe we just added witness intimidation and a dozen extra years to your sentence. We need Jeffrey dead,' I said.

I pulled the phone from my jacket pocket and speed-dialled Logan. It rang only twice before he picked it up.

'Is he Hovis?' he asked before I had a chance to speak.

'No he's not. The bastard's gone out. I don't know where.'

'You what?' Logan replied. 'He's gone out and you don't know where he is?' he said, repeating what I'd said almost word for word. I thought they only did that on the telly to let the audience know what had just been said on the other end.

'Did all the others go all right?' I asked before Logan had a chance to collect his thoughts.

'To a man,' he told me.

'Good. Get them on the blower and turn them around. I want this area covered inch for inch. All his usual haunts, pubs, takeaways and whatever. Tell them to take it nice and easy, don't attract attention to themselves, keep their eyes peeled and the first team to spot him plugs him. We'll take Craig's favourite boozer, The White Lion, as that's probably most likely. We'll phone you if he's there.' I gave the phone to Craig and put my foot down. I guess it was only half a mile at best from his house to the pub on foot, but the area was funnelled and criss-crossed with one-way systems so that we had to take a massive detour all around the houses before we came to a halt under the pub's swinging sign.

Craig regarded the pub's exterior for just the briefest of moments before pulling down his mask. He looked exactly what he was – a criminal returning to the scene of the crime.

'If I do this place much more I'll have to start hanging me gun up with the tankards,' he said, climbing out.

'Wait here, I'm going to look through the window, see if he's in there,' I told him. I kept my mask rolled up like a woolly hat as I peered through the window and sure enough, sat by the end of the bar, was Jeffrey. By rights he should've been home. Everyone else had been. See, we'd phoned all seven and told them that we were the police and that we wanted to come round and see them at blahdy-blah o'clock to check something in their statements with them. It was very important and it would only take a minute, so could they please make sure they were in. All seven had happily agreed, including Jeffrey. Now here he was having a pint and doing the crossword when he should've been home.

What an unreliable arsehole! No wonder his marriage failed.

'What are we going to do then, go in all guns blazing?' Craig asked.

'No, I'm not sure they'd appreciate the irony,' I replied. 'We'll have to wait for him to come to us.'

'But that could be hours. We can't wait around out here all night, someone's bound to see us.'

Craig might've had a knack for stating the obvious but he was right for all of it. We couldn't hang around indefinitely waiting for Jeffrey to call it a night. He was single, he lived alone and he had a crap life. He wasn't quitting this pub until closing, and he probably wouldn't want to even then. We had to get him out of there somehow.

'We could wait for him in the bog,' Craig suggested, demonstrating the very limit of his tactical thinking. 'Well, what are we going to do then?'

'I don't know,' I replied, racking my brains.

'Why don't we just give him a bell and ask him if he'll be so good as to step outside for a moment?'

I was just about to tell Craig to keep his gob shut if he couldn't think of anything sensible to say when he suddenly gave me an idea.

'Give me the phone,' I said.

'Eh. You're not really are you? I was only joking.'

'Look, this one's yours. I'll get him out here, you shoot him.

Can you handle that?' I asked, remembering how he'd reacted after Claire.

'Yes.'

'Are you sure? I'll do it if you're not sure.'

'I can do it,' he insisted.

'All right, but you better fucking had, this is your neck on the line, not mine,' I told him to add a little incentive, just in case he found he needed it when the time came.

'You just get him out here and leave the rest to me,' he said. 'How are you going to do it?'

'You ever heard of Norman Collier?'

'No. Who's he?'

'I'll explain another time, you just pull your mask down and get your arse over behind those bushes. When he comes out, shoot him. And make sure you put one in his head.'

And with that, I climbed back into the car and pulled my mask down. The street was off the main road so it was fairly quiet, by London standards at least. People and cars were going about their normal business but no one had walked by us this side of the street while we'd had our masks up and nobody was paying us any attention. That was probably about to change.

I checked Jeffrey's number on the list and dialled his mobile. It rang three times and I was just about to start worrying that he'd left it at home for the evening when he answered.

'Hello?'

'Hello, is that Paul Jeffrey?'

'Yes.'

'Hello, this is DS Pratchet of the Serious Crimes Squad.'

'Oh, hello Sergeant. I did telephone this evening to let you know that I probably wouldn't be home until later but the officer I spoke to didn't seem to know what I was talking about.'

I bet he didn't.

'That's quite all right ...ister ...frey, this is ...m ...ing different but ...ery important.'

'Sorry, you're breaking up a little, could you say that again.'

'Yes, I ...ed this is very ...tant. Can you ...ear me?'

'Yes, I think I got most of it.'

'We need to ... ...at ... ...in ... ...the ...elephone.'

'I'm sorry, I didn't catch any of that.

'I said, ...e ...eed to ... ... at ... ...in ... ...the ...elephone.'

'What? Hang on a second, I'm just going outside to get a better signal, I can't hear you,' he told me in a loud and clear voice. I started the engine, waved at Craig and pointed towards the pub door.

Jeffrey emerged from the pub a moment later with a phone in one ear and his finger in the other. He stepped out on to the pavement and I watched as Craig slipped from behind the bushes and tip-toed up behind him.

'Hello, Sergeant, can you say that again?' Jeffrey asked.

'Yes, I said, Craig Fisher says hello.'

'What?' he asked but I never got a chance to explain. Two quick 'phhuts' in the back and Jeffrey dropped to the pavement like a puppet that'd had its wires cut. Craig stepped over him and fired a last silent shot into his brain, permanently ending Jeffrey's evening. The first screams caught both of our attentions. A couple of young girls across the road, teenagers by the looks of them, opened their larynxes when they saw Craig deliver his coup de grâce prompting everyone within a hundred yards of us to look, first their way, then ours. I revved the engine to remind Craig that escape was the second part of the plan and by the time I had the motor in first gear and moving he was slamming the door shut and leaning across me to stick two gloved fingers up at the girls across the road – rather childishly, in my opinion.

We were two hundred yards down the road and doing fifty before people started spilling out of the pub to look at the mess we'd left on the pavement, and by that time, that's all they could do.

'Get on the blower and tell Logan the job's done. Also, tell him we're going to have to ditch the car and we're going to need picking up, so tell him to get Eddie or Felix or one of them to meet us round the back of Safeways. I've got an incendiary in the boot, I'll set it for two minutes once they're here.'

Craig made the call and a couple of minutes later we were off the road and waiting around in the dark behind the supermarket for Felix to arrive.

We kept our masks on in case there were surveillance cameras so it was difficult to judge Craig's mood, but I noticed he was pretty quiet. I concluded that it was just nerves, though to tell the truth I'd expected him to be all hyper and annoying after the hit. Instead, he actually seemed lost in his thoughts. I hoped that he wasn't having another attack of conscience, especially considering who we'd just rubbed out and what the purpose of the exercise was, so I asked him how he felt.

Craig thought about this for a little while before answering.

'Not guilty on all counts,' he smiled.

16. It's not my party so I can moan if I want to

Despite the amount of witnesses, it turned out that nobody saw a thing. Not even the drinkers sat at the pub windows seemed to recall seeing Jeffrey executed gangland-style four feet away. I guess they must've all been looking the other way at the time. 'I'd had too much to drink,' one of them told a national newspaper. 'A man can't be expected to remember every little detail from a particular night when he's in that sort of shape.'

I loved that line.

He was about the only person the press managed to get anything out of. Everyone else, it seemed, had been in the toilet or at the bar when it had happened so that was that.

All of Craig's remaining witnesses were questioned by police and dutifully withdrew their testimony to a man. A week later Craig surrendered himself for questioning and was released after two days with all charges dropped.

'We are not looking for anyone else in connection with the murders of Roger Laidlaw or Paul Jeffrey,' DI Leonard told assembled reporters, 'but instead we'd like to make an appeal for fresh witnesses to come forward. May I reassure the public that all information will be handled in the strictest confidence.'

Best of luck.

Incidentally, I was right about his wife. She looked great in the papers and on the telly at the funeral.

Craig wasted no time moving out of my place and threw himself a big party at The Aviary the next night. Despite Logan's reservations almost all the organisation turned up for it, including myself. It was like one big underworld jolly-up with loads of retired old-timers and active hard cases there all cracking open the champagne and sticking their fingers up at the Old Bill. And I don't mean metaphorically either, the police were camped in force outside the club, taking pictures of everyone as they rolled up. Naturally, everyone that rolled up gave them something to take a picture of.

Except me. I'm not that photogenic so I arrived via the back entrance of the restaurant next door which shares a cellar with The Aviary. This was the A-list entrance, Sam Broad had told me, reserved for only the most important of guests. There was definitely something in the way he'd said it that bothered me but I couldn't quite put my finger on it.

I think he was taking the piss.

Anyway, Logan told me if I wanted to come along I'd have to use it and keep out of the limelight. And the funny thing was, for once I did want to come along. I never got invited to any such parties and probably wouldn't've to this one had Craig not absolutely insisted I attended. I don't mean to sound like Cinderella or nothing, I'll be the first to admit to feeling like a bit of a spare part at discos and parties and stuff, but then, perhaps that's just because no one had ever insisted I attend before.

I even bought some new clothes, all black. Black shirt, black jacket, black trousers, shoes and socks. I even had black pants on… just in case.

'You going to a funeral or something?' Felix asked as I emerged from the cellar and entered the club.

'I dunno, say something else and we'll see,' I replied and walked through the crowd towards the bar. I sat down on one of the stools and smiled to myself at how cool that had sounded, then George came over and asked me if I was going to a funeral or something.

'Just get me a drink,' I said, then wondered what I should have. An alcoholic drink looked to be the order of the day, but this felt like neither the time nor the place for that. You might think a party would be the perfect time and place for an alcoholic drink but I hadn't been surrounded by this many villains since I'd been in the nick and thought it best I kept my wits about me. 'Just a lemonade,' I told him.

'You want vodka in that?' George asked.

'No George, that would then make it a vodka and lemonade, whereas I only want a lemonade. That's like a vodka and lemonade without the vodka.' George told me that he'd heard of it and went away to have a go making one, leaving me to check out the other guests. As this was a private party I reasoned that everyone here would be connected in one way or another with the organisation, though I never knew the company had so many young and attractive girls working for it. I figured they must be the girlfriends of some of the hard nuts here tonight but dismissed that as I watched no less than eight of them slobbering all over Craig as he whooped it up in the middle of the dance floor.

They were Crystal's girls. I suddenly recognised half a dozen of them from when I used to call in on her. I looked around the club and saw that it was absolutely packed with skirt. And short skirt at that.

'Won the roll-over did he?' George asked, indicating towards Craig with a flick of the head.

'You might say that,' I told him as two leggy beauties sandwiched Craig between their bodies and rubbed up and down against him. The other girls around Craig closed in at this point and soon they were all smooching with him and each other as a sea of laughing faces clapped along and cheered all around.

'He's mad,' George said after a moment or two. 'They're only interested in his money, you know that don't you?' I told him I did. 'What a waste!' he said shaking his head sadly.

'Not your style then?' I asked.

'Me? No!' then he laughed. 'I've got more sense than him. Wouldn't touch it I wouldn't. Wouldn't touch a penny of it,' he said. 'Stick it all in the bank and try and carry on as if it hadn't happened.'

I've heard George say this sort of thing before but it didn't matter because I never tire of the utter insanity behind his thinking.

'You'd give up your job though?' I suggested.

'Give up my job? Of course I wouldn't. A man's got to work you know. Got to pay the bills.'

'But if you won, I mean, won big. Millions I'm talking about.'

'No, I wouldn't touch it. I'd just stick it in the bank. You start dipping into it and before you know it you're penniless and living on skid row. I've seen it happen. Happened to this bloke in the paper the other week. He went out and bought helicopters and a big house and...'

'Oi George, can I get a drink down here sometime tonight?' someone was shouting from the other end of the bar.

'Be back in a sec,' George reassured me and wandered off. I wondered if he'd always been like this or whether the instinct to hoard had been born from a lifetime of having fuck all. Either way, he was still clearly bananas but I guess it made sense to him. And I guess Craig's attitude towards life made sense to Craig too. One of the girls now had her legs wrapped around his waist and was riding his back topless. As busy as he seemed Craig still had time to spot me and give me a wave and a salute. The girl clocked this and did the same much to the amusement of Craig.

'Look at all the fucking birds in here,' Eddie said as he sauntered up. 'There's stacks of it!'

'They're just prostitutes Eddie.'

'I couldn't give a shit what they do for a living, I'm not exactly what you'd call a career man myself. All I know is that I've been walking around with a hard-on for the last hour.'

I edged away slightly.

'You going to get some?' he asked. 'It's all paid for.'

'I don't think so.'

'Well I am,' he said and stood where he was for the next twenty minutes telling me about it. In the meantime Craig had given the girl straddling his shoulders a piggy-back to the men's toilets and returned ten minutes later looking very smug with himself indeed.

'They're just begging for it,' Eddie was saying, hopping up and down on one leg slightly while behind me George continued to mutter to himself.

'Mad he is! Mad!'

How the hell did I get stuck with these freaks, I began to wonder to myself. A horrible notion occurred to me that maybe the rest of the club were viewing us as a trio. I ordered another lemonade and made my way to the other side of the dance floor.

The music was louder over here and most of the people around me were dancing. I stood motionless for a few minutes, feeling like a bit of a sore thumb, so I decided to have a little dance, then felt like a whole septic hand. I stopped. One of the girls close by was staring at me so I gave her a smile. She returned my smile and strolled over. She danced in front of me provocatively, enticing me to join her, then leaned closer and shouted in my ear,

'You want to party?' This confused me a little because I thought we already were. Then I got what she meant.

'No, I'm fine at the moment,' I told her. But I didn't want to be rude so I added, 'My name's Ian.'

'Good for you,' she said and walked away, leaving me twisting half-heartedly by myself. I finished my drink and returned to the safety of the bar. Eddie called me an old dog while George asked me if I wanted another vodka and lemonade. I sniffed the glass and told him to forget about getting me any more drinks.

What was I doing here?

I wasn't enjoying myself that was for sure. It was about this time that I remembered the other reason I didn't go to discos and parties – I hated them. No one ever talked to me (and by that I mean the people I wanted to talk to me never talked to me), I didn't like dancing and I wasn't a social drinker. Standing in the corner of a very noisy, very hot and very disorientating room, where everyone around you is having a good time – and you don't understand why – is just not my cup of tea. I usually remembered this and stayed at home where I could relax but Craig managed to lull me into thinking this might be different, this might be fun. I think I was just flattered that he asked me and, fearful of what I might miss, I came along.

I should've listened to Logan.

Eddie was now dancing over in a dark corner, behind a large pillar and just next to the toilets and doing about as good a job of it as I had. There was a pathetic kind of desperation about Eddie, who couldn't even seem to summon up the courage to proposition a hooker. I didn't feel sorry for him, but I did feel like shooting him, just to put him out of his misery and because he was beginning to make me cringe. Did I look like that? The oddball who wasn't joining in?

No, I was different. I didn't want to fuck a hooker. I could if I wanted to but I didn't. I've had hookers before. They do a job. They sort you out (temporarily), and that's about the nicest thing I can think to say about them. But I didn't want sorting out. I wanted…

…oh, I don't know, what did I want?

I was becoming more and more miserable by the moment. I watched Craig back on the dance floor and surrounded by hookers again. He looked to be having the time of his life. What was he doing differently to me? I thought as I stood at the bar on my own without a drink. Craig had said this was going to be the party to end all parties. And as far as I was concerned, he was right.

I wondered if people realised I was a killer…

'You waiting for a drink?'

I turned around, it was JB's son and 'downstairs' bar manager, Sam Broad. He was leaning over the bar just behind me.

'A drink? What do you want?' he repeated.

'I don't want anything,' I said, then thought. 'Unless you've got a cup of coffee.'

'We don't serve coffee,' Sam told me, but then his face softened a little. 'But I can put on the kettle out back if you want.'

'That would be good. Milk, no sugar.'

Sam disappeared through the door and reappeared a couple of minutes later with a mug of coffee. He must've used powdered milk because he'd somehow got some in his moustache.

'Cheers,' I said and sipped the coffee.

'I don't think I've ever seen you here at night before.'

'No?'

'No.' He leaned forward a bit closer. 'Are you working tonight?'

'No,' I told him. 'Are you?'

Sam forced a smile.

'That's a good one, I like that. You're a surprisingly funny man,' he informed me, then got serious again. 'You know the Old Bill is outside in numbers. I don't want any "business" in my club, I don't care who your target is.'

He continued in this vein for several minutes and I let him because he was cheering me up a little. Sam liked to think he was some kind of a big shot. He loved ordering people about and sticking his nose in where it didn't belong but really all he was in charge of was the downstairs bar. And seeing as the downstairs bar was about half the size of the main bar upstairs that should tell you what kind of vital cog he was.

'As long as we understand each other,' he said. 'So, who's your target?'

'Why do you always assume it's not you?' I asked and for one immensely satisfying moment he looked like he was going to have a heart attack.

Craig emerged from the throng at that moment with a couple of hookers in his arms. 'Hey, anyone need a hand-job?' he announced. 'If so, you'll have to ask one of the girls as mine are a bit full at the moment. Here Bridges, here, have a wank on me,' he said and pushed one of his girls into my arms, then looked at Sam. 'You'll have to sort yourself out, I'm almost out of whores.'

The girl in his arms objected to this.

'Oh don't say that, that's horrible. I hate that name.'

'Shut up. You want paying, you're a whore. You want to do it for free, then we'll rethink your job title. All right?'

'All right,' she said.

'Now what are you?'

'I'm a whore,' she said reluctantly.

'You sure about that?' he asked, humiliating her further.

'Yes,' she said. 'I'm a whore.'

'Aren't we all,' I ventured in an attempt to defuse the moment.

'Really?' Craig asked. 'How much you charge for anal?'

That was a nice little ice-breaker and we all had a good laugh at this until Craig announced that these two did it for eighty quid.

'Are you drinking coffee?' Craig asked me.

'I don't really drink.'

'Jesus! Did I ever tell you about the time I gave up drinking?' Craig asked. I said he hadn't. 'Worst five minutes of my life. Hey, bartender, get me a bottle of your finest champagne. I'm having a drink with my friend Bridges.'

'No really, I'm fine,' I told him.

'Nonsense. Come on, you've got to have a drink. Come on, at least have one,' he urged. I tried to object some more but Craig didn't take in a word of it and went ahead and asked for four glasses.

'I'm the bar manager actually, not the bartender,' Sam objected.

'I didn't ask for your life story mate, just get me my drink and fuck off.'

Sam's eyes burned with fury and for a moment I thought he was going to lose it, but instead he simply ordered George to serve us and stormed off out the back.

'You know, I'm related to him somehow. Cousins or second cousin, or is it cousin twice removed or something? To be honest I haven't looked into it that deeply. Nice bloke though.'

George cracked open the champagne and poured it into four glasses for us. Craig nagged on at me to pick one up and after a little indecision I did. Would one kill me? Probably not. Besides I'd had two vodka and lemonades already thanks to George. Perhaps I should try and join in a bit more. If I made more of an effort, maybe I might even end up enjoying myself. The girl in my arms rubbed her legs against mine and smiled as I looked down at her…

'And have one yourself,' Craig told George but George just laughed and shook his head.

'You can throw it all away if you want but don't ask me to help you.' Craig looked at him somewhat confused then ordered us all to raise our glasses.

'Bridges, your health. Ladies, bottoms up,' and we all drank. 'Another,' he told our flabbergasted barman. 'Just keep 'em coming.'

'One's enough for me, really,' I insisted but Craig wrestled my glass away from me and topped it up.

'You need to chill out Bridges. You look like you're going to snap in half. Hey, hey, hey, remember all those months I had to learn to trust you, well now it's your turn. Relax. Enjoy yourself.'

'But I was.'

'Standing at the bar drinking coffee and sizing up how many of my guests you could take out before they get you isn't enjoying yourself.'

Yes it was.

'So, you're going to have another drink,' he said tipping my glass up to my face, 'and then you're going to take this lovely young thing out back, I'm sorry, what's your name?'

The girl in my arms thought for a moment. 'Whore?' she asked.

'Er, yeah, whatever. And you're going to do whatever comes naturally.' Craig thought for a moment then whispered in my ear. 'And that doesn't mean strangling her.'

'No, really,' I started to say but Craig and 'Whore 2' were dragging and pushing me towards Sam's office behind the bar and causing such a fuss that a dozen people around us all turned around to watch the spectacle. In the end, just to get away from all those mocking eyes, I hurried through the door, dragging 'Whore 2' with me.

Sam jumped out of his skin and looked up at us through a veil of cocaine dust.

'I need your office,' I told him and he stared at the girl in horror.

'Jesus Christ!' was all he could say before stumbling out through the door.

'I guess he doesn't get it all that often,' 'Whore 2' said as she locked the door behind him and dropped to her knees.

She did her job and I felt bad.

Efficient, painless and relatively quick, I didn't give her so much as a backward glance and I made my way out of the office, feeling a bit like a cow leaving the milking stools.

I instantly chastised myself. Why had I let her? Why hadn't I just put my foot down, been strong and said no? I could've killed her if I'd wanted. I could've and gotten away with it. Logan knew that. Craig knew it. Even Sam knew it. Now they'd all be looking at me and sniggering and nudging themselves and laughing about what Bridges had got up to with a whore.

At that moment I hated them all.

The motherfuckers!

Christ, I really just felt like pulling the trigger and blowing someone away. Someone. Anyone. I didn't care, just to restore the equilibrium. I'm the guy you don't fuck with. I'm the guy who kills people. And I don't do whores!

Craig was gone, much to my relief, though Sam was stood at the end of the bar looking wide-eyed and white. His expression changed only when he saw 'Whore 2' emerge from the office behind me and say cheerio. The relief was etched all over his face and as he passed me he said only, 'Please knock next time you want to use my office.'

George asked me if I wanted another glass of champagne but I told him to make it a triple scotch, straight up.

'You want lemonade in that?'

'Oh for fuck's sake, just get me my fucking drink,' I snapped. 'Just the one,' I told myself. 'Just to sort myself out then I'll go.' George brought me my scotch and quickly retired to the far end of the bar, leaving me alone with my thoughts.

Why had I come here? I asked myself again. What did I think I was going to find? This wasn't me, I hated this scene, so what the fuck was I doing here? I knocked my scotch back in two and it burned my throat, making me wince and wheeze.

I looked around and clocked Craig once again, dancing in the middle of the dance floor, this time with two new hookers. What was he playing at? I'd have to have words with him the next time I saw him. He couldn't carry on with women like this, not in our business. Not if he wanted to keep his streak. Logan had told me that, and he was right, it was true. Women were weakness. Christ, I should know that better than most. Almost every woman I've ever known has tried to fuck me over one way or another. In fact, if it…

'Hi, is anyone sitting here?' I spun around. It was that hooker who'd been riding Craig's back earlier in the evening. I told her as far as I knew the seat wasn't taken. 'You're a friend of Craig's aren't you?'

'Yes,' I said, 'sort of.'

'I'm Debbie.'

'Look, you're a bit late, I've already had a hand-job off that hooker over there.'

'I'm very pleased for you but I'm not actually a hooker.'

'Oh well, whatever it is you're calling yourself these days.'

'I just call myself Debbie. I don't have another name for myself.'

'Well, if you like, I've already had a Debbie tonight and I didn't bring that much money with me anyway so…'

'No, no, I don't think you understand. I'm not a hooker, I'm not a prostitute, I'm not an escort, or a model or a P.A. I don't do sex for money – not unless you count my old man, I suppose – and I'm not making you any offers.'

I looked at her long and hard before pointing towards the dance floor.

'But I saw you riding around on his back with your tits out!'

'A girl can have fun, can't she? I just got carried away, that's all. I didn't even know the other girls were hookers.'

'Oh,' I said. 'Sorry.'

'That's okay. How was it anyway?'

'What?'

'Your hand-job.'

'Um, yes. Very nice thank you.'

'Good. Is this anyone's champagne?'

'No, help yourself.'

'Way ahead of you. You want one?'

'No, I have to be going.'

'Oh really, but it's so early. Running home to the wife are we?'

'If I had a wife I very much doubt I'd be here…'

'Getting hand-jobs off hookers?' she said finishing a sentence I didn't really want finished. 'Of course you would. Half the guys here have wives at home.' She looked around the room. 'The other half have brought them with them… if you know what I mean?'

I didn't, but I didn't ask, assuming it was a married thing.

'I'm married myself, but my husband's so boring I'd go off my head if I stayed in with him every night.' She gave me a sly smile. 'I'm with my sister tonight,' she said, then chuckled, or giggled, one of the two. Either way it was very becoming. She held my gaze for a little longer than warranted before looking away.

'What's your name?' she asked.

'Ian.'

'What do you do for a living, Ian?'

'I work with computers, building websites and search engines.'

'Really! Sounds fucking boring.'

'Doesn't it? It's not though, it can be pretty exciting stuff,' I said, then added after a little reflection, 'if truth were to be told, I have a pretty exciting job.'

'Aren't you adorable,' she said wrinkling her nose and jumped down off the stool and wrapped her arms around me in a warm embrace. I held mine aloft as I tried to decide whether or not she'd flip out if I did the same before bringing them to rest around her slender little waist.

'Ian?'

'Oh sorry, I thought…' I started to say ripping my arms from her body.

'No, no that's fine, you keep them there, they feel nice. I just wanted to ask you a question.'

'Oh, okay,' I said and replaced my hands, albeit slightly lower.

'All I was going to ask is this, why would a computer geek carry a gun?'

It took a moment for the penny to drop. She wasn't hugging me, she was frisking me. I pulled away again and this time I broke free. Debbie looked at me all smiles and satisfaction.

'You're one of JB's boys aren't you? It's okay, don't go. Ian, please, just stay and chat, I don't mean any harm. We're just having a drink together. And it's always good to know who you're drinking with.'

I stood my ground, uncertain of what to do. Normally I would've taken her out back to Sam's office – knocked on the door – told Sam to piss off and put a couple of bullets into her, but this wasn't a normal night at The Aviary. This place was full of villains tonight. I mean, who here wasn't a fucking villain? Of course I wasn't going to be a web designer, not in this company, not when she's just seen me hob-nobbing with a man who's just beaten two murder charges by mass witness intimidation. Christ, where were my brains?

I'll tell you where, they were down the toilet with two vodka and lemonades, two glasses of champagne and two slightly tingly balls. Now that's what I was talking about; you can't keep your wits about you in this line of business with booze and birds.

Saying all that though, if she was here and she knew JB, then she was probably a villain too.

'So, what is it you do for a living?' she asked. I thought for a moment but couldn't think up anything clever or coy so I said nothing. 'Did you help out Craig last week? You two seem to know each other quite well.' Again I said nothing. 'You don't want to say anything, and I can understand that. We've all got to be a bit careful these days. Take my old man for instance, I can't imagine what he'd think if he knew half the things I got up to behind his back,' she laughed, then leaned in a little closer and lowered her voice. 'You could imagine though, couldn't you. You could imagine everything. I bet you're even imagining one or two things you'd like to do to me now, aren't you? Because if you're not, I sure am.'

She leaned closer still so that I could feel her warm breath on my face.

'And hand-jobs are only for starters…' I felt her hand wrap itself around my weapon and I'm not talking about the one under my arm when all of a sudden Logan came out of nowhere and interrupted.

'Oh, Danny!' Debbie jumped. 'How are you?'

'I want a word with my man here,' he said in no uncertain terms.

'Oh, sure, cut right in.'

'I don't think you understand girl, I want a word with Ian alone so sling your arse. Go on, fuck off, but don't go fucking off because I'm going to want a little chat with you before the night's out.'

'Sure Danny, I didn't mean…'

'You still here?'

Not for much longer. Debbie spun on her heel and rushed off as Danny had ordered, giving me just the merest of backward glances as she ran up the steps.

I waited for Danny to go into one but he was calmness personified. In fact, the only change in his tone came when Debbie disappeared from view and he remarked, 'The arse on that is fucking criminal.' Then after a quick rethink, 'Well, it's certainly seen its fair share of villainy anyway.'

'You know her?' I asked.

'Oh yeah, that's Debbie, she used to be one of our dancers, years ago this was. Over here, over at Benny's place, Stringfellows, she did them all, and I mean that in every sense of the word,' he said and gave me a wink.

'She's a hooker?'

'Oh no, nothing like that. She's more, the good time had by all, if you know what I mean. And she's a scheming, manipulative little cunt with it.'

'How do you mean?'

'How do I mean? I mean she's got a body to die for, and she knows how to use it. She'd have you in the palm of her hand in no time at all.' He was spot on with that one. 'And that's no dig at you, she's done it to plenty before.'

'I think Craig did her.'

'Yeah, I wouldn't be surprised, but Craig's different.'

'How's Craig different? He got a licence or something?'

'No, but let's just say he just knows how to use women and not let himself get used,' which meant that previous comment *was* a dig at me. 'I can't tell you how to live your life Bridges, but I can tell you the best way to keep on living it, and that's stay away from Debbie Benson, she's bad news.'

17. Mother's day

'Oh, don't give me that!' I shouted at her.

'All I said was I'm always there for you,' mum said.

'I know, that's the fucking problem, you're always there. Why don't you fuck off somewhere else for a change and just leave me alone?'

'You know, when I was a little girl I always wanted to be on my own too, but when I grew up I realised that I'd wasted so much of my life and what I really regretted most was not spending more time with my own mother. You can never get those days back you know, Ian.'

'Thank Christ for that!'

'I guess what I'm trying to say is that I didn't have a very happy childhood. That's probably why I spoiled you so much as a child. Probably too much now that I come to think of it, and I regret that.'

'Spoiled me? Spoiled me?'

'You always had the best toys,' she pointed out. 'And you remember that bike I bought you. Brand new it was. I never had a new bike when I was a little girl. Nobody did.'

'What do you mean nobody did? Somebody must've had a new bike. What did the factory do, make second-hand ones?'

'Nevertheless, yours was brand new.'

'Yes, I remember that bike. You only bought it for me because Uncle Brian rode my last one to the pawnbroker's. Come to think of it, he rode my new one there too and we never saw either of them again.'

'Yes, he broke my heart, not that you cared at all. I cried for days and days but you weren't interested in that, were you? All you ever cared about was yourself. You always were selfish.'

I remembered when Uncle Brian left. I had only been about twelve when it had happened and the following two weeks were some of the worst of my life. And that's saying something. Mum blamed me for driving him away and beat me black and blue every day for a fortnight until I couldn't take any more and ran away from home. I was gone for a week and almost starved by the time the police picked me up and took me back. Mum told the police my bruises had been made by Uncle Brian and that's why I'd done a runner, but everything was okay now because she'd kicked him out. I heard all this from my bedroom. She told this same lie so many times to so many people she actually ended up believing it herself. After the police left she locked me in my bedroom so that I couldn't run away again and kept me prisoner for a whole summer.

She'd make sure I never left her again.

'Sometimes, I hate myself so much,' she said.

'Hey, I'll second that.'

'You've always been selfish.'

'I'm not selfish.'

'You are. All you ever think about is yourself and doing what you want to do. What about my happiness, did you ever think about that?'

'You did enough thinking about that for the both of us. This is my life, not an extension of yours!'

'You wouldn't even have a life if it wasn't for me. I sacrificed everything for you and what thanks did I get? None. Me, me, me, that's all you ever thought about.'

'That's a fucking lie you bitch! You never did anything for me except hold me back and ruin my life.'

'Ruin your life? You're my little boy. You don't have a life without me. I am your life and you are mine. I've listened to you, now it's your turn to bloody well listen to me…'

Listen to her? That's all I'd done for the best part of six weeks and I was coming to my wit's end. Craig's party had been that long ago and I hadn't seen or heard from him since. According to Eddie, he was still out celebrating, making up for lost time, which galled me a bit. Nice to know the time he'd spent learning from me he considered 'lost time'. And the simple fact is he would've lost a lot more of it too if it hadn't've been for me.

Now I was all alone again.

Well, almost.

'I didn't want it to come to this but you've left me no choice. I'm sorry, but if you'd have listened to me in the first place this wouldn't be necessary. As your mother I am ordering you to give up this silly killing business and get a proper job.'

By Christ I can laugh when I want to!

My sides hurt so much I almost couldn't take it but every time I thought about those nineteen words I collapsed again.

'Did you hear what I said?'

'Please don't. No more, stop it,' I begged her as the tears ran down my face.

'THAT – was an order.'

'Ahhhhh, ha ha ha ha ha ha! Court-martial me you fuck!'

'I MEAN IT!' she screamed at me. 'I am your mother and you will do what I bloody-well tell you to do!'

'NO!' I screamed back. 'I'm not listening to you any more. Go away! Go away!'

'You listen to your so-called friends, thieves and murderers and whores but you don't listen to me. What sort of a boy are you? I am so ashamed. You shame me. You shame me.'

'You shame yourself. You were the worst mother in the world. You are nothing to me and I'm glad you're dead!'

'No-ho-ho,' she bawled. 'You don't mean it. You can't mean it. I've never…' but mum was cut off by a sound at the front door.

I spun around, dropped to the floor and quickly pulled out my gun.

Silence.

I listened again. Nothing. I even held my breath and listened but all I could hear was my own heart pumping hard inside my chest. I let out a slow breath then quietly drew another and just as

I did I heard it again. There was definitely someone at the door. They hadn't rung the bell or knocked or announced themselves in any way but they were there all right. Waiting. Listening. Trying to get in? I turned my attention to the back of the house but heard nothing from that direction, just footsteps on concrete out the front and a slight brushing on the door. I aimed my Glock at the top left-hand corner of the door and readied myself. My pistol was silenced. When I'm at home my pistol is always silenced just in case of this sort of thing. Well, no sense in bothering the neighbours with gunfire is there?

I shot the door three times in quick succession, the top left-hand corner, the bottom right-hand corner and again at the top.

I didn't know who it was out there and didn't particularly want some bashful Jehovah's Witness to dispose of unnecessarily, so I fired to panic them away from the door. I jumped up and charged to the front window to get a look at who it was and a possible clean shot if it was necessary.

'Don't shoot! Bridges, fuck, it's me, it's only me,' shouted Craig as he stumbled back and dived into my hedgerow.

I yanked open the front door waving my hand and telling him to 'Shhhhh!' I live in London. My neighbours might not have batted an eyelid if my house had been on fire and I'd been trapped in the upstairs bedroom screaming for help (and there'd been a ladder in the front garden) but there are some phrases that'll still get the curtains twitching. 'Keep your voice down,' I said and pointed to the silencer on the end of my gun. 'Come on, inside.'

Craig followed me into the house and while I didn't keep the gun trained on him, I didn't put it away either.

'What were you doing out there?'

'Eavesdropping,' he said all matter-of-fact. 'I was just coming up to see you and I heard you rowing with someone.'

'You were listening to me?'

'Yeah,' he said. 'But only from the end of the street. Who were you rowing with?'

'No one, it's not important.'

'It sounded like it was your mum.'

'Forget about it.'

'I thought you told me your mum was dead?'

'She is.'

'Oh, I can see why you was having to shout then,' he said. 'Put your shooter away and stick the kettle on, Bridges. I could murder a cup of tea.' He followed me into the kitchen and I filled the kettle and reached for a couple of mugs. The gun I left tucked into the back of my trousers. 'So,' he said, 'what's this with your mum then? You want to talk about it?'

'Not really,' I told him.

'Are you sure, because I'd love to know.'

'Your concern is touching.'

'Go on, tell us.'

'It's private.'

'Look, you don't have to tell us if you don't want to but I would if I was you because at the moment I think you're nuts so you might as well put me straight about it.'

'I'm not nuts.'

'Well then tell us about it.' He paused for a moment then shored up his argument with, 'Go on Bridges, don't be a cunt. Just tell us.'

'All right, all right, just give me a moment here.' This was embarrassing. Being overheard talking to yourself is always embarrassing but being overheard rowing with yourself… explain that one. I should've just told him he was right and I was nuts and had done with it but I felt the need to explain. And not just for Craig's benefit but for mine.

'I had a bit of a shit childhood,' I told him. 'My mum resented me and blamed me for not being able to hold on to a bloke. You know, who wants to get lumbered with a single mum? Especially in the seventies. She used to take all her frustration out on me, which just got worse the older we both got. My teenage years were just… just horrible.' I filled the mugs with boiling water and stirred the tea bags around a little before continuing. 'Sounds stupid doesn't it, you think if they were that bad why didn't I just leave? It wasn't like that though, my mum was a fucking expert at emotional blackmail. She'd feed me through the ringer and back and make me feel guilty for feeling bad about it. That kind of thing. You know what I'm talking about?'

'Yeah. Sort of. I think.'

'Anyway, I did try and leave, dozens of times, but every bloke she'd been involved with had left her and she sure as fuck wasn't about to be left by her own flesh and blood. Oh I don't know, there's just no rhyme or reason to it. She used to turn up everywhere and cause a scene, at school, at work, if I was down the library, she'd freak out, think I was trying to leave and hunt me down. Oh man, she even turned up at prison and insisted I came home with her.'

I squirmed inwardly as I remembered that day. I'd only been inside a short time when they told me I had a visitor. It was mum. The first thing she said to me was, 'I've had enough of this, come on, we're leaving.' I thought she'd gone bananas. I didn't know the half of it.

'Mum, I'm in prison, I can't leave.'

'Oh yes, well we'll soon see about that, you're coming home this instant, mister. No arguments,' and she dragged me to my feet. 'Come on, let's go.'

'Mum, I can't.'

'Er, excuse me madam, what are you doing?' asked Mr Emery.

'I'm taking my little boy home.' Cue much laughter from my fellow prisoners.

'I'm afraid you can't do that,' Mr Emery smirks.

'Can't do it? I'm his mother. He's my baby and he's coming home.'

'In a little while perhaps, but don't you worry, we'll take good care of him while he's here.'

'I'm not having it. I'm not having it. Ian, come along.'

'Bridges, you stay where you are.'

'I ain't going anywhere.'

'IAN! You're coming with me now!'

'Perhaps I can get you a cup of tea and we can sit down and have a little talk about this.'

'Get out of my way.' Mum grabbed my arm and started dragging me towards the door. Mr Emery was trying to separate us both while blocking my mum's kicks and every prisoner (and his wife) in the visiting room was falling about in hysterics. 'He's my little boy, he's my little boy, not yours,' she kept on shouting as three guards finally dragged her off me and towards the door. 'I'm his mother, he belongs to me. Get your hands off me!'

By Christ, I got a good kicking that day.

'You know the irony about that though,' I told Craig, 'was that she was the one that turned me in in the first place. I think she thought they'd just have a word with me, give me a slap on the wrist and tell me to do as my mum told me in future. I don't think it even occurred to her that they'd send me down. Well, I was just a little boy wasn't I. If a little boy needs punishing who better to do it than his mother.'

'She died while you were in the shovel?'

'Yes, I never saw her again after that day. I banned her from coming to see me and she died after I got life for Breen. I don't know why I still argue with her. I mean, I'm not nuts, I don't believe she is still alive and talking to me, it's more knowing what she would've said had she still been alive and here. And I can't help but hear her criticise me and everything I do because that's what she did in life.'

'Yeah, well I guess we're all a bit fucked in the head to one extent or another. So argue with your dead mum if it makes you happy, I don't care, but do you know what the bad thing about it is?'

'What?'

'You sounded like you were losing.' Craig took a sip of his tea and smiled. 'If I was going to have imaginary arguments I'd make sure I at least won them.'

'You're a great comfort.'

'Tell me something – just while we're getting all this out in the open – there's something I've always wanted to ask you.' There was a certain sly smugness to his tone that immediately got my guard up.

'What?' I asked cautiously.

'What did you go down for, in the first place I mean?'

How did I know this was coming?

'Assault,' I told him.

'Really?' he replied, unconvinced. 'Look, I'm not being funny or anything but that's not what I heard.'

Fucking Logan! I told him I didn't want anyone knowing. Some people just can't keep a promise.

'Honestly, I'm not taking the piss or anything, I'm just curious. I heard you used to steal knickers.'

'Did you?'

'Yeah. I just wondered if it was true. I mean, I don't care or nothing, I was just, you know, curious. Hey, what we do when we're young doesn't matter a toss. Past is past. All that matters is what we do today and you're a top man today, so I was just wondering why you did it.'

'I've got a gun you know.'

'I'm not taking the piss, cross my heart and mum's the word and all that old bollocks.'

'What can I tell you, I had issues.'

'Yeah I heard, more than 250 pairs of them. Fucking hell, what d'you want all them for?'

'Oh I don't know, it was a long time ago. I was confused, I couldn't help myself.'

'Eddie reckons you used to get them off lines, out of launderettes, even break into people's houses and steal them right out of the drawer.'

'Eddie knows? Oh fucking hell!'

'Everyone knows. That's all right, isn't it? I wouldn't've brought it up if I thought it was a secret.'

I dropped my face into my hands, rubbed my eyes and moaned. That was my past. Something I thought I'd left far behind, but you never can leave your past behind because your past is what makes you today.

'Don't worry,' Craig said. 'Logan reckons everyone's known for years. I don't think anyone thinks anything less of you.'

'I don't think they can, can they?'

'Hmm. So, what I wanted to know was, what did you do with them all? I mean, did you wear them or something, or sniff them? I mean, what do you do with 250 pairs of pants?'

'You can stop asking me questions any time you like you know?'

'Oh yeah, I know that, I'm just interested. I've got ten quid says you used to wear them.'

'I didn't. And I didn't sniff them either.'

'Look, we've all done it, I'm just comparing notes here that's all.'

'I don't know why I took them, all right. It was just a compulsion. The act of stealing them was the thing itself.' This had been explained to me at great length by the prison psychologist. 'I didn't want them or anything and I didn't do anything with them, I just kept them in a bag under my bed.'

'And your mum found them?'

'Yes. She didn't know where they'd come from at first but she took them to the police all the same so that the police would tell me to stop doing it.'

'And they did?'

'Yes, they did. But because there were so many pairs and because half of them had come from houses they viewed it as a very serious crime. More than fifty burglaries. A lot of the women didn't even know their... thingies had disappeared. I was branded a sex offender, but because I hadn't attacked anyone – and never would've – I wasn't sectioned.'

'Gave you a hard time did they? The other lags?'

'Yes. They did,' I told him, remembering those first hard months.

'Oh well, these things happen. Think about it though, you probably wouldn't be here today if you hadn't've done all that weird stuff. Makes you think, doesn't it?'

'Thank you Sigmund Freud. Always a pleasure retracing old footsteps,' I said and finished my tea. 'So, aren't you going to say it?'

'Say what?'

'That I'm nuts.'

'Fuck me Bridges, do you think I need to? You're a fruitcake. Ah, don't take it the wrong way, we're all a bit loopy one way or another. You know what your problem is today though don't you? You need to get out a bit more. You spend all your time cooped up in your house with nothing to do all day but argue with dead relatives, you're bound to lose the plot a bit.'

'That's what comes of spending half your life in prison. And the other half with no friends.'

'What are you talking about, I'm your friend – although don't get any ideas,' he said shooting me a sideways glance. 'Me and my dad.'

'Your dad?'

'Yeah. Haven't I introduced you? He's over there in the corner drilling your mum at the moment.'

I looked over at where he was pointing and said, 'I wouldn't be in the least surprised,' at which we both laughed.

'His name's Harvey.'

'Craig, what are you doing here? I haven't seen hide nor hair of you for weeks.'

'We've got a job,' he told me.

'A job? What is it?'

'Well, you ain't going to believe this but…'

18. When your number's up

Unbelievably, George's ship had come in. Unfortunately for George, it turned out to be the *Titanic*. Five numbers and the bonus ball had netted him around £250,000 and while George didn't want to touch a penny of it, there were plenty of people who did. It might not have been a lot of money considering JB's total worth, but it was just too easy not to take it.

George had won a couple of days after I'd seen him last and JB and Logan had spent the intervening weeks milking him.

George'd had plans to put it all in the Post Office or some such account but JB 'insisted' George invested his winnings in diamonds and bogus trust funds.

Poor old George, what was he to do? He figured he was going to get stitched up for the interest and possibly even lose a chunk as it was siphoned off here and there, but he could never have dreamed JB actually planned to take the lot.

The lottery advisers and George's bank manager pulled their hair out as George sunk his loot into one shaky investment after another but what could they do? It was George's money, he could wallpaper his house with it if he wanted to.

As part of the plan, and to lull George into a false sense of optimism, he was instructed to have a good, strong wall-safe fitted to keep his diamonds in.

'Diamonds keep their value George. Better than any ISA. You'll double your money on them in no time.'

Once the funds were set up and the safe and diamonds and everything else were in place, it was just a question of removing George and his next of kin.

And this was where Craig and I came in.

We blindfolded George and Lucy before we started slapping them about. I've worked over people before and it's harder when they're looking at you. Especially if they know you.

'Come on, let's just kill them and do this afterwards,' Craig said, slapping Lucy around the face. 'They're making too much noise.'

'It sounds loud to us but I promise you their neighbours won't be able to hear them. Not through their gags and not in a detached property like this. Besides I told you, the injuries can't be post-mortem, they have to look like they were alive.' This was JB's plan; take George and his wife back to their place, give them a going over and then top them to make it look like they'd suffocated on their gags. It was your classic robbery gone wrong.

And who'd take the fall for this?

Well, Nigel of course. George's greedy and unscrupulous only son, who'd returned from university to rob his own parents. He'd be the first person the police would call on (particularly after they found the clues we were going to leave them), unfortunately they'd be just too late. In a fit of remorse, when Nigel suddenly realised that he'd actually killed them both, he'd top himself back in his little student flat. Some cash would be found next to his body, maybe even one of the smaller diamonds, some clothes and some rope – all covered in forensic. A nice little open and shut case for the police to file away and forget and £200 for the *Evening Standard*, for running an ad for a new barman in their Situations Vacant column.

George's trousers darkened with terror and his muffled screams increased several octaves when Lucy's gag was knocked off and she was able to call out his name before Craig smothered her again.

'Sorry George,' Craig said as he stuffed the handkerchief back into her mouth.

'Don't apologise to him,' I told Craig. 'Have a little respect. We're murdering them, the least you can do is allow them to hate us for it. Don't try and appeal to his sense of pity, just be his worst nightmare and simplify things for him in what is obviously a difficult time for them both.'

'I'm sure you meant that to make sense,' Craig said, thinking about it.

'Don't feel, just do,' I told him. 'Look, just a little bit more then we'll finish them off. Okay?'

'Okay,' Craig agreed.

'All right then, tighten those ropes around her wrists. Make it look like a real amateur job.' Craig went to work while I opened the safe.

We already had the combination, the torture was just meant to make it look like Nigel had had to beat it out of them. 'JB wants you to make them look stubborn,' Logan had told us, 'but just use your common sense, all right.'

This might've seemed like a first-class nightmare but it was an easier option compared to JB's initial plan for George. Originally he'd planned on getting George to invest all his winnings in jewellery so that he could torture it out of him. In that plan though George was to have been kept alive so that he could've claimed on the insurance, bought another lot of jewellery and then had that tortured out of him too. I'm not sure how many times JB had envisaged pulling this stunt but I'm glad for George he was talked out of it by Logan. Can you imagine? 'Hello George, what's your job?' 'Me, oh I get tortured once every six months then have to do a lot of paperwork.'

Lucy had passed out and I was happy to leave her that way. George, in the meantime, was fighting to breathe. He'd never particularly struck me as the last word in physical fitness and the little punishment we'd given him had started to turn his body against him. Craig and I hadn't touched him in over two minutes but he was still flinching like a man on the rack, when all of a sudden he went limp. I held my fingers to his neck and felt for a pulse but there was no pulse to be found. I checked his wrists and drew a blank there too.

'Dead?' asked Craig.

'Yes. Heart attack. Glad in a way. Means I don't have to do the actual killing,' I told him. 'Less suspicious too. Look a bit iffy if they'd both died from asphyxiation. Looks too deliberate.' I turned to where Lucy was lying on her side on the floor. 'Okay, get on with it. Nice and quick, just like we agreed.' Craig pushed the gag further down her throat then tied a towel tightly around her face. Lucy's toes quivered and kicked for more than a minute before finally going limp.

'Tough old bird,' Craig commented. 'You've got to hand it to her.'

'Yes. Still, never mind.'

Nigel put up less of a fight than his mum and swallowed the sleeping pills voluntarily after I'd shown the alternatives. It's easier when it's like that. Easier for everyone. I left a little evidence here and there, made sure the coast was clear, then slipped out into the night. Craig picked me up at the end of the street and we drove back to London, arriving back at mine before dawn.

'Bad business,' Craig said pouring another large flavoured vodka.

'No. Just business,' I told him and sipped my tea. 'You know what's really weird though, it says here in George's Post Office book that he had a £61, 243 nest egg already before he even won the lottery. Don't you think that's weird? He could've retired in comfort and never had to worry about bills, the lottery or working at The Aviary again.'

'Some blokes live to work.'

'Fucking mad!' I said. 'I believe him now, I don't think he would've given up his job if JB'd left him alone. Hard to understand isn't it?'

'Different generation.'

'Yes.' I thought about this while Craig sat across from me in the kitchen and got slowly drunk by himself. George had a wonderful wife, a son he loved and no money worries to speak of, so why did he spend every evening serving drunks and being bossed about by Sam? It truly didn't make any sense. If that had been me I would've stayed home with my wife and made love to her every day and every night. I would've never let her out of my sight, not for a minute, not even for a second, and I would've still been alive today to enjoy all that. Instead, all he did was dream about winning an enormous sum of money that he never planned to use anyway. Didn't he appreciate what he had? Didn't he understand that there were some people in this world who thought he was a rich man already? What a waste!

What a fucking waste!

I got more and more depressed as I thought about it and my mind inevitably turned to Angela, as it usually did on occasions like these. I was just thinking about her sad little smile and helpless limp when a woman came on the radio between records and proposed to her boyfriend. Craig had wanted a little music to accompany his drinking and take his mind off the events of last night.

'Paul, I know you'll be listening at work and I warned you I'd do this, you didn't believe me did you but here goes. I love you like crazy and want to spend the rest of my life with you, Paul, will you marry me?'

'Give us a call, Paul and let us know your answer and we'll even chuck in a CD player,' the DJ urged him.

'Let's phone up,' Craig suddenly said. 'Pretend we're him and tell her to fuck off.'

But I wasn't listening to him, I was too full of anger. Before I knew I'd done it I pulled out my Glock and shot the radio to pieces.

'So Bridges, tell me something, how's your love life these days?'

'I don't have one,' was all I could tell him. Other people had love lives, other people had lovers, I had no one. I would never have anyone. I would die alone. This was my destiny, this was my curse and it wasn't fair.

'See, this is like I tell you, you need to get out a bit more. You'll never meet anyone stuck in here all day. Trial and error, that's what it takes. Go out, have a good time, meet some girls, sooner or later you'll get one you click with and that'll be that. Don't sit around thinking about it, just go out and do it.'

'It's so easy for you isn't it? I don't like doing the things you do. Clubs, bars, fucking discos, it's all just bullshit. I'm not into all that. I hate it.'

'It's where you have to go if you want to meet girlies,' he told me. 'Where else are you going to meet them? Work? You're not like everyone else, you're not going to meet girls at work, or the ones you do you generally kill – not the basis of a good relationship – so you have to go out there and do all that bullshit. Everyone does. It's just the way it is.'

'It's so easy for girls, all they have to do is stand around and wait for it. We have to do all the talking and I'm just no good at that.'

'What? You're no good at talking? All you've got to do is believe in yourself and act the big man. You're a fucking killer, and you can't even say hello to a little girl. Bridges, listen to yourself. Anyway, you're wrong about it being easier for girls. Oh, it's probably easier for girls to get an indiscriminate shag, but it's just as tough for them to meet Mr Right as it is for us to meet Mrs Right – or should that be Miss Right? I don't know. Anyway, know this, girls are like spiders, they're just as scared of you as you are of them.'

'What a load of bollocks!' I told him.

'Hey, believe what you like but put it this way, who gets more girls, you or me?'

'But that's not what I want, I want to meet Miss Right.'

'Yeah, but you're so intent on her being the one that you'd probably scare her away the moment you met her anyway. You've got to relax a bit, play the field, have a few laughs and stop worrying about whether she's the one, all the time. The more birds you have, the more your confidence'll increase and the more you'll be able to spot Miss Right when she comes along.'

'It's Catch 22 though isn't it, how do I have a lot of women when I find it difficult getting one?'

'Ah well, this is where I come in. I'll help you out, give you a few pointers, I'll soon have you filling your boots. Trust me on this one.'

'Why should I?'

'Well, let me put it this way, if I stuck all the birds I'd ever shagged into one room, the floor would cave in,' he said and gave me a cheeky wink.

'Me too,' I replied. 'And by that, I don't mean there'd be a lot of them.'

We talked into the morning, Craig making less and less sense as the bottle evaporated, until eventually he passed out on the sofa. I think our conversation had helped take his mind off George, Lucy and Nigel but all it had done for me was depress me even further. I'm sure he meant well but I just couldn't do what he did, and I wasn't about to go trawling around nightclubs and bars with him being Mr Confidence. That wasn't me and I had to find my leukaemia girl my own way.

When Craig came to a few hours later he told me that he'd had some great ideas on how I could meet birds while he'd been asleep, all of which sounded very promising.

'Why don't you use your computer, get on the old internet. Stacks of despo's meet each other that way these days, you're always reading about it in the paper.'

'I'm not desperate,' I told him.

'Well, you know what I mean. Why don't you give it a go?'

I told him no.

'Why not, you never know what you might turn up? And it's not like you've got to put your hand in your pocket and buy them a drink or anything is it? Go on, let's have a look.'

I told him no again and he wanted to know why, so I told him. A few years ago, when I first went on-line, I spent a long time trawling through all the chat rooms. It was a thoroughly depressing time. Thousands of lonelies all around the globe with nothing to say for themselves except 'what time is it where you are?' There were quite a few women on there too, in America, Australia, Germany, but by and large they're not what you'd call desirable – or at least, I don't remember desiring any of them at the time. We'd sometimes exchange phone numbers and pictures (one woman in Italy sent me some extremely pornographic pictures of herself, which I showed Craig) but I never found anyone who lit a spark in me. Sure I wanted to meet someone, but that didn't mean I'd settle for just anyone. Why should I have to be the one who lowered my standards?

The whole thing came to a bit of a head when I met a girl called Florence in Kansas. She was gorgeous. We both had webcams and could see each other as we spoke. Suddenly Florence started flirting with me and talking dirty to me and I couldn't help but get turned on. She suggested that we both, well you know, did things to ourselves in front of the camera. I was a little reluctant at first but she talked me into it with some very frank remarks. I was halfway through going first when a dozen frat boys hoved into view laughing at me.

I was ready to get on a plane for Kansas, track them down and kill every last one of them.

Instead, I just got drunk and gave up chat rooms as a bad idea. Some people might meet each other on the internet, but I didn't want to be one of those people. Like Craig had said, it all smacked a little too much of desperation.

'You know what your problem is?' Craig said.

'Oh, I do hope you're going to tell me. Please, please, I'm begging you, don't keep it to yourself.'

'That is, other than sarcasm, of course, your problem is that you have one bad experience with something and you don't want to know any more. You should've stuck with it, you'd've probably been shacked up with someone by now if you had.'

'Not for me,' I told him.

'There's a lot that's not for you isn't there?' he said.

'The same goes for dating agencies and lonely hearts columns, I don't want to do it that way.'

'But why?'

'Why? Because I don't want to find my wife off the scrap heap. I'm sorry, but I won't do that.'

'All right, all right, then let's at least see if we can get some bird in America to get her tits out for a laugh. I wouldn't mind seeing that.'

We spent about an hour trying before Craig got bored and said he was going to go home. Just as he was putting his coat on he had a thought.

'Adelaide.'

'In Australia?'

'No, she's a bird I know. Well, sort of.'

'You sort of know her or she's a sort of bird?'

'I used to knock off her flatmate, Jackie. Oh man yeah, Jackie was nuts about me, a bit too keen actually so I gave her the elbow. Know what I mean?'

I didn't. I didn't have a clue what he meant.

'Anyway, her flatmate Adelaide was single and I'd put fucking money on it she still is. We should get them out. You could give her the once-over.'

'Oh, she sounds great,' I said shaking my head.

'No, no, don't get me wrong, she's not a moose or anything, she's all right, she just don't do herself no favours that's all. She's all a bit, well, you know?' he said leaving out any form of description whatsoever.

'Not a chance.'

'Oh go on. Nothing ventured, as they say. She's all right really. Fucking hates me though.'

Hmm, perhaps she didn't sound that bad after all.

19. Date hate

Adelaide Harrison stared at me as if I'd just interrupted her meditation to tell her something vitally important.

'So, do you go out with Jackie a lot?' I asked her.

Craig had made his phone call. Jackie was thrilled to hear from him again and he told her a few things she wanted to hear, then suggested we all met up. 'I'm not sure if Adelaide will come but I'll definitely be there,' she'd told him.

'No, Adelaide's got to be there. My mate's coming out with us and we don't really want him tagging along with us all night now do we? Get Adelaide to come out and we can pair them off together and have some fun on our own.'

'Well, I'll ask her but I don't know if…'

'Look, if she's not there, then I can't make it either. Sorry, but there's just no other way around it,' he told her.

We met them at a bar in town which played live music. It was very busy and very loud, but Craig and I had got there early and grabbed a table, so that was something at least.

'I said, do you go out with Jackie a lot?' this time shouting it into her ear. Adelaide visibly deflated as she let out a long, long sigh before answering.

'Sometimes,' she shrugged, then went on watching the band.

Craig and Jackie hadn't stopped giggling and whispering to each other since we'd arrived, but Adelaide had barely looked at me. She had a scowl plastered all across her face that made me wonder if I'd wronged her in a past life or something. I scratched my head for a bit, sipped my Coke and wondered what to say to her next.

I knew her name. I knew she was a teacher (and that she had

work tomorrow). I knew she lived with Jackie somewhere in Kensington and had done ever since they'd both graduated from teacher training college together a few years ago.

What else was there to ask?

'Do you come here often?' I muttered under my breath and frowned. Adelaide hadn't heard me, or if she had, she wasn't letting on.

I looked over at Craig as he urged me on with his eyebrows. Jackie turned around momentarily, joy and happiness smashed all over her face, though I don't think I actually registered as an image to her.

'Would you like another drink?' I asked Adelaide.

'What?'

Oh for fuck's sake! 'I said, would you like another drink?' She shook her head and took a minute sip of her fizzy mineral water. 'Noisy, isn't it?' I shouted in her ear.

'Actually, I think they're good,' she replied.

'I wasn't saying anything against the band.'

'What?'

My shoulders sagged and I felt a couple of tears well up in my eyes.

'I said, I wasn't saying anything against the band. I think they're good too.' We'd been here only an hour and I was already hoarse. 'Have you seen them before?'

'A jumper saw lemon another lace,' she shouted back, evidently not loud enough.

Whatever.

'Right, who wants another drink?' Craig shouted climbing out of his seat.

'Me, me, me,' Jackie said.

'I'm fine,' Adelaide replied.

'I've still got this,' I told him.

'Right, so it's just you and me then, is it? Hey Ian, would you give us a hand at the bar?' which we all saw through.

'So, how's it going with you and Adelaide?' he asked after we'd fought our way through the crowd.

'Oh just dandy. She can't hear a word I say and even when she does she couldn't give a shit.'

'Yeah. She's all right though, isn't she? See I told you she weren't no boiler.'

And he was right, she was quite nice. She wasn't as attractive as Angela or Rose or even half the girls here tonight but she certainly had something about her. Although that just made it harder. If she had've been a boiler, I could've said anything I liked to her and not worried about whether she found it interesting, informative or unbelievably insulting. It wouldn't've mattered. But her being nice meant that it did matter. I wanted her to like me and for us to get on. She was definite leukaemia material.

'How come she doesn't have a boyfriend?'

'I don't know, she never has all the time I've known her. I don't think she likes blokes very much.'

'In that case, what the hell am I doing here then?'

'Well, you never know, you might crack her. Just give her a bit of the old bullshit and try and get a few drinks down her neck. Here look, I'll order a couple of bottles of champagne if you pay for them. Then we'll all have a drink and you can get her steaming.'

'But she's got work tomorrow.'

'Oh, who cares about that when there's free champagne on the go? Here, before I forget, cop hold of this.'

'What's that?'

'It's her ticket from the cloakroom. You should always check a bird's coat for her when you take her out.'

'Really, why's that?'

'That way she can't leg it or run off with some other fella without leaving her coat behind.'

Craig took the glasses through while I followed up with the champagne. Adelaide spared us a quick glance before continuing her vigil on the band.

'Bubbly?' Craig announced.

'I know I am,' Jackie laughed. 'And you can pop my cork any time you like you cheeky bastard.'

Craig gave me a wink so I tried the same thing on Adelaide.

'Bubbly?'

'No thanks.'

'You sure?'

'What?'

'You sure you don't want any champagne?'

'I don't want any.' I set the bottle down on the table and fell back into my seat.

'Go on, Adel, have some,' Jackie urged her.

'I've got work tomorrow.'

'Just have a little then, it's not going to kill you.'

'No! Look, I've still got books to mark. It's all right for you, you don't even have to go in till twelve but I've got to take bloody assembly tomorrow morning.'

'Really?' I asked. 'What are you doing it on?'

'What?'

Oh, please God please, let her hear me, just once. 'I said, what are you doing it on? Assembly, I mean?'

Adelaide stared at me and for a moment I thought she was going to say, 'The joy of celibacy' but instead she told me she was going to do a talk on pet bereavement.

'Good subject. Ever had any pets that died?' I asked.

'No,' she replied sarcastically, 'what's it like?'

'Here, I remember the day we found Goldie dead in his tank,' Craig shouted over. 'My old man tried to flush him down the shitter but it got stuck half-way. Yeah, take it from me, never try and flush a golden retriever down the bog,' at which point Jackie creased up, especially when Craig added, 'What he was doing driving a tank I have no idea.'

Adelaide looked at me and for the briefest of moments we were on the same wavelength.

'More champagne?'

A little while later, Craig and Jackie disappeared off for a dance leaving me and Adelaide by ourselves. I tried a few more times to shoehorn a conversation out of her, taking in such topics as where her parents came from; did she have any brothers or sisters; did she like *Only Fools and Horses* and had she ever been to the Aquarium, before I finally blew myself out. I looked up and saw Craig just in front of us checking Jackie's teeth for cavities, then I looked over to Adelaide, and saw her flinch noticeably.

What was I was doing wrong? Hadn't I made an effort? Hadn't I worn my smart black funeral clothes again and had a shave? All this and I was acting about as friendly and as non-threatening as I could, so what was the fucking matter?

What was wrong with me?

If she didn't like me then fine, she didn't have to elope with me, but couldn't she at least give me the fucking time of day? There was such a thing as manners. Should I say something to her? Let her know what a rude ignorant cow I thought she was being? Make her feel as bad as she was making me feel?

Fuck it! Fuck it! Fuck it! Fuck it! Fuck it! Fuck it! Fuck it!

I was just about to try a different tack when Adelaide got up from the table and disappeared off towards the toilet. I let the smile fall from my face and picked up the glass of champagne in front of me; then I put it down again. I looked at my watch – it was just gone ten o'clock – and made up my mind to leave the moment Adelaide got back from the loo. This was about as good as it was ever going to get between us, and I didn't think it would stay this good for all that long. It was hard facing up to the reality of the situation but she just wasn't interested. And that was a shame because I'd warmed to her from the moment she'd walked through the door. For a short while after Craig had introduced us I'd felt like I was on a date with an attractive yet unassuming woman. Now, I just felt like a pest.

Well, I'd had enough. I wasn't about to sit around here all night desperately trying to squeeze a few words out of her in the hope that she might finally acknowledge my existence. So what if she was attractive? So what if she was available? I had better things to do than grovel at her feet and pamper her ego all night. In fact, I wouldn't even give her the chance to sit down. As soon as I saw her approaching I'd just get up out of my seat, toss her her cloakroom ticket and walk. No, better still, I'd be perfectly pleasant to her. I'd say it had been very nice meeting her but I had to rush off to be somewhere else. Then I'd just leave. I wouldn't give her any ammunition to justify her behaviour, that way when she woke up tomorrow she'd realise she'd acted like a complete arsehole. She might even want another chance to make it up to me, but I wouldn't let her. 'Fuck off,' I'd say. 'You blew it, and there's nothing you can do about it now.' But then, maybe if she was really, really sorry I'd let her make it up to me. I'd make sure she knew what a bitch she'd been but then I'd forget about it and she'd see that I wasn't petty-minded. She'd probably had a lot of bad experiences with guys in the past but I'd be different and she'd see that. I'd make her see that I wasn't like Craig, or all the other blokes she'd met. I was different. I'd take care of her and do the things she was interested in. I'd be there for her when she was down and provide for her so that she wouldn't have to work any more. With me, she could drink champagne every night if she wanted. With me, she wouldn't have to be single any more. With me, she could be happy.

There was just one problem.

Where the fuck was she?

She'd been gone more than twenty minutes and I'd shunned her, dumped her, made her grovel for my forgiveness and grown old with her in the time that she'd been gone. I tried to spot her in the crowd but the place was packed. In fact, the only space in the whole bar was around me. I kept three empty chairs company for another five minutes before Adelaide reappeared.

'I thought you'd fallen in,' I joked.

20. Shooting stars

If you've wondered what it must be like to meet a celebrity, try to imagine what it must be like killing one. It does your head in just thinking about it. There they are, someone famous, known and loved (to a certain extent) up and down the country by millions of ordinary working people – and you've just ended all of that.

It's always news when a celebrity dies, but when one dies in mysterious circumstances it only adds to their fame. Just look at Marilyn Monroe. Sure she was a big star in her day, but then so were a lot of actresses. Would Marilyn Monroe be the legend she is today if she hadn't died so young and under such suspicious circumstances?

By the way, that's not a confession. I was way too young back then.

And then there was Ted Allen. Whatever happened to that guy? Newspaper reports would have you believe he's been living under a pseudonym in Paraguay or that he'd retired to South Africa with a girl of fifteen and the production budget for the new series of *The Brain Game*. He did neither of those.

You can take that from me.

I remembered him from years back, from when he used to do *The Comedians* and *Sunday Night at the London Palladium*. I would've had my bath, had my tea, then it was in front of the telly in my pyjamas to watch Bruce Forsyth, Jimmy Tarbuck, Jim Bowen, Danny LaRue, Kenny Lynch and Ted Allen as they joked, tap-danced and sung their hearts out in a star-studded spectacular.

Fuck me that used to be depressing!

I hated it. If it wasn't bad enough that we had school the next day there was that load of old bollocks to end the weekend on.

Then there was his catchphrase: 'Oh my gawd, the wife'll never believe this one!' He basically built a career out of those nine words. All his Palladium pals had ability or talent or women's clothes to fall back on but all Ted had was nine words and a reputation for drink. Ted bumped along for twenty years opening supermarkets and doing *Celebrity Squares* and the occasional advert (if he was lucky) before achieving cult status by nonchalantly joking 'Oh my gawd, the ex'll never believe this one' during a radio interview just two weeks after his wife had walked out on him. Soon, everyone wanted him on their show and Ted found he could get a new laugh every time, simply by replacing the word 'wife' in his catchphrase with 'old cow', 'bloodsucker', 'change of locks', 'CSA' or 'research assistant', though he almost shot himself in the foot with 'new Taiwanese child bride' and was forced to make a series of humiliating public apologies in order to save his new-found popularity. These have since become cult-TV classics. Still, he'd caught the public eye enough to get himself his own weekday afternoon quiz show, *The Brain Game,* which kept him in regular employment and, according to Logan, cocaine, prostitutes and stockings and suspenders.

It was probably for one or more of these reasons that he found himself trussed up on the deck of my boat and heading out to sea.

We'd gone out about a mile when Craig removed his gag to talk to him. I wouldn't normally allow this but then it's not every day you get to meet someone off the telly is it?

'Right, you're going to talk,' Craig told him.

'I haven't got the money, but I can get it. All I need…'

'Shut up!' Craig interrupted. 'I'm not interested in that. Your mates, Brucie and Tarby and Saintsie and Greavesie and all them lot, I want to know who's bent, who's on drugs, who's banging who, who likes doing it with dogs and all the rest of the dirt. And if you hold out on me I'll do your fucking kneecaps.' Craig took a hip flask from his pocket and gave Ted a drink. 'Right, let's hear it.'

What followed was one of the most fascinating hours of my life; the last time this many beans were spilt was in the war when the Heinz factory got bombed. Craig and I listened intently, only interrupting occasionally to go, 'No way! Not him,' or 'Every presenter she's ever worked with?' or 'Up the arse with a big stick?' and things like that. In fact, we were so engrossed that we didn't hear the fishing boat until it was only fifty yards away.

Ted raised his arms and started to shout for help but Craig silenced him with a whack to the head.

'Cover him up quick. Use the blanket.' Craig did as I said as the boat drew level. Four angry fishermen in yellow waterproofs stared at us with suspicion.

'What are you doing out here?' one of them shouted over. I held up a couple of rods and a tackle box and told them we were planning on a day's fishing.

'Bullshit, at this time of the morning? In this water?'

'What's wrong with this bit of water?' Craig shouted back. 'Looks just as good as any other bit to me.'

'Those are our pots down there. Now what are you doing here?'

'Skinny dipping, what's it look like?'

'Poaching our fucking lobsters, that's what it looks like,' he replied, drawing the boat closer. 'What's under the tarp?'

'Beer,' I told him, wrapping a hand around my Glock.

'Show us.'

'Why don't you fuck off?' Craig suggested.

'Yeah, why don't you fucking make us? Brendan, go and call the Coast Guard, tell them we've caught a couple of suspected poachers.'

'Wait,' I shouted. 'Wait a minute. Hold on. Look, all right, you win, chuck us a rope and we'll show you.' Craig looked over at me and read my expression. The fisherman nearest the stern threw us a line and we pulled ourselves towards them until there was only a couple of feet between us. All four stood at the stern staring down at the tarpaulin, three of them holding poles and lumps of heavy rope.

'All right Craig, all of them, okay.'

We turned and drew at once, firing into the wall of yellow. The shocked surprise showed in their eyes as our muzzle flashes lit up the darkness like camera flashes. Two of them went down immediately, while the others stumbled back under a hail of bullets. Craig emptied his clip into a big guy with a beard while I sent their spokesman falling sideways into the water with his head spilling brains.

'No! No! No!' Brendan screamed in terror as he ducked and dived the length of the boat and towards the cabin.

'Stay here,' I shouted at Craig and leapt the short distance separating the boats as the engines started. The acceleration nearly knocked me off my feet and into the water but I managed to steady myself against a stack of lobster pots. I knew I only had a matter of seconds before he was speaking to the Coast Guard and raced forward as the boat swayed from side to side until I could see him through the cabin windows. I yanked open the door and the radio fell from his hand in surprise. I guess he thought he'd got away.

'No wait! No wait!' Brendan screamed as I raised the gun and fired into him three times.

'Repeat, over. Do you read me, over?' the radio asked. I looked at it for a few seconds and wondered what to do. One thing was for sure, these four fishermen couldn't be found riddled with bullet holes. And neither could the boat.

We hadn't got long. I was still motoring away from my own boat so I turned the wheel and headed back towards Craig. I was pleased to see that he'd used a bit of initiative and had snared the captain with a pole and pulled him towards the boat.

'We've got to hurry. See how much rope and how many weights we've got,' I yelled over as I drew level. Craig did a quick stock-take and announced that we probably only had enough for three. 'We can stretch it to four. I'll see what we've got over here.'

I turned up enough rope and weights to sink ten fishermen and we quickly got to work attaching lines, puncturing lungs and tossing our catches overboard so that we must've resembled some sort of macabre murderous trawler. We couldn't've taken more than twenty minutes but it seemed like an eternity what with the voice on the radio and the lightening skies.

'All right, that's the lot,' Craig said dumping the last of them overboard. 'What are we going to do about the boat?'

'I've got a couple of large calor gas bottles stowed below. Go and get them and get my spare petrol can as well.'

While he was gone I located the fishing boat's fuel tanks and removed the caps. By the time I'd finished the whole boat was an explosion waiting to happen. We clambered back across on to my boat and pushed off.

'Go and start the engine but don't hit the accelerator until I say so.' I waited until we'd drifted about ten yards away from the fishing boat before tossing across a couple of lit pieces of rope doused in petrol (a couple because I missed the first time). 'Go!' I shouted as the deck went up in a huge fireball. We'd put about fifty yards between us when the tanks and the bottles went up, lighting the dawn sky and blowing half the boat to matchwood.

I watched as the burning vessel fell further and further away until it was just a pinprick of light and then nothing at all. Craig was going full throttle and the surf was splashing about in our faces. It was at about this moment that I suddenly remembered Ted. I pulled the tarpaulin back and saw him lying still with his head leaking out over my deck. Craig looked back at me.

'Is he dead?'

I felt for a pulse. 'Almost,' I replied, then gave him a couple of good whacks and felt for a pulse again. 'Yep. He is now.'

'Wow,' Craig said. 'Ted Allen. I wouldn't've minded getting his autograph first. Still, never mind.'

'Let's put a good ten miles between us and the fishing boat, then dump Ted overboard and head in. I'll get him ready.'

I stripped Ted off, punctured his lungs and stomach and tied on the weights before popping a somewhat smaller mouth bomb into his mouth and rolling him over the side.

'See ya, Ted!' Craig called after him before adding, 'Nice bloke actually.' I watched as a small amount of bubbles broke the surface from where the mouth bomb had detonated, then told Craig to head for home. 'Where is it?'

'That way.'

The sun had broken on the horizon and it looked like it might turn out to be quite a nice day, although that really depended on whether or not we were arrested on five counts of murder.

'Piracy you know,' I told Craig. 'That was what that was. Get charged with that and we could get hung.'

'Really?' replied Craig.

'Yep. It's about the only thing you can still swing for these days.'

Craig mulled this over for a while before commenting, 'Smart!'

Actually, I didn't know whether this was true or not. Britain did still have the Death Penalty for piracy, treason and setting fire to Her Majesty's docks (for some reason) up until pretty recently (and even had a working gallows in Wandsworth nick in case Long John Silver was ever caught in Portsmouth with a can of petrol and a box of matches) but they may well've scrapped it and not informed me. I didn't know. It didn't really seem to matter to Craig though, he seemed all made up by the idea that he'd just committed a capital crime and could get his neck stretched for his morning's work. To be honest, I wished I hadn't mentioned it, that way I might've at least been spared all the salty sea dog impressions all the way back to shore.

I was just scrubbing down the deck to get rid of the last of Ted when I heard my mobile ring. This was odd as it was new, bought especially for this job and nobody had the number except for... shit!

JB.

How the hell had it slipped my mind? I guess all those stories about Harry Secombe and then that silliness with the fishermen had made me clean forget, but before we did Ted JB had wanted a word with him. I'm not too sure what he wanted to say, something along the lines of 'nobody fucks with me' or 'look who's laughing now' or whatever but JB had been quite adamant in his instructions. And he wasn't a man who took disappointment well.

'Oh bollocks, you know who that's going to be don't you?' Craig said as the penny finally dropped.

'Yes, thank you switchboard, I have remembered too.'

'Fucking hell, I wouldn't want to be in your shoes.'

'My shoes? You were the one who smashed Ted over the head!'

'Yeah but you were the one who finished him off. He would've been all right if it hadn't been for you.'

What sort of logic was that? He would've been all right if it hadn't've been for me? He was trussed up like a Christmas turkey with his head bashed in and pouring blood, heading out to sea with a couple of hitmen who had orders to dispose of him! How the hell was he ever going to be all right?

This was all fairly academic anyway as what was done was done regardless of who struck the final blow. And I wasn't just saying that because it was me.

'What are we going to do?' Craig said.

'Well look, you can do a pretty good Ted Allen impression, I'll answer the phone and you pretend to be Ted.'

'Fuck off!' Craig snorted. 'Are you out of your mind?'

'Look, he isn't going to want a half-hour television special out of you, just grunt, cry and try and sound like you're too scared to talk.'

'And what if he wants to know anything specific? What if he wants to know Ted's account numbers or who's got the microfilm or whatever else?'

'Well, I don't know, just tell him to fuck off, defiant to the end, that was Ted. Then I'll just tell him he made a break for it and we had to shoot him.'

'Made a break for it? What did he do, build another boat out of his hair while we weren't looking?'

'No choice,' and despite Craig's continuing objections I answered the phone. 'Yes?'

'You didn't phone. Everything go okay?'

'Yes, great,' I replied.

'All right then, put him on,' JB told me. I held the phone out for Craig but he refused to take it. I mouthed at him to take the fucking thing but he waved his hands and stuck his fingers up at me until I was forced to talk into the phone again. 'Won't be a minute, just untying his hands,' then I thrust the phone at Craig again but this time I brought my Glock out to keep it company. Craig stared at me in disbelief for a moment so I held the phone to my chest to cover up the mouthpiece and explained. 'The man wants to gloat at someone before they're killed. He can either gloat at you as Ted or he can gloat at us as us, now take the fucking phone.'

Craig finally took the phone and after a little more gesticulating held it to his ear.

'Hello?' he said, almost as if it was Aunty Pat calling him up on his birthday. I suddenly saw what a bad idea this was. 'Yeah, yeah,' he continued and I slapped him and growled at him to cough and splutter more like he meant it. He eventually got into the swing of things and ended up doing a half-arsed impression of Ted Allen throwing a sicky.

'What?' he said after a while and looked at me in shock. 'You... er... okay, okay, okay, okay.' He grimaced at me a little, cleared his throat then said, 'Oh my gawd, the wife'll never believe this one!'

I turned away and shook my head a few times as Craig repeated it twice more. 'Yeah, yeah, okay. He wants to talk to you now,' Craig said holding out the phone for me to take. Reluctantly, I accepted it off him and braced myself for JB's wrath.

But it never came. All he said was, 'Okay, do him now and hold out the phone, I want to hear.'

I almost couldn't believe it. No, in fact there was no 'almost' about it, I couldn't believe it. Craig's was the worst impression of Ted Allen I've ever heard in my life and it had got worse each time he'd done it as he tried to put more and more emphasis in the 'gawd', but JB had bought it. He'd believed that the guy with the New Delhi accent had been the same Ted Allen he'd obviously come to know. What an idiot. But then, why wouldn't he believe it? He had no reason to suspect that he wouldn't get to talk to Ted this morning and people are always sounding different when they're under duress, so why shouldn't that be Ted? Who else was it going to be?

I held out the phone and my Glock to sea and I fired a couple of times.

'It's done,' I told him.

'Good work,' he replied then the phone went dead. I stared at it for a moment then tossed it into the water.

'Well?' asked Craig.

'Oh my gawd, the wife'll never believe this one!' I said, exaggerating his bad impression. 'You really are a cunt.'

'He wanted to hear it one last time, him and whoever else he was with, so I done it for them. They seemed happy enough. Believed it didn't they? I didn't think it was too bad actually.'

'You see those waves over there,' I said pointing out across the water. 'Those little ones just breaking over there.'

'Yeah,' said Craig squinting out towards where I was pointing.

'That's Ted Allen, spinning in his fucking grave.'

21. Bit of a turn-up for the books

Craig wanted to come back to mine and have a drink again but I felt that this was on the verge of becoming a bad habit so I told him to get himself home and take a few sleeping tablets. Besides, I had other plans.

I had a date.

'With who?' Craig wanted to know.

I merely tapped the side of my nose and said, 'Never you mind.' That sort of thing works in the movies but it never really works in real life. Craig wouldn't leave it at 'Never you mind' and badgered me all the way back into shore and then all the drive back up to London until I was ready to kill him.

'Go on tell us. Go on, don't be a cunt. Who is it? Bridges, just fucking tell us. Go on. Go on. Go on.' Imagine that non-stop for two hours.

It was Adelaide.

'How the fuck d'you manage that one?'

Complete coincidence really. I'd bumped into her the week before while I'd been following Ted around. He had a flat in Kensington and I'd been surreptitiously circling the neighbourhood for a few days to keep an eye on his comings and goings when Adelaide had happened along and seen me. Naturally, the moment I spotted her I'd immediately looked away and tried to ignore her in the hope that she'd treat me likewise, but instead she'd come over and rather awkwardly said hello. I think she must've taken my attempted evasion for embarrassment over our failed date and she apologised for how she'd behaved that evening.

'She apologised?'

'Yes, she said she hated you and felt she'd been strong-armed into going on a date that she didn't want to go on. She thought I'd be an obnoxious arsehole too and had made up her mind about me before she'd even met me.'

'What's obnoxious mean?'

We'd talked for a few minutes on the street corner but I'd had difficulty paying her my full attention as I was expecting Ted to emerge from his front door any second. I was short but polite with her in the hope that she'd go away and not distract me further and this probably combined to make her feel all the more guilty over her previous conduct because she asked me out.

'What?' I'd said to her.

'Let me make it up to you. I'm not really a bitch. Let's just go out by ourselves and see how we get on.'

This was, as you can imagine, a little unexpected. What was it with women? Why couldn't they stop trying to catch me by surprise all the time? Be predictable. Please, just once, let me have some kind of idea what you're going to be doing, thinking or feeling five minutes from now, for fuck's sake!

'And what did she say to that?'

'I didn't say that to her, I just… oh, whatever.'

I'd agreed to give her a call in a week or two's time when I was less busy at work though she'd looked at me rather doubtfully as we said goodbye and I went back to hanging around on a street corner. But call her I did. I knew I'd be finished with Ted Thursday night / Friday morning so I'd asked her if she wanted to meet up Saturday. To my continuing surprise she'd said she did so we'd made a date to meet by the ticket office of London Waterloo at midday.

Craig argued that if I wasn't meeting her until the next day I was safe to have a 'bit of a drink this morning', but I disappointed him again. I needed a good wash and a soak and a scrub and an empty day's relaxation to rid myself of the stink of death. It was coating me at the moment – up my nostrils, in my hair, under my fingernails, in my pores. It didn't matter whether it was a proper physical smell or not, the point was it was there and that was no way to go out on a date.

Mind you, that was no way to come back after a date either, but then that was another matter.

It would be fine.

As I've explained before, I'm not much of a drinker and people are probably the safer for it, so I suggested to Adelaide that we caught the train and made a day of it down in Brighton. Adelaide made a few positive noises so twenty-eight hours later we met as arranged at London Waterloo.

The journey down was a pretty uneventful experience. We attempted a little unarmed conversation and made a few pointless observations about things that were whipping past the windows as we attempted to find some common ground. Adelaide had brought a big flask of coffee with her for reasons I couldn't understand, and rather thoughtfully handed me a flimsy plastic cup filled to the brim with 120°C molten caffeine so that I could empty it into my lap as we rocked along at 90mph. About the only other thing worth noting was when Adelaide mentioned Ted Allen.

'Haven't you seen the news? He went missing the other day, didn't show up for his programme and all the papers reckon he's done a runner. He lives just around the corner from me and Jackie and there were loads of police outside his place this morning.'

'Hmm,' I mused. 'Bit odd isn't it?' and left it at that.

As it turned out it was a lovely warm day. I'd decided against my all-black funeral clothes in favour of something a little more casual. Although I looked smart in black I couldn't help feeling a little bit conspicuous, like I was actually trying to look like a hitman or something. So, I'd opted for jeans, a blue cotton shirt and a new blue jacket I'd just bought when it occurred to me that I'd just exchanged all one colour for all of another and you weren't meant to do that. Or were you? I decided I didn't know. I hated clothes and was no good at dressing. Everybody else seemed to manage it fine. Why did I have to look like Coco the fucking Tramp all the time? I'd spent most of the morning staring long and hard at myself in the mirror until I'd decided that I couldn't see anything wrong with the way I looked, but that didn't stop me being plagued by a sense of ill-dress all day long.

'Where do you want to go first?' Adelaide asked.

'Let's have a look at the pier.'

We strolled down the hill towards the seafront and swapped a little more conversation. Adelaide asked me again what I did for a living and I told her again that I used computers. She tried to look interested this time and even asked me a few polite questions on the subject but all too quickly the subject was dropped and never came up again. This was good in that it worked as a cover story but was bad in that there was suddenly one less reason for Adelaide to be interested in me. I'd originally chosen computers as a cover story as I'd had a little working knowledge of them and found that people who didn't rarely pursued the subject for long. But just recently it had occurred to me that this was because they found them dull. And if they found them dull, then it would follow that there were suddenly things about me that they found dull. So, how was I meant to hook a woman's interest when I was deliberately trying to come across as dull so as to discourage deeper interest in me?

All those years I'd been telling women that I worked with computers I'd just been shooting myself in the foot.

What if they knew what I really did for a living? How impressed with me would they be then? How exciting and interesting would that make me seem?

But then there were the specifics.

If they knew specifics they'd probably be terrified. They'd probably fear for their lives and run and tell the police. But I couldn't let them do that. I'd have to make them disappear long before it ever came to that. It was the only way to be safe. I wouldn't have a choice.

And that was why I had to tell them I worked with computers.

But then, did it have to be computers? Couldn't I reinvent myself. Get another fantasy job? An exciting one? It wouldn't be difficult, I could have any job in the world.

I could be a... a... a... how about a reporter?

'What paper do you work on?'

Well how about an actor?

'What films have you been in?'

I only do stage plays.

'Can I come and see your next play?'

I test racing cars.

'I'd love to see you race.'

I'm a photographer.

'Take my picture.'

I search for dinosaur bones.

'Can I see your fossils?'

I'm a deep-sea diver.

'Take me swimming.'

I work with computers.

'Did you see *Dawson's Creek* last night?'

Hmm.

I couldn't allow any interest in my job. Well, unless I started dating someone in IT, then presumably I'd have to tell them I worked on the bins or something.

Adelaide and I walked along the pier and shared an enormous sticky bush of candy floss until our faces and hands were covered in sugary glue and we gave it up as a bad idea and dropped it in the bin. Once we'd cleaned up in the toilets we resumed our stroll.

'How do you know Craig?' she asked.

'I was doing some work at his solicitor's and met him there.' Then added, 'computer work. His solicitor's database was down.'

'Yes but, I don't get it. You're nothing like each other so what I think I mean is, why do you know Craig? I mean, you don't go out drinking, you already said, and you don't seem like a flash

Harry like most of his friends so why? I just can't seem to put you together.'

'The attraction of opposites?' I ventured.

'You're gay?'

'NO! No, no, of course not. I was only joking. God no! No,' I said shaking my head and she broke out into a smile. 'No, no, no. I just meant we got along even though we don't have anything in common. Or much in common, I should say.'

'Oh really? What do you have in common then?' she asked.

I thought about this for a moment or two.

'Computers,' I told her. 'Craig's really into them.'

'Really?' she said doubtfully.

'Well, not really, but he's trying to learn. I'm teaching him.'

'Somehow I never thought of Craig as being much of a computer geek.' She suddenly stopped herself in her tracks. 'I'm sorry, I didn't mean, you know, that you were or anything. You don't seem like a geek either.'

'That's okay. And thank you.'

'I just meant,' she said and thought carefully for a moment. 'I just meant I never thought of Craig as intelligent enough to be interested in computers.'

'Yes,' I said, then wondered if that meant she didn't think I was intelligent enough either.

'What does Craig do for a living?' Adelaide suddenly asked. 'I've always wondered. He never seems short of money or anything so he must do something.'

Computers? I considered saying, then thought better of it. 'I think he's got a rich family somewhere.'

'Oh, that figures. Doesn't look like someone who's ever had to do a day's work in his life.'

'No,' I agreed. 'Lucky bastard.'

'Lucky? No thanks. I'd rather work for my money, thank you very much, than turn out like Craig.'

'You really don't like him do you?'

'Not really, no.'

'Why don't you like him?'

'Lots of reasons, but mostly because of the way he's treated Jackie over the... well not years but, you know. She's absolutely mad about him but he really treats her like shit. Rolls up whenever he wants, disappears without a word for months on end. Two-times her. Steals money from her! Bosses her about, and other things,' she said letting that go. 'I hate girls who use this word but he is a cunt.'

'A cunt?' I said.

'And a wanker. And a bastard and a shit and a... a...'

'An arsehole?'

'Yes,' she said enthusiastically. 'He's an arsehole.'

'Well, I don't understand that sort of thing. Jackie seemed lovely to me. I don't think I could ever treat anyone like that.' I felt an overwhelming urge to apologise to Adelaide, but I wasn't sure what for. We leaned against the rail at the end of the pier and looked out across the glittering sea.

'No, no I don't think you could. Which is why I find it really surprising that you and Craig are friends.'

'Friends?' I said quickly. 'We're not friends, I'm just teaching him computers, that's all. Personally, I think he's a cunt.'

'You do?' she smiled.

'Oh yeah, a real cunt. And a wanker.'

'What else?'

'A bastard and a shit...'

'And an arsehole?' she interrupted. 'Do you think he's an arsehole?'

'I think he's a fucking arsehole,' I reassured her. 'A fucking total cunt of an arsehole.'

Adelaide laughed.

'I love it when you talk dirty.'

You know, it was one of the most truly touching moments of my life and I loved her deeply at that moment.

We were strolling back along the pier feeling so much more at ease in each other's company when we passed a shooting gallery.

'Two please,' I said and slapped down the money on the side.

'Oh, I'm not very good at this,' Adelaide objected but I forced the rifle into her hand.

'Come on, it'll be fun,' I told her. I made a bit of a mental note not to completely show her up and to miss a few too, but I thought it would be fun to win her a cuddly toy. The man gave us our pellets and we fired the first couple of shots at two rows of passing metal ducks. The sights must've been way out because I didn't hit anything except the back of the stalls. My second shot went equally astray though I knocked over a duck with my third and winged one with my fourth, only to waste my fifth in the ceiling as I loaded the rifle.

'Never mind folks, better luck next time,' said the old crook manning the stall. Adelaide gave me a sheepish 'oh well' look but I was far from amused. I'd been handling rifles for longer than I remembered and could take a man's nose off at two hundred yards so a few tin ducks shouldn't've been a problem.

'Two more,' I told him in no uncertain terms and put the money on the counter.

'Don't waste your money,' Adelaide said, but I assured her we were just having fun and I was going to win her a bunny rabbit. My first shot hit a target and knocked over a duck. As did my second and third. My fourth, however, disappeared into thin air and my fifth hit square and true but the duck didn't tumble. I looked up from the sight and saw that the duck had a mark on it where I had hit it and told the stall owner so.

'Yeah well, sometimes if you hit them at a slight angle they don't go down.'

'I didn't hit it at an angle. I hit it straight on. That one's glued in place, I know it is.'

The duck came round again and he tapped it lightly with his finger and it toppled over.

'Sorry mate, but we don't glue the ducks. They just sometimes don't go over.'

I reached into my wallet and was about to pull out a £10 note when Adelaide squeaked with delight.

'Yes!' she cheered, waving her rifle about excitedly. 'That's five.'

'That's five for the young lady, what prize do you want? Choose anything from the middle shelf.'

'The elephant,' she said and pointed at this big pink monster the same colour as the candy floss we'd ditched.

'There you go my darling, looks just like you.'

Adelaide accepted the elephant triumphantly and held it aloft like it was the FA Cup.

'I got five,' she told me and before I could explain about my superglued tin duck she handed me the elephant. 'Here, he's for you.'

'What? No.'

'Yes come on. I won him for you. I want you to have him,' she insisted. I tried to graciously object but Adelaide wouldn't hear a word of it and pushed the elephant into my chest until I was forced to take him. I didn't want the fucking thing but I didn't want to appear impolite either. Adelaide set off towards the town with a spring in her step leaving me to look back accusingly at the stall owner, but he just gave me a smile and raised his eyebrows.

And the worst part? We'd only been here half an hour and suddenly I was stuck with carrying a big fucking pink elephant around for the rest of the day.

We made our way down on to the beach and clattered along the water's edge for a little while chatting and laughing as we went. Adelaide took off her shoes and socks and waded out to her knees before rethinking the whole idea. 'It's cold,' she announced. 'And the pebbles are hard on your feet.'

'Yes, I expect they are. That's why I didn't do it.'

'Have you ever skimmed stones?' she asked.

We spent the next five minutes competing to see who could skid little flat stones furthest across the surface of the water and I'm glad to say this time it was me.

'See that? That was an eight.'

'That was never an eight,' Adelaide protested. 'That was about a six at best with a bit of a splash at the end.'

'What are you talking about, that was an eight. Didn't you see how far it went out?'

'I'm not disputing the distance, I'm questioning how many times it skidded and it didn't look like an eight to me.'

'It was an eight. Here look, I'll do it again,' but try as I might I couldn't do any better than a seven. 'It was an eight, though.'

'Okay, I'll give it to you.'

'No, you don't have to give it to me, I got it. It was an eight.'

'I'll believe you, thousands wouldn't,' she said with a teasing little chuckle. This narked me a bit. I'd rightly thrown an eight and she was patronising me like I was making it up or something but I wasn't. Why would I do that? I'm not that petty-minded, but I'm telling you this, it was a fucking eight.

'I once threw an eleven,' she told me.

I considered going, 'Oh yeah, bullshit!' but I didn't. I let her have her eleven as it was no skin off my nose.

'It was across a really flat pond. The surface was like glass and my stone skidded right across to the other side of the bank. You know I reckon it would've been more than an eleven if the pond had been wider.'

'What, like a thirteen or something?'

'I'm afraid we'll never know. It was just one of those moments now lost forever. You know, much as I think of it as a fantastic achievement, an eleven and all that, sometimes I do find myself hoping that that won't end up being like the highlight of my life.'

'Yeah? Reckon you've got a fourteen in you or something?'

Adelaide smiled.

'On the right day with the right conditions and the perfect

stone, I reckon I could manage a sixteen.'

'That's just madness talking,' I told her. 'I want no part of this. You're crazy.'

'Are you hungry?'

We found a little café that did typical seaside food and settled in for a late lunch.

'Ah, cod and chips,' Adelaide announced as she dug into her batter. 'Is there anything better than cod and chips at the seaside?'

'Yes probably,' I replied. 'Lots of things.'

'I like to peel back the batter and eat the white flesh separately, and then eat the batter with my chips,' she told me.

'Really?' I remarked. Why did women always have to have a method for eating food? I tried it for myself but it all seemed a little overcomplicated, especially with a little wooden fork, so I gave up and ate normally.

'Why aren't you married?' she asked me all of a sudden. 'Or why don't you have a girlfriend?'

'Er. Erm. I don't know. Just… things I guess. I haven't met anyone.'

'You haven't met anyone? You must've met someone before.'

'Yeah but not anyone who liked me.'

'Girls don't like you? Why not? What do you do?'

'I don't do anything,' I told her.

'You must do something to turn the girls away?'

'No nothing. I don't know.'

'Hmm,' she said looking at me long and hard. 'You know, a friend of mine used to say that you should always be a bit wary of any man who seemed perfectly okay yet didn't have a girlfriend or a wife.'

'Well what sort of chance does that give me?'

'… her logic being that if he really was okay then there was no reason he wouldn't have a girlfriend or a wife and the fact that he didn't meant that there was.'

'That all seems very fair,' I said.

'That wasn't me who used to say all that, that was my friend, Elaine. She'd only ever go out with attached men because they obviously had something that single men didn't. Or, that's what she used to say anyway.'

'Catch 22.'

'No, I think she caught a lot more than that,' Adelaide said quick and cracked up laughing at her own joke.

What sort of fucked-up ideology did Elaine ascribe to? As if meeting women wasn't hard enough already without this sort of prejudice going on. Did she only send food parcels to overweight Ethiopians too? I really wished I knew this Elaine and that there was something I had in abundance that she desperately wanted just so that I could deny her it, say life-saving medicine for one of her relatives or a frogman suit on a downed submarine. The truth of the matter was though there probably wasn't anything. People like Elaine, in my experience, rarely wanted for anything important. I bet she'd never even known a lonely night in her life.

Adelaide stopped laughing and saw me brooding on these thoughts.

'It's okay, I don't think that. It was just something Elaine always said.'

'Some friends you've got – Jackie who can't get enough of being treated like shit and Elaine who's only interested in adulterers and cheats. Doesn't being a nice guy count for anything these days?'

'Oh you shouldn't take it all so personally, they don't even know you, well, Jackie a little bit but not much.'

'No, and the fact that I won't steal money off them or that I haven't got a wife to desert means that I probably never will.'

'Well then you're better off already,' she said dismissively and I saw that there wasn't any point in blowing this up into an argument as Adelaide wasn't talking about herself and even if she was it wouldn't do me any favours whatsoever.

'Yes,' I simply said and tried to push it all to the back of my mind to screw over later.

'So, why aren't you married then?'

'I don't know, it's an impossible question to answer. It's like asking someone why they are married. They are married because they met someone and settled down. I'm not married because I haven't.'

'You must meet women when you're out?'

'Why must I? It's not easy talking to women you know. You try walking up to a perfect stranger in the middle of a pub or a club when they've got all their friends around them, tapping them on the shoulder and saying, "Hello, hope you don't mind but can we make some boring small talk for a while to see if we like each other enough to become life partners? Oh go on, I'll buy you drinks all night and give you and all your friends a lift home if you'll just give me a false telephone number at the end of the evening." Sorry, but I spent a year doing all that when I first got out of prison, I've got no intention of putting myself through it all again.' Adelaide was staring at me intently. 'What?'

'You were in prison?'

'What?' I said as my heart jumped into my throat. I thought about what I'd just said and felt the colour drain from my face. 'No, I... er...'

'What did you do?' she asked.

'Nothing. Oh shit, I'm sorry. Shit, shit, shit! I'm sorry, I'm sorry, I'm sorry.'

'That's okay, it's okay. I didn't mean to upset you, I was just curious that's all. You don't have to tell me if you don't want to. It's your business.'

I couldn't believe I'd let it slip. How fucking careless! Why didn't I just tell her I killed people too? Okay, think, think, think. Adelaide was still sitting across from me, she hadn't run away screaming yet. And by the look of utter fascination in her eyes it didn't look like she was about to any time soon. But then why should she? It wasn't a crime to have been in prison was it? Plenty of men had, though it wasn't the sort of thing you should go around telling people, especially women.

What must she think of me now?

I didn't know but I suspected it wasn't good. And that was such a shame because we had been getting on so well up until this point. I was so disappointed with myself. Why couldn't I've watched what I was saying? Why did I just let my mouth run off like that?

Not that there was any point worrying about that now, the damage was done and with it any chance I'd had for getting to know Adelaide. I wouldn't see her again. But then, maybe that was for the best.

At least I didn't have to kill her. Or did I?

I thought about this quickly and reassured myself that I didn't. So I was in prison, so what? She might not want to have children with me any more but it wasn't like she had anything to go to the police about. Which was something, I supposed.

Bollocks!

Adelaide continued to plead with me with her eyes for information so I decided to tell her. What further harm could it do?

Not about the knickers mind, I still had some pride.

'Manslaughter.'

'Manslaughter? You killed someone?'

'I didn't mean to,' I lied. 'I got into a fight when I was younger and it just sort of happened.'

'My God! How? I mean, what?'

'I'm sorry, but it's not something I want to talk about. It was a long time ago. I just want to forget about it.'

'Of course, I'm sorry, how thoughtless of me,' she said, as it was now her turn to apologise once again. 'It kind of explains things though.'

'Like what?'

'Like why you find it tough talking to women. Just what it is you have in common with Craig. And why you always seem, just ever so slightly, sad.'

'I don't, do I?'

'You do, but it's kind of becoming.'

'Er, thank you,' I said and pushed my half-eaten lunch away from me. 'Look, if you want to call it a day and go home now, I'll understand. I won't try and follow you or anything.'

'Go home? Ian, don't be so silly. I don't care if you've been to prison,' she said loud enough for the next table to hear. 'I honestly don't. I'm not going to sit in judgement of you or run a mile just because you've made some mistakes in the past, we all make mistakes, that's what life's all about. I mean, I take it you're not planning on making a habit of it?'

'Er…'

'Well exactly. You know, I think you're the nicest and the most sensitive man I've met in a long long time. I'm glad I've met you Ian, I really am. And, if you'd like to, and if the prospect doesn't fill you with utter horror, I'd like to see you again if I may.'

'You would?'

'I would.' Adelaide smiled at me then went back to operating on her cod. I sat there watching her eat for a few moments in silent disbelief though I still couldn't quite get my head around what she was telling me. As a successful computer programmer, I was a bit of a yawn, chuck in the odd murder though and suddenly she was ready to start leaving a toothbrush around my place. 'I'll tell you what though,' she said after a while, 'I'd better not tell any of this to Jackie or Elaine.'

'Why's that?' I asked.

'Because you'll be fighting them off with a stick if I do.'

I shook my head and furrowed my brow some more.

Women, just how fucked-up did they want to be?

22. Accounted for

Logan was in my house.

But Logan was never in my house, I always saw him at The Aviary. He was today though.

I wondered what he wanted.

I decided to listen to him and find out.

'I've got a little job for you,' he told me, though I'd guessed that part already. 'You and matey boy.'

'Craig?' I said giving matey boy a name. Call me pedantic if you like but I always prefer specifics when it comes to jobs; expressions such as 'we want you to "you know" old whatsis-name down the road' can so easily be misconstrued.

'Yeah, Craig,' Logan confirmed. Craig wasn't here at the moment, it was just me and Logan.

But it was never just me and Logan?

'He doesn't know who's calling the hit or anything else about this except what he's got to do though, you got that?'

'Just the plan, I've got it. Who is it?'

'Connolly.'

'Connolly?' I said expecting to be handed a picture and a dossier. It took a moment for me to recognise the name. 'Connolly? JB's accountant?'

'That's the same Connolly.'

'Fuck! Why? Sorry, sorry, I take it back.'

'Listen kid, I'll tell you this much; he's just about to turn me, you, JB and every other cunt in this organisation over to the Old Bill. That's why we've got to stop him. And we've got to move quick, and I mean like tomorrow quick. You ain't got time to go sniffing around for weeks on end like you normally do, I'll give you a time, a place he'll be tomorrow and you take care of business. Are you with me?'

'Yes, sure,' I said, completely unsure in fact.

'I want it done as quickly and as quietly as possible. Do him from a mile away if you have to but I don't want no comeback on this at all, from anyone, not the Old Bill, not any of the lads, not JB, no one.'

'Not JB?' I asked a little confused.

'JB collects the money, I make the tough decisions. If it wasn't for me he wouldn't have no organisation,' he said, though I still didn't understand. I know that's not all that important in the great scheme of things, I just do as I'm told, but Logan elaborated. 'JB doesn't know I'm calling in this hit. He doesn't know and he must never know.'

'But why then?'

'Let's just say I've got connections in the Old Bill – high-up connections – that look over us and tip us the wink when it needs to be tipped. Connolly's going to blab, I have that on good authority, but my connections don't want to deal with anyone but me. They don't even want JB knowing they exist, and neither do I.'

This made sense; Logan was more brains than Broad. Where he'd see opportunities to buy information, JB would see opportunities to extort it. This was no basis for a healthy business relationship.

'None of our fellas must ever know, not now, not ever. That's why it's got to be done quiet.'

'Okay Danny.'

'The most important thing though is that it must be done. You'll get one chance and one chance only. If you blow it that'll be that and we won't ever have another crack at him again 'cos we'll all be doing bird.'

'I've got it, Danny.'

'I fucking hope so. Now, believe it or not, some of our fellas are going over with him. This is people we know. If they get in the way, take them out too, spare no one. We can't afford to.'

'Who's going over?'

'I don't know yet but they won't be able to prove a thing without Connolly, he's your main target. Kill the others if you have to, but just make sure you get Connolly. You got it?'

'He's already dead.'

'Good. Right, what'll you need?'

I couldn't've been more than 150 yards away and with a clear line of sight. I was positioned at a first-floor window across the road from Connolly's house and could've probably put a bullet through his letterbox if I'd wanted to. Craig was waiting by the side of the road another half a mile past his place with a Beretta Model 12 sub-machinegun tucked underneath his coat in case Connolly managed to bolt in that direction. As well as my M12 rifle, I also had an Uzi (Craig had wanted it instead of the Beretta but rank still counts for something in this man's army, as they say) and of course my Glock. Logan had also sorted me out with a couple of grenades in case things got really interesting, but by and large I was rather hoping I wouldn't have to use them. I'm sure most of Belgravia was with me on that one.

Connolly was in his house, I'd seen him through the window getting dressed. I'd even half thought about taking a pop at him but decided to be patient and wait until he was out on the street in plain view.

It was almost twenty-past nine; they'd be here for him pretty soon.

From behind me she started whimpering again. I turned to look at her and put a finger to my lips to signal her to be quiet. He was still out for the count with a lovely purple lump throbbing away on his head but she'd come to. I wondered if this meant she had a thicker skull than him or whether I'd subconsciously smacked her softer because she was a woman and I was all a bit wobbly with thoughts of Adelaide. I didn't know, but I didn't want to smack her again in case that left her with any permanent damage, and I had no desire to hurt either of them. I just wanted to use their bedroom for a bit.

Neither had seen my face as I'd had a full-face crash helmet on when I'd entered and both were blindfolded now, but I didn't particularly want them listening to me if I needed to speak to Craig. I'd only kept them in the bedroom with me because I'd wanted to keep an eye on them but that was more than two hours ago. There were only a few more minutes left until things got underway so I was fairly confident I could stick them next door and wash my hands of them.

The woman struggled and kicked out at me a few times as I tried to lift her so I gripped her shoulders and pushed her harder back against the wall.

'Keep this up and I'll just kill you,' I whispered to her, disguising my voice. 'Sit still and shut your mouth and you'll live.'

When she'd quietened down, I picked her up and moved her into the bedroom across the hall and flopped her down on to the bed. This prompted a momentary return of histrionics but these soon subsided when I left her by herself and returned with her husband a few seconds later.

'Behave,' I told her and shut the door.

When I moved back to my position Craig asked me through the headset who I was talking to.

'Who do you think? How many women prisoners have I got in here?'

'What's she like?' he asked.

'Very pretty, a bit posh, perfect skin. Lovely and tanned.'

'How do you know?'

'Well she's still in her nightie and stuff, isn't she.'

'Is she? See-through is it?'

'What?'

'Her nightie, see-through is it?'

'If you like,' I told him though this wasn't true. I mean, she'd answered the door in it and who answers the door in a see-through nightie, especially while her husband's still at home?

'You lucky bastard. You want to steam in there.'

Yes, that was just what I wanted to do; try and woo a female hostage at gunpoint while her unconscious husband lay next to her just after I'd opened fire from a first-floor window on to a busy urban street. I couldn't see anything wrong with that.

'If you're collecting any of her knickers while you're up there get me a pair will you?' he said, then turned serious to tell me that the car had just passed him. 'Get ready, they're coming.'

I looked through my scope and watched as the Merc approached and stopped right outside his door. Someone got out from the passenger side and I recognised him and one of JB's men from his dockside warehouse – Jules, I think his name was.

Was he one of the snitches too?

Jules walked up to the door and rang the bell. After a few seconds the door opened and Connolly looked out. I poked the rifle barrel out of the window and fixed him in my sights, but Connolly disappeared back into the house leaving Jules on his doorstep to stand around and jangle his change. I withdrew the rifle from the window and waited for Connolly to reappear.

It must've been about only six or seven yards from his front door to the car but with this rifle I could turn that six or seven yards into a killing zone before he made it half-way.

Connolly reappeared and I slid the rifle out again and fixed him through the scope. I wanted to wait until he pulled the door shut before I opened fire so as to give him nowhere to run, but the moment he did my vision was blocked. I looked up from the sight and saw an open-topped double-decker bus full of open-mouthed Japanese tourists staring back at me with interest.

Not that that mattered. Chances are people were going to know about it as soon as I pulled the trigger anyway, the only important thing was that I no longer had a clear shot.

By the time the bus finally made it past Connolly's car,

Connolly himself was already inside and Jules was just pulling the door shut. The time for pin-point accuracy was gone, as quick as I could I found the roof of the car and started popping the trigger. The peace and quiet of this expensive Belgravia street was suddenly shattered along with the back and side windows as I criss-crossed my fire across the black roof.

Once my rifle was empty I would need to run across the road and put a bullet into everyone's brain but it didn't look like I'd get the chance because suddenly the Merc wheelspan forward and away.

'He's coming your way,' I called to Craig. 'The car's shot to pieces but make sure you stop it and do them all.'

'Got it,' Craig called back.

I stuffed the rifle into its bag and slung it over my back as I ran down the stairs and outside to my waiting Honda 550. The traffic in London's so bad that I always make sure I use a motorbike if I think I'm going to need a quick escape. Before I left the house I pulled on my crash-helmet and made sure my other weapons were reachable then slung my leg over the seat.

Somewhere up ahead I heard the rattle of machine gun fire together with a number of single pistol shots. I started my bike and was roaring off towards the sounds before my feet were off the ground.

'Bridges, no good, he got past me. I shot the fuck out of his motor but he didn't stop.'

'Get after him,' I shouted into the mike though I was practically on top of him by the time I'd finished that sentence. Craig was running, Beretta in hand, towards his own bike while passers-by were scattering and screaming. 'Go! Go! Go!' I shouted to Craig as I whipped by.

A lot of traffic had come to a halt. Cars were slewed across the road and vehicles were backing up behind them. Several, I noticed, had bullet holes in the bodywork but none of them were Connolly's Merc. I pulled on the brake and slowed enough to mount the kerb and drive around them.

'Which way'd he go?' I asked Craig.

'Straight on up,' replied a little tinny voice in my helmet.

I pulled back on the accelerator and tore off in the direction of the river.

If it had been the afternoon the main bulk of the traffic would've been headed south out of London clogging the roads and halting Connolly's flight. As it was he'd made good progress veering and chicaning his way through the flow so that he'd reached Chelsea Bridge by the time I caught sight of him again.

The Merc had been caught by the lights and was surrounded on all sides by either cars or oncoming traffic. A head poked out from the back window and obviously saw me coming up fast because the Merc suddenly started ramming and reversing its way past the car in front.

Three shots fired out from the back window towards me though all were so wide I didn't even hear the whiz.

'Chelsea Bridge! He's stuck by Chelsea Bridge,' I shouted into the mike, but by the time I'd said it he was free again and driving straight through moving traffic. A dozen cars suddenly tried to brake or swerve with little or no warning and several smacked straight into Connolly's Merc, spinning it round ninety degrees. More shots were fired in my direction as I skidded to a halt behind a couple of stalled cars and pulled out my Uzi.

'I'm right behind you,' Craig told me as a couple of bullets skidded off the bodywork just three or four inches from my head. The Merc's tyres started to screech as Connolly's driver fought to get the car moving again. The sudden motion cost the shooter his accuracy though and gave me a chance to swing an arm over the boot and empty half my clip into the Merc. I was caught in two minds as to what to shoot, the tyres or the shooter, and in the end managed neither. Before I had a chance to aim properly the car was out of range and half-way across the bridge.

This renewed machine gun fire must've terrified the innocents running in all directions as the screaming and the running went on long after the firing had stopped.

Craig suddenly appeared and screeched to a halt beside me.

'Are you all right?'

'Get after him! Don't let him out of your sight!' I told him and in a flash he was roaring across the road and on to the bridge. I pulled my bike up off its side, slipped it into gear and was flying after Craig just a few seconds later.

The traffic heading north was already backing up across the bridge, unaware of the chaos ahead of them, but the road south was clear. Craig was way off in the distance but I could hear him in my ear as he gave me directions.

'Roundabout; straight across. Heading for Clapham. He's a dozen car lengths in front of me and driving like the clappers. Hang on, he's coming up to some traffic now.'

'Can you get a shot?'

'Not if I want to stay on the fucking bike. Whoah! Someone's shooting out the back window. Cunt! Hang on.'

I had to slow a little for the roundabout but found a gap in the traffic and motored my way through to much skidding, beeping and finger-raising.

'He's stopped. Now he's going again. Hang on, I think I can... wanker! Fucking wanker.'

'What is it?'

'I can't get my gun out and ride my bike and the bastard keeps shooting at me. How much ammo does he want anyway? He can't have that much left.'

'I'm almost with you. You still on the same road?'

'Coming up to the Common now. Fuck me he's all over the place. There goes another one.'

I rounded a long sweeping bend and found myself looking at a dozen cars piled into each other, the drivers shaking their heads and looking at their bumpers. I twisted and turned my way around them then pulled back the accelerator and shot off along a long straight. More cars were stopped and blocking my route further up the road and I was forced to make a small detour on to the pavement at one point to get around the worst of it.

'Fuck, I think I've just shot someone else,' Craig told me.

'Don't worry about it, just try and stop Connolly.'

Craig and the Merc were now close enough for me to see. A number of oncoming cars were slewed across the road and there were people all around on the pavements hiding from bullets. A clear road opened up in front of me so I accelerated further still until I was almost up with Craig.

'He's turning right at the Common, right at the Common.'

'I see him. I'm right behind you.'

Craig turned his head and saw me closing, then swung his bike on after Connolly's Merc. I waited until I'd made the turn too before pulling out my Uzi with my left hand. I still wasn't close enough to get an accurate shot and Craig was veering and swerving in front of me but I kept it in my hand as I resumed my grip on the handlebars.

Whoever had the gun in the Merc was no longer firing, which meant he was either out of ammo or running so low that he wanted to make them count. Either way it allowed Craig and me to creep to within twenty yards.

More traffic up ahead made the Merc mount the kerb and drive on to the Common to get around it and I saw a head poke up from the backseat and watch us as we did the same. I couldn't recognise it as Connolly but I wasn't discriminating so I levelled my Uzi and fired four quick bursts at the back of the car until the clip was empty.

The Merc rejoined the road where the Common ended and the shooting from the backseat resumed with a couple of shots in our general direction, though these were so hopelessly off-target that they could only be counted as warning shots.

I dropped back and slowed right down so that I could let go of the handlebars altogether and reload before setting off again.

Craig looked back to see where I'd got to then screamed, 'Old Bill!'

I turned my head and saw two flashing lights way off across the other side of the Common.

'Do you suppose they're for us?' Craig pointlessly asked. I didn't bother wasting any of my valuable breath answering him.

'Put your foot down and get him. Get him now,' I told him. 'We haven't got long.' I twisted back my accelerator and overtook Craig in a matter of seconds so that I was right up the Merc's arse. A hand appeared and an automatic fired but this time there was no sign of the head. I brought the Uzi up again and sprayed the back window with lead. The driver must've been doing his best to keep out of sight because I couldn't even see him, but I did my best to centre my fire towards his seat.

The Merc swerved at a right angle and ducked down a side road, just beating an oncoming saloon for the space. The move had been too quick for me and I was going too fast with only one hand on the handlebars to make the turn and overshot it by a couple of bus lengths. Craig had no such problems though and carried on after Connolly's Merc.

I managed to bring my bike to a dead stop and slotted in my final Uzi clip before spinning around the back wheel and getting on after my target. And not a moment too soon either. I'd just made the turn when an angry police car appeared in my wing mirrors and invited himself along on my chase.

'Cops, right behind me. Take him down now.'

'Almost on him. Shit! Fucker! He's still shooting.'

'Then get shot, but just fucking get him!'

I could just see Craig's tail-end disappearing around a new corner each time I turned into a street. The Old Bill were no longer in my mirrors as I hurtled round the suburban streets and over speed bumps with hardly a let-up on the accelerator. Connolly had to be done now otherwise the police would have a helicopter here soon making escape almost impossible. Not that we'd leave before we'd got him.

'He's crashed! He's crashed!' Craig yelled into my ear.

'Do him now, I'll keep the cops off you.'

I rounded the next corner to see Connolly's Merc crumpled into a Post Office van at the T-junction of a main thru-road. Craig was off his bike and running towards the steaming mass of metal firing short bursts into the windows as he went. I skidded to a halt and quickly jumped off mine just in time to see the police car screeching its way around the corner towards me. I raised my Uzi in both hands, aimed towards the bonnet and windscreen and pulled the trigger. Sparks and glass sprayed out in all directions for several seconds from the front of the Panda before it ploughed headlong into the side of a row of parked cars. I continued to fire into the Old Bill in case either had made it through my lead storm and were unclipping their Heckler and Kochs and it was only when I moved closer and saw all the carnage that I let up. I turned around just in time to see Craig yank open the Merc's back door and open fire. He criss-crossed his line of fire about inside until everything in the Merc was turned to jam then told me about it over the radio.

A line of traffic had built up behind the Merc and people were leaving their vehicles and running for their lives creating noise and confusion all around us.

'Let's go. If we have to split up, put a bit of distance between them and you and lose them on the Tube like we talked about.'

'Too late for that,' he suddenly said looking down past a row of abandoned vehicles. He dropped behind the Merc and opened fire towards something around the corner that I couldn't see. 'Cops, on foot, with guns.'

'Well then let's not wait for them to surround us, get on your bike and let's get going.'

'I'm right behind you,' he said, then fired his Beretta empty at the approaching trouble and made a run for his bike. I still prob-ably had half a dozen rounds in my Uzi but killing was no longer the priority, escape was, so I slung it when I climbed back on my bike, along with the cumbersome rifle still strapped to my back, and headed for deepest suburbia.

It wouldn't be long before the place was swarming with cops – swarming? Yes, that was an appropriate word. Firing a machine-gun in a London street was like poking your nose into a bee's nest; the stripy bastards just didn't like it.

Craig was right behind me and going like the clappers by the time we spotted the first (of many) police cars. This one flashed across our path a little way ahead but failed to see us. The second appeared behind us and announced he'd found us to the whole neighbourhood by turning on his rooftop disco.

'Brixton's a couple of miles away. You know the route?' I asked Craig.

'I know it.'

'All right. Go for it, and I'll see you in court.'

'Not me pal, I'm a fat man at the dinner gong. Lots of luck.' Craig peeled off at the next turning and roared off towards Brixton.

It wouldn't be long, I thought to myself, before they had the street up ahead blocked off. Luckily, I wasn't going that way and jumped on the brakes and skidded 180 degrees so that I was facing my pursuers. Without pausing for breath I pulled back the accelerator and flew past them before they were able to close the gap, leaving them facing the wrong way down a narrow car-filled side street. I said a quick prayer to whoever was listening then put my life into God's hands as I flung myself around three dozen tight corners as I attempted to put as much distance as I could between me and the police.

Tooting was maybe only two miles away on the map but by the time you took into account all the twists and turns as I tried to lose myself and the Old Bill in the suburban labyrinth, I'd probably clocked up closer to four. I finally emerged on the high street just a short distance from Broadway station and jumped off the bike. A handful of tired old drunks and restless youths watched as I hung my helmet over my wing mirror, pulled a baseball cap down over my eyes and legged it towards the station – leaving my bike ticking over by the side of the road.

'Take it you thieving bastards, it's yours,' I muttered to myself as I disappeared through the entrance and used my travelcard to get past the barriers. I didn't know how long my bike would have to sit there before one of these little geniuses plucked up the courage to take it for a spin. Not long, I was hoping. They'd also find one outside Brixton station if they went up there looking that way.

Nice areas, Brixton and Tooting. Nice and crowded. Nice and dodgy.

I pulled the cap hard down over my eyes as I passed the security cameras and jumped on the first train to roll into the station. As it turned out, it was heading north.

The carriage was half empty, or half full depending on how you look at these things. I lost my jacket and left it beside the door when I jumped out at Tooting Bec and caught the next train south. Ten minutes later I was walking out of Morden station and hailing a cab to the other side of Wimbledon. There I tossed my gloves into a bin, caught another tube into town, found a bar and waited for Craig to call.

I heard from him within fifteen minutes.

'You make it?'

'I'm in a boozer on the Old Kent Road and I think I'm all right, though I keep expecting them to come crashing in through the windows any second.'

'You changed?'

'No, I'm sitting here trying to look inconspicuous in me fucking crash helmet, aren't I?'

'Let's just save the sarcasm for now, can we?'

'I'm changed, don't worry.'

'Keep moving about. Get a cab into town, buy a new hat and a new jacket, then get yourself home and stay out of sight. I'll phone you tonight to make sure everything's still okay, so stay sober, and call me if you need anything. Don't go phoning anyone else and don't answer the door under any circumstances. You got all that?'

'Yes, I've got it.'

'You sure you're fine?'

'Yeah, I'm okay. I've just got the shakes a bit that's all.'

'It's just adrenaline. You're probably pumped up to the eyeballs with it. This is why I don't want you talking to anyone, you're overdosing on your body's own Coke, don't trust yourself around anyone else, otherwise you might not be able to stop yourself from shooting your mouth off. Do I make myself clear?'

'And what about you?'

'Don't worry about me, I've been practising not talking to anyone for years.'

23. Meal deal

I've never been able to take my own advice. I tried to sit still at home but I just couldn't. All I could think of was Adelaide. We'd seen each other three times since Brighton though this was the first time I'd called round on her unannounced and uninvited. I'd thought about waiting for her outside the school gates until I'd remembered that I was trying not to get myself noticed so I waited until seven then knocked on her door.

'Hi!' she greeted me, a little surprised.

'Hello. Look, I hope you don't mind. I was just passing so I thought I'd knock and say hello. Seemed silly not to when I was just passing.'

Adelaide thought about this for a moment, looked less than convinced, but agreed it would've been silly not to have called – if I was just passing.

'So, what brings you to the neighbourhood?'

'Work,' I told her.

'You've been working around here?'

'Yes, up on the factory estate about a mile from here, installing software and such like.'

'They let you go in dressed like that?'

I looked down at my jeans, running shoes and sweater.

'They don't mind, as long as I can do the job. Perks of working for myself, you see.'

'I do. Are you hungry? I was just about to make myself some dinner.'

Hungry wasn't the word for it.

'I do apologise again, I'm afraid I'm not used to eating in front of people.'

Christ, what a fucking animal! Fingers, thumbs, sleeves and wisdom teeth had all come into play as I'd shovelled it into my mouth without a second's thought as to what I looked like. And the noises? *Wildlife on One* Jackie had called it. Wellies stuck in mud Adelaide had reckoned. Of course, I'd been happily oblivious to all this while I'd been doing it and only paused for thought when I'd seen the looks of horror on their faces.

It wasn't my fault.

I was hungry. No, I was fucking starving. The adrenaline from this morning had given me an appetite that only Robinson Crusoe could've appreciated. Coupled with the fact that it had been so long since I'd eaten in front of someone else I'd plain forgotten how and that'll give you some idea of what Adelaide and Jackie witnessed that evening.

About the only things around me not covered in gravy or brown sauce were my knife and fork.

'Honestly, I'm sorry. It's been such a long day that I think I forgot how hungry I was.'

'Well then just forget about it again. I'll take it as a compliment on my cooking.'

'Yes, yes, just think of it like that. It was delicious, really delicious. I don't think I've ever had anything as lovely.'

Jackie laughed at this as Adelaide cleared away.

'You utter arse-kisser,' Jackie grinned. 'Keep it believable or you'll blow your play.'

'What? What do you mean?'

'Don't listen to her Ian, she's just jealous because no one's ever been able to finish one of her meals without shitting blood the next day.'

Jesus!

Jackie continued to eye me knowingly with a little wry smile. She lit a cigarette and blew the smoke up in the air then turned her gaze back towards me.

'So, you two seem to be getting along very nicely just lately.'

I didn't know what to say to that so I just nodded and stuck my bottom lip out. Adelaide looked over at Jackie and shot her a look I couldn't read. 'All I'm saying is you seem to be getting on well…' Jackie broke off laughing as Adelaide gave her the daggers again and I sensed that there was a previous conversation at work here.

I began to question my judgement in coming. What was I doing here anyway? Okay, I'd wanted to see Adelaide. No, that's not quite right, I'd longed to see Adelaide. But why? What did I want?

I didn't know. I'd just acted on my feelings and given little thought as to what I was going to say or do. All I'd known is that I'd wanted to see her and that was the long and the short of it. Topics of conversations or planned social activities were of secondary importance.

Now I was here though, with nothing to say for myself and no reason for calling round, I felt pretty awkward.

It had been the adrenaline. That was what it was. I felt like I was burning up to tell Adelaide something, but I didn't know what. I was pretty sure it wasn't 'I love you' and I knew for a fact it wasn't 'I just killed some cops today', so what was it? Perhaps I was being paranoid about the events of this morning. Perhaps I was subconsciously fearful of being arrested and just wanted to see Adelaide one last time.

Was that it?

No, it couldn't be. If I was fearful of being arrested, even subconsciously, I'd be half-way across the Channel by now.

Wouldn't I?

'Oh my God, yeah, did you see that thing on the news tonight Ian?' Adelaide said, trying to divert the conversation away from whatever Jackie was getting at.

'Oh yeah, wasn't that unbelievable?' Jackie agreed.

Please let them be talking about monetary union, I quickly prayed.

'These two maniacs on motorbikes shot a load of people today in Clapham. They had footage of them and everything.'

'Machineguns, they had. You saw it on the news, them shooting everywhere. What is it they said, five people, was it five?'

'Yep, five people killed so far, loads more in the hospital either shot or hurt in car crashes.'

'And that's only like five miles or so from here. Imagine if that had been me walking down the road and that had been round this way, I could've been one of them that was hurt,' Jackie exclaimed excitedly. 'Or even killed.'

'Yeah Jackie, you were really in the thick of it weren't you?' I said with a roll of the eyes.

Imagine if… imagine what? Some people loved to see action by proxy didn't they? There are eight million people living in London. So we killed five, so what? Three of those we'd meant to kill, two were policemen who'd risked their lives to stop us and paid the ultimate price and the rest of the casualties, none of which were fatalities, were just accidental. Sorry about that. And I really am, but what could I do about it? The point I'm trying to make is that the chances of Jackie being killed walking down the street today were nil but that didn't stop her trying to come across as a bit dangerous because she lived in the same town as a shooting incident. No, to be honest and thinking about it for a second, she stood more of a chance of getting shot sat in here with me tonight.

'I didn't see it,' I told them.

'Oh you have to, it's incredible. Stick the news on when it comes on next,' Jackie said.

I promised I would watch it with great interest.

'Well okay, I think I'll leave you to it,' Jackie announced looking at her watch. 'Maybe I'll give Craig a ring, see if he wants to take me out.'

'I don't think you'll be able to get him,' I told her quickly. 'I spoke to him tonight and he said he'd gone to bed.'

'Gone to bed? It's only eight.'

'He said he's not well.'

'Drunk more like.'

Drugged, actually. I'd told him to take three sleeping pills and put the phone off the hook and get a good night's rest. I'd told him it was the professional thing to do. Craig had reluctantly agreed.

This again made me question my own actions.

Perhaps it sounded hypercritical but I knew myself and trusted myself not to say anything to anyone while my blood was still up, but I couldn't vouch for Craig, so I'd taken no chances and taken him out of the equation. A good night's sleep and it would all seem a little less real the next day and a little easier to ignore. Sometimes I thought that this was the hardest part of the job, not being able to tell anybody about the things I had done.

Craig would learn. But tonight he'd sleep.

'Well, I'll go round and see Carol then. I'm sure you two don't want me around under your feet.'

'We don't mind,' Adelaide said.

My silence spoke volumes.

Jackie clattered about for a bit longer before finally leaving. A little nattering went on at the front door before I heard it shut and finally Adelaide and I were alone.

'Coffee?'

'Please.'

We sat around the table sipping coffee and making the odd remark to each other but there was no real danger of conversation breaking out. I couldn't understand what was wrong, we normally got on so well, but suddenly neither of us could manage to string three words together.

My caginess I could understand, I was trying not to confess to being on the news. I wondered what Adelaide had done today.

'So, tell me, what brings you around here tonight?'

'Like I said, I was just working in the neighbourhood and…'

'Come on, really, tell me why you came around.'

What did she know? Had Craig already phoned and told them what we'd done today? Was that why they'd brought up the news earlier?

Which pocket was my silencer in?

No, stop that, stop that! Don't even think about it.

'I just really wanted to see you, that was all. There was nothing sinister in my motives. I had just been thinking about you all day and…'

'And what? What did you want to see me about?'

'I didn't want to see you about anything. I just wanted to see you,' I assured her. Christ this was awkward. Couldn't I call round and see someone for no apparent reason? Other people did it didn't they?

Adelaide let a small smile break out across her face.

'God, you're not very good at this are you?' she said and leaned over and planted a little kiss on my lips.

Good at what? my brain screamed. What was it I was meant to be doing and wasn't?

Was she talking about sex?

I felt a hot flush come over me. Like I'd said, we'd seen each other four times now (not counting our first meeting) but we hadn't been intimate with each other yet. In fact, we hadn't even touched tongues. It's not that I hadn't wanted to or anything, it just hadn't come up that's all.

Was Adelaide mistaking my post-homicidal agitation for a case of the schoolboy jitters?

If she was then it seemed fitting. Most of our relationship to date had been built on mutual misunderstanding. It seemed like the natural way forward.

'I'll make this easy for you if you want?' Adelaide said. 'Would you like to stay the night?'

I thought about this carefully and picked her words apart a dozen different ways to make sure we were both finally on the same wavelength and that I wouldn't be waking up on the sofa before I answered.

'I would.'

Then we touched tongues.

24. Logan's run

JB was in my house.

But JB was never in my house. In fact I'd only ever met him in person once before.

I wondered what he wanted.

I decided to listen to him and find out.

'What the fuck did you do?' he shouted at me.

It didn't sound like good news. 'What the fucking hell did you do?'

Craig looked edgy next to him. As did Felix and some guy whose name I couldn't remember; he looked like a shooter though. I'd stuffed my Glock into the back of my belt before I'd opened the door and I started to wonder if I could get to it before they got to me.

I wondered if I needed to.

'Things got messy I know, but we took him out and got away clean. The damage is minimal,' I tried to explain.

'No! No! You don't start half-way through a fucking story. I want the whole chapter and verse you motherfucker. Now what did you do?'

I looked at Craig and he threw me an expression that I took to mean, 'don't look at me, I only work here'.

'We… we took out… Connolly.'

'I know you took out Connolly, Action Man here told me all about it. What I want to know is why. On whose fucking authority did you whack my accountant? Or was it something you just fancied doing on your own time?'

There was no point trying to enlighten him with explanations as to the whys and wherefores, that was Logan's job. I was merely doing my job. And, as my boss, JB had every right to know who called in the hit. They could argue the right and wrong of it between themselves, this had nothing to do with me, so I told him.

'Yeah? And why the fuck would Danny ask you to do that?' he shouted at me and for a moment I thought he wasn't going to believe me.

'I don't know JB, it's not my job to ask questions, I just do.'

'You just do? And what else have you been fucking doing lately? You take down my crew in Hatton Garden? Huh? Huh? Did you?'

'No JB, I don't know what you're talking about.'

'You don't huh? What about my lorry and my goods? Logan get you to take them from me too?'

'No JB, I haven't touched any lorry.'

'You fucking lying to me?'

'No, honestly. I work for you, anything you want to know I'll tell you.'

'You work for me? What the fuck d'you kill my accountant for then?'

'Orders Mr Broad, I was told to. Logan said Connolly was going to the Old Bill.'

'Bullshit! BULLSHIT!'

'I swear it's the truth, you can ask Logan.'

'Oh I fucking intend to. Just as soon as I can fucking find him. Now where is he?'

The discussion that followed got a lot more heated before it got any cooler. I really thought my number was up and even had the order worked out as to who I'd take down first, though I hadn't been able to make up my mind whether or not to include Craig in there somewhere. As happy luck would have it, I didn't need to. JB eventually believed my story and believed me when I told him I didn't know where Logan was. Actually, I think he probably believed me right from the start, or at least, I don't think he ever believed I was anything to do with the whys and wherefores. I was simply following orders, same as I always had. It wasn't my fault if those orders weren't JB's orders. How could I be expected to tell the difference?

I couldn't, could I?

The simple fact that I was never involved with the 'whys' and JB knew that was probably what saved my life – and JB's and Felix's and the shooter's and possibly Craig's, though I still hadn't made up my mind about that.

He stayed in my living room for a little under an hour and before he left JB gave me and Craig some new orders. I'm sure you can guess what they were.

Logan was gone; he'd packed a couple of suitcases and disappeared taking his wife and kids and passport with him. We searched his house for clues and we searched the office for the same. We even searched the West End flat I'm sure Mrs Logan didn't know about but we found nothing. Well, I'm not a detective am I?

The word was out and London was suddenly all eyes but none of them gazed upon Mr Daniel Logan or any member of the Logan brood. His wife's brother turned up, and that was just too bad for him. He didn't seem to know where Danny had disappeared to, or at least wasn't saying, and so that was the last anyone saw of Logan's wife's brother.

A great many people upped and ran after that, friends, relatives, lawyers, and I can't say I blamed them. JB had instructed us to leave no fingernail unturned in our search for his former trustee.

Rumour was that he'd scarpered to where the skies were blue and the water emptied the other way down the plughole and that was probably right. I imagine he had some quick getaway money stashed around the house or the office and just decided to put a planet between himself and JB. He'd return after a few years (they always do) and JB would have his pound of flesh then. In the meantime everyone kept on their toes. The organisation had come in for some bad luck just lately and JB was taking it all very personally. Much of it was laid at Logan's door, including the murder of Brian Faulkner, one of the guys who sorted Craig's witnesses with us, that night. I'm sure a lot of heads in the organisation turned my way when his body was found down by the river in East London, but JB knew full well that my bodies were never found, so I was never in the frame.

I still didn't know why Logan did what he did... or rather, got me to do what I did. Maybe he had told me the truth. Maybe Connolly had been a rat and he was just looking out for JB's best interests without compromising his sources. It sounded plausible to me. But then why had he run? That didn't make sense.

So, perhaps there was another reason.

You can never know for sure, not in an organisation like ours, but there are always a lot of theories floating about. Some people reckoned that Connolly was fucking Logan's wife. I didn't believe that. Other people thought Logan was positioning himself to take over the organisation and that Connolly was just the first unfortunate victim of an unsuccessful coup. I didn't believe that either. Yet more people thought that Connolly and Logan had been partners in something and that Connolly had ripped Logan off. Or maybe Logan was ripping Connolly off. Hmm, I didn't know, possibly, but that one had holes in it too.

For me the most plausible explanation came from Eddie of all people. He reckoned that Logan had been siphoning off company money into his own account for years and that JB's numbers just weren't adding up. Not that JB would've noticed this, of course, he had more money than he could keep track of, but his accountant might've spotted something. He might've even taken the books to Logan to look at, not realising it was Logan who was doing the siphoning. Again, I can't be sure, but it holds water for me. Maybe Danny'll send us a postcard from wherever he is and let us know. I hope so, because I'm dying to know.

Not that any of this matters. All I know for a fact is that Logan had wanted Connolly dead real bad, and that he'd used me to do it.

This placed me in a precarious position. Once you were tarred with suspicion in this organisation, you were tarred with it for life.

And all the assurances and understanding in the world wouldn't change that.

25. Hitman and her

The next few weeks were marked by tension and mistrust. Logan had been a linchpin of stability within the organisation and his disappearance unsettled everyone. You have to understand that a set-up like JB's is made up of people who are inherently greedy, dishonest, manipulative and wary of everyone around them.

Basically they're crooks.

And to run and maintain an organisation where every member of staff is a greedy, dishonest and untrustworthy crook is some kind of feat. I don't think ordinary people truly appreciate this.

That's why you need a guy like Logan. Logan was the eyes and ears. JB might've been the brains but Logan was the heart. No, that's not right, Logan was the brains too, JB was probably just the stomach or something, I don't know. Anyway, my point is, the smartest thing JB ever did was to take Logan on and Logan was the reason JB became JB. Unfortunately, when Logan disappeared, a lot of things started going tits up. Payments weren't made, money wasn't collected, goods were lost, people were nicked and deals were soured. JB couldn't possibly know every little detail behind every little scam after such a long time away from the helm, though he was fucked if he was about to take advice from anyone again. As I've said, it was all tension and mistrust.

I won't bore you with the details of every little piece of misfortune, mostly because I don't know them myself, but I was kept in the picture largely by Craig (who seemed to relish the day-to-day involvement a lot more than me) and Eddie, who just liked to drop by every now and then for a gossip, which was useful information. According to Eddie, JB had started a 'clean this mess up' operation and a couple of faces had disappeared already. This spooked me considerably; not that the boss had disappeared a couple of his own boys, I didn't care about that. What spooked me was that he hadn't used me to do it.

Now, what did that tell me?

I looked through my strongbox to make sure my passports and identification were still in order and started withdrawing large amounts of cash from my different accounts. I didn't know where I was going to go, all I knew was that my days were numbered here so anywhere would be good enough for the moment.

Adelaide?

What did I do about Adelaide? We'd gotten pretty close over the last couple of months, closer than I'd ever dared hope for. Oh, we weren't there yet, or even half-way, but we were on the right road and I'd started to believe that my years of loneliness were over. And suddenly all that was for nothing if I had to go the way of Logan. There was only one thing for it, she would have to come with me. In fact there wasn't even a decision to be made.

But then, the decision wasn't mine to dismiss.

'…so the Headmaster says he'll see to it that every teacher does the same thing. Isn't that good?'

'Great!' I replied less than enthusiastically. I can't tell you what had been said before that, for all I know she could've put forward a proposal for pupil/paedophile nature walks, I hadn't been listening.

'Are you with me at the moment? You seem to have something on your mind.'

I looked at her across my dining table and ran my fingers over my stubbly head a dozen times until I decided I couldn't put it off any longer.

'I've been wrestling over how to ask you this and I just can't seem to find the right words.'

'Oh my God! Wait, Ian, don't say anything else please. Let's not rush into anything okay, this is nice how it is at the moment, isn't it? Let's not get carried away.'

'What?'

Adelaide put her hand on mine.

'I like you a great deal. In fact, I think it's more than that, but let's get to know each other before we go rushing headfirst into anything we might both regret.'

'What?'

'What I'm trying to say is, let's take it nice and easy. We're friends aren't we? Let's stay friends, good friends, and see where time takes us.'

'I don't think you understand…'

'I do, I really do. More than you could ever know. You see, I've been there before.'

What, you've had a relationship with a hitman whose life was in danger and you had to change your identity and flee the country to get away from an underground organisation bent on murder? – I wanted to say, though I didn't. I thought I'd break it to her a little more gently than that.

'No, I really think you've got your wires crossed, I ain't proposing to you or anything.'

'You're not?'

'No, this is something else entirely, this is… this is really difficult for me as I've never done this before but… I want to tell you a few things about myself, but I'm scared of what you'll think of me. And I… I don't want to lose you.'

'Oh my God! You're married!'

'I'm not.' Jesus, what was it with her today, she really had wedding bells on her mind? 'Listen, please, hear me out.'

'What is it?' she asked rather unnecessarily, like I was just going to go 'Oh nothing' after all that build-up.

'I'm not a software installer,' I told her.

'A what?'

'You know, computers.' I noticed her eyes start to glaze over as an instinctive knee-jerk reaction to the word 'computers' so I quickly moved on. 'I don't really do that for a living. I only told you that, and in fact, I only tell that to everyone because I can't tell anybody what I really do.'

'You're a secret agent.'

'Do you want to stop guessing for a minute? No, I'm not a secret agent. I'm a...' Hmm, how did I put this? '... I'm a... a sort of gangster, I guess you could say.'

'A sort of gangster? What's a sort of gangster do when he's sort of gangstering?'

'Well, I belong to an organisation and the things we do are... oh, what's the word?'

'Organised?'

'No! Well yes, but mainly illegal. You know, handling stolen goods, gambling, property, racketeering...'

'Drugs?'

'Yes, I suppose so, but I have nothing to do with that side of things at all,' I said trying to defuse the expression on her face which looked like it was just about to go off.

'You handle drugs?'

'No, no, the people I work with do, I just deliver stuff, make payments, act as a go-between, that sort of thing.'

What utter lies!

Adelaide stared at me with incomprehension blazing away in her eyes. 'What are you telling me, that you're a drug dealer? That you work for drug dealers?'

'Look, just get the drugs out of your head. I have nothing to do with drugs and I never have. I'm just an organiser, a fixer, if you like. The organisation has a problem and I'm called in to solve it.'

'I don't understand any of this. What do you mean you're a fixer?'

'Look, I love you,' I told her.

'Oh, don't say that. Please, don't say that. People who say "I love you" at moments like this almost always follow it up with something really bad.' She stared at me for a while waiting for me to answer. 'You are, aren't you? You're going to tell me something really bad now aren't you?'

'Not necessarily.'

'Is this to do with you being in prison?'

'Sort of.'

'There are those words again, "sort of". What's "sort of"?' Adelaide cleared her mind of further questions and braced herself. 'Okay then, I'm waiting. Let's hear it. Let's hear what you've got to "sort of" say, and no more beating about the bush.'

'How would you like a holiday?'

'You're still beating about the bush.'

'Okay. It's like this; I want out. I want to leave the organisation and settle down and have a normal life like everyone else, but I can't. You don't just quit a job like mine and stay in the same town. That's not done. So, I've got to go away, somewhere a long long way away, and I might not be coming back.'

'How far is a long long way away? Are we talking Scotland here?'

'Maybe, but I was more thinking about somewhere where the water runs down the plughole the other way.'

'Australia?'

'Could be, I don't know yet, it's up to you.'

'It's up to me? Why is it… Oh no, you can't mean…?'

'I want you to come with me.'

'This isn't for real. I mean, this is all just a joke or something isn't it?'

'No joke. I only wish it were. Look, how about it? We can see the world, go anywhere we want, do anything we like. I've got over three hundred thousand in cash to take with us and we can live in the lap of luxury for years. We could even go to Adelaide if you wanted.'

Adelaide's mind was overrun with a thousand questions and for a few seconds she was unable to say anything as she attempted to pin one of them down. When she finally did, it was a typically 'practical Adelaide' question.

'And what happens when the money all runs out? Three

hundred thousand might sound like a lot but that's nothing these days.'

'Then we come home, but not to London. Somewhere quiet, Cornwall maybe or Cambridge, or even Scotland, somewhere like that. I'll leave enough behind to set ourselves up so that we won't have to worry about anything except getting normal jobs and settling down. You'll be doing what you're doing now, only somewhere else and after seeing the world. Please, I don't want to go without you.'

'But, you're a gangster.'

'Only sort of. I'm not wanted by the police and we won't be doing anything illegal, we'll just be travelling, that's all. Thousands of people do it every year, the only question is whether or not you want to come with me. Please think about it, it's the chance of a lifetime, how many opportunities like this do you think will come along?'

'Are you in trouble or something?'

'No, no I'm not. I just want to leave. Once we disappear they'll probably forget all about me in a couple of weeks, but I can't just stroll up to them and hand in my notice like I was working in a bank or something, they wouldn't let me leave. I know too much about them.'

'Are you in danger? Or more to the point am I in danger?'

'No, don't worry about that. Besides, I can protect myself.'

'Don't worry about that? What are you fucking joking or something? "Darling, I work for drug dealers and have to go on the run. You want to come with me? It's not dangerous or nothing."'

'It's not like that.'

'And what do you mean you can protect yourself? Up until five minutes ago you were a fucking computer nerd, now you're telling me you're Robert DeNiro. Wait a minute, have you got a gun?'

'Er… yes,' I said and could've added, 'I've got a safe full of them upstairs – and some grenades.'

'Show me it.'

'No. It's not appropriate.'

'I don't give a shit what's appropriate. Show me it.'

When I failed to produce my gun Adelaide's face softened. 'I knew you were full of shit. You can't con me, I'm not that naive,' she laughed.

'I'm not conning you, this is all for real,' I told her but a big smile spread across her face and she shook her head vigorously.

'You should've said you were a secret agent, that one would've been better. You almost had me going there for a minute.'

'Oh for God's sake,' I said and reached under my sweat-shirt, pulled out my Glock and laid it on the table in front of her. That was a moment I'll take to the grave with me. You know how people say that time stood still? Well it really did. I laid the Glock on the table with a big thunk and then all the clocks and watches in the house stopped for a small eternity as Adelaide fought to keep her jaw attached to her face.

'Is that thing real?'

'No, it's a mirage and this is all a dream. Of course it's real. I told you, I work for gangsters.'

'You only said "sort of" gangsters.'

'Well, they are... "sort of",' I said, confusing myself now.

'And you've got a gun?'

'I know. Look, that's it just there.'

Adelaide suddenly stood and backed away from the table sending her chair crashing to the floor.

'Oh my God. Wait a minute? Oh my God,' she kept muttering to herself over and over again.

'It's not as bad as all that,' I tried to reassure her. 'Just think of it this way. We're getting on well together and I've just told you I'm well off and asked you if you wanted to come on an all-expenses-paid holiday around the world for a year or two. That's all this is.'

Adelaide screwed up her face as she listened so that I couldn't tell if she was going to laugh, cry, throw up or start talking dirty to me.

'Are you out of your fucking mind?' she shouted at me. 'You've just pulled out a gun on me and you want me to pretend you're Tony Curtis. Hang on a minute, is this how you know Craig?'

'I… sort of… well, it's how…'

'I bloody knew it. Computers my arse. He has enough trouble with calculators. Hang on a minute.' Adelaide's eyes continued to dart between me and the gun and I said nothing for a while as I could see she was putting two, three, four, five, six, seven, eight and nine together and slowly coming up with… er… er, the right answer, whatever that would be (two and three is five, plus five and four is fourteen… six is twenty, twenty-nine, nine plus seven is… er thirty-six plus er… er… eight, that's forty-two, no forty-four! – Oh what does it fucking matter?). Anyway, the point is, I sat quietly and didn't interrupt her while she thought things through as I thought it was better that these things occurred to her while I was with her than have her go off and agonise over them alone. At least while I was here I could answer her questions and do my best to set her worst fears at ease. In fact, I found it pretty reassuring that she hadn't tried to leg it the moment she started taking me seriously; at least that showed she was actually considering my proposal and not just ready to dismiss the whole notion out of hand.

I don't know what I would've done if she'd tried to run. I like to think that I wouldn't've killed her, that I would've just let her go. After all, I myself was getting ready to leave the country any day so what difference would it have made what I'd told her? She didn't have anything solid that could've sent Interpol after me or even made things difficult for me when I eventually returned. So I was a gangster? So I had admitted as much? No one could lock me up for that.

There was still the problem of JB. Could word reach him?

Could my flight endanger Craig and the rest of the organisation? Before I'd even invited her round to have this talk I'd come to the conclusion that if she had've run and had've talked I would've been long gone by the time the Old Bill got round to paying me a visit and that Adelaide would've marked her own card as far as JB was concerned.

But then, that would've been her own fault if she'd talked. And there was nothing I could do about that.

Adelaide suddenly made another connection.

'You're a fixer?' she asked.

I nodded.

'You fix problems?'

Again I nodded.

'Problems like the ones Craig was having.'

My head stayed perfectly still, though I think I betrayed myself with my eyes.

'Have you ever used that thing?'

'Once or twice,' I told her. 'Though that wasn't me who pulled the trigger that night.'

I waited and waited and waited for her to hit the roof (shouldn't that be the ceiling?) but she never did. Instead she just disappeared off into her own mind again and thought about this.

'But you have used it before? Once or twice, you say.'

'Yes,' I told her.

'Have you ever killed anyone?'

'You know I have. That's what I was in prison for.'

'I mean, have you ever killed anyone else? Since? And with that?'

I stayed silent for a moment and looked at my Glock. I wasn't so much struggling to find the right answer as wishing the question had never been asked. But it wasn't going to go away. It had to be answered and answered honestly if we were to take things forward.

Well, this was all my own fault. If I'd just looked after number one and ran I wouldn't've had to answer any of these questions, but that wasn't what I wanted to do. I wanted to take Adelaide with me and honesty and trust was the price.

'Yes,' I told her. 'I have.'

'How many?' she asked, incredulous. 'How many have you killed?'

Again I stayed silent, then told her: 'Four.'

Well, there's honesty and there's honesty and four sounded like a respectable figure to me. Not too many to freak her out, not too few to prick her suspicions.

'Including the one you went to prison for?'

'Okay then, five.'

'Five? You've killed five people?'

'Yes, but they were all gangsters too.'

'And that's an excuse?'

'No. That was just my job. And I'm tired of it. I don't want to do it any more. I want to be with you. I meant what I said when I said I loved you, because I do. Please... please, give me a chance and I'll make every day of your life the best day of your life.'

'Oh will you? Well, I must say this one's been a fucking corker.'

'Please...'

'Ian, stop and listen to me. Do you know what you're asking? Do you have any idea of what you've told me? I'm trying to take this all in but my mind is spinning. Ten minutes ago we were having dinner, now you're asking me to make a life-changing decision in... how long have I got?'

'Er...' I looked at my watch.

'No, I mean, when were you planning on leaving?'

Again, I looked at my watch.

'Tuesday.'

'Tuesday? Fucking Jesus!'

'You know, you don't half swear a lot when you're stressed.'

'Fuck! Fuck! Fuck! Fuck! Fuck! Fuck! Fuck! Fuck! Fuck! Fuck! Fuck! Fuckiddy fuck, Ian. Tuesday? I've got a class to teach. I've got notice to give. I've got...'

'None of that matters. None of it. Not in this life. All that matters is that you say yes and come with me. Please, I've waited all my life to find someone like you… No, that's not right. What I meant to say is that I've waited all my life to find *you*. I have to go, but I don't want to go without you. Come on,' I implored her, wanting her so badly to say yes that it almost hurt. 'Please, come with me.'

'What if I say no?'

'Don't say no.'

'But what if I do? Will you kill me too?'

'No. I wouldn't. I'd be heartbroken, but I wouldn't hurt a hair on your head.'

'Even though I now know about you?'

'There's a difference between knowing and being able to prove. You're not a danger to me at all, though one word of advice: my boss might not take the same point of view. If you decide not to come with me, though I hope you don't, you'd be better off not going to the police. For your own safety. And that's just advice to someone I love because I care about you, nothing else.'

Adelaide stood her ground and looked into my eyes.

'There's a lot I don't know about you isn't there?'

'There's a lot I don't know about you! But there's nothing I don't want to know.'

Only now did she stand her chair back up on end and retake her place at the table. She was slow and methodical and sat quietly for a long time without speaking. She didn't look at me and she didn't ask any more questions, she just sat and thought.

Hours seemed to pass, though I knew they were only really minutes and finally I had to say something. I knew cajoling her would only disturb her inner thoughts but I couldn't bear the silence any more, I had to say something.

'Adelaide? I know it's a lot to take in, but do you think there's a chance you might consider it? Please, give me that much. Is there a chance, even a little one, that you might come with me?'

Adelaide looked up at me and gave me a half-smile.

'I'm still here aren't I?'

I let out an enormous sigh of relief and smiled back at her.

'I'm sorry to spring all this on you, I really am. I wish we had years to get to know each other but we don't. It's either this or never see each other again, and I so don't want that. Look, no pledges or commitment or anything, if you don't like it – or you find you don't like me – you can just come home. It might be a bit awkward with your job and all that but I promise I'll give you enough money to tide yourself over until you got back on your feet. That's the only risk you'd be taking, a slight blot on your CV, nothing more than that. Even if you only stayed with me a year, what a year we'd have! It'd be the best year of your life and then some, and we'd get to know each other and maybe you might want to stay another year. And maybe another after that. But even if you didn't, then no problem. At least you would've given it a chance. At least we would've known for sure. Can you imagine how you'd feel if you said no and I went away Tuesday and we never saw each other again? You'd always be asking yourself… what if? And it might be something you end up regretting your whole life. Of course it might not, but you can't know that, not here, not now. Isn't that what life's about, about taking risks? Living life to the full? Grabbing…'

'All right, all right, you're laying it on a bit thick aren't you?'

'I'm sorry, I know I am, but that's just because I really want you to come with me.'

'So I gathered,' she replied, then looked down at my Glock. 'What about that? You won't be able to take that with you.'

'I know, don't worry, I'll get rid of it. I'll chuck it in the sea. No one will ever find it.'

'Okay,' she said. 'Okay.' Her features softened again and her hand reached for mine. She was shaking ever so slightly and she grasped my hand firmly to disguise it. 'Ian…?' she started then stopped.

'What?' I asked.

'Nothing,' she said but I persisted.

'Come on, what is it? Tell me.'

Adelaide paused for a moment, then smiled sheepishly and asked: 'Well, before we do chuck it away… can I have a go on it?'

Of course, there was never a doubt in my mind that she'd agree to come with me, though that surety only materialised after the event. At the time, I think I was expecting, and readying myself for, a big heart-sinking disappointment.

If only she'd said no.

I agreed to postpone my departure by another five days to give her a whole week to tie up her affairs. She wanted to come with me, but she didn't want to burn her bridges. What difference would another few days make?

I laid low and didn't answer the door or the phone except when Adelaide rang (I have a machine that flashes up the number calling) in case JB had a job or a hole dug for me somewhere and spent the next few days cleaning the house from top to bottom. I didn't want to leave my prints or hair fibres or anything else that JB could've used to set me up with once I'd gone. Not that I thought he would, but it kept me busy and kept my mind occupied otherwise I think my mum would've driven me crazy.

That's my dead mum, talking to me in my head. And I was frightened she was going to drive me crazy? Hmm…

That was the longest week of my life and I hated it. I'd never really feared death before, perhaps because I had never really had anything to lose except my life, but now it mortified me. I couldn't die, I couldn't, not when I was this close to actually having what I'd always dreamed of. I just couldn't. I became utterly paranoid and the closer we got to Sunday the more Bogeymen I saw lurking for me in the shadows. I almost took someone out in my local supermarket on the Wednesday because he'd followed me around the store. Every time I turned into an aisle he wandered round with me or was there waiting for me already. He even smiled at me once as I squeezed past his trolley. What did he want? Bread, milk, eggs, chicken, washing powder, the usual stuff of course, because he was just there doing his shopping. It wasn't his fault he had similar tastes to me. In fact, it was probably only his love of chocolate biscuits that saved him from becoming just another motiveless, unsolved murder as he spent so long trying to decide between Jaffa Cakes and Penguins that he was still there when I left.

I wonder which he went for in the end?

It got to Friday evening and I phoned Adelaide to see how her last day at work went but all I got was the answerphone. Reluctant to leave any sort of message I simply repeated 'Pick up Adelaide, it's me' a few times until the phone was answered.

Tears and crying.

'What's up? What's the matter?'

'Who is this?' sniffed a voice I recognised as Jackie's.

'It's Ian. Is Adelaide there?' I wasn't too alarmed at first because Jackie was always crying about one thing or another.

'Oh Ian, I'm so sorry…' she said and trailed off.

'What? What's the matter?'

'It's Adelaide… Oh Ian…'

The blood drained from my face yet my heart began to race as all my paranoid fears suddenly rushed to greet me.

'What is it Jackie? Tell me. What's happened to Adelaide?'

'She's in hospital… in intensive care… I don't know how she's…'

'What happened?' I demanded, and had to repeat myself several times before Jackie got it together enough to answer me.

'She was run over… by a car… leaving the pub this evening.'

'The pub?'

'We went for a quick drink to say goodbye, me and the other teachers, but she only stayed for an hour, and then she said she had to go. And she was run over getting into her car… Oh Ian, I'm so sorry.'

26. Clockwork psychopath

I was drunk.

I was *really* drunk.

I didn't know how much I'd drunk or even what room I was in, all I knew was that I was roaringly drunk... and the reason why I was drinking. That was the annoying part. I was drinking to forget and it had worked because I had forgotten everything except the one thing I was trying to forget. That was just too big. Too *unforgettable*. I was in so much pain. All I wanted was a brief respite from it. Just an hour or two, that was all. After that I'd pick up where I'd left off. I promised myself I would. Just an hour or two. Not even that. Just to get her out of my mind. Just...

I came to in the kitchen and felt the physical pain before the real stuff kicked in. That was easy to deal with, I just started drinking again. Within minutes I was drunk again. Then sick. Then drunk. Then sick. Then drunk. This was how I passed the night, not knowing what time it was, or whether it was day or night – and not particularly caring. All knew is that I had to drink, I had to. Every time I sobered up – or at least, came close to it – I opened up another bottle of scotch and drank.

We had been so close, so very, very close, it wasn't fair. If only I'd insisted we left on Tuesday instead of giving her a week, she'd still be okay and I'd be with her and we'd be...

Drink! DRINK! Don't think, just drink!

I did as I told me. It wasn't fair... it wasn't fair...

'What is fair?' Mum asked me. 'You don't care about anyone except yourself. Isn't fair? You don't know the meaning of fair, all you know is gimme gimme gimme. You're selfish! You always have been. Don't think about anyone except yourself. "It's not fair,

I don't have anyone to go on holiday with. It's not fair, nobody loves me. It's not fair, Adelaide went and got herself run over and now she's ruined my plans." Listen to yourself. You're not even thinking about her are you? All you're thinking about is yourself and how it affects you.'

'That's not true, I love her.'

'Huh, love! Huh! You don't love anyone except yourself. You're an evil little boy who only ever thinks about himself.'

'I'm not! I'm not.'

'Oh you're not, are you? I suppose you're going to tell me that you love me too now.'

'Fuck that, I hate you.'

'Yes, of course you do. You hate your own mother. Someone who gave you life, someone who gave you everything, who sacrificed everything for you and you hate her.'

'No, you made me hate you. I used to love you but you made me hate you.'

'I made you hate me? And how did I do that? By slaving my guts out for you? By never being happy for you?'

'Stop lying to me. Stop torturing me!'

'Torturing you! All I ever did was do my best for my little boy, so that he would be happy. That's all I ever wanted for you.'

'I'm not a little boy! I'm a man.'

'A man? Of course you're not. Men care about people. Men look after people. Men love their mothers. You're just a little boy. An ungrateful, spiteful, nasty little boy. And that's all you'll ever be.'

'That's not true. That's not true.'

'Is he talking about love again?' Angela sneered.

'He says he loves Adelaide,' my mum scowled.

'Love? Huh, what does he know about love? Do you love her like you loved me?'

'More. So much more… I love her so much,' I said and tried to kill them both with another swig but it didn't work.

'Yeah, I bet you do. Just like you "loved" me. Just like you "loved" Rose. Just like you "loved" Breen and Harry and Mr Ashton and Ben and Alex and Sue and their next-door neighbour and Foster and Adrian and Matt and Tom and Katrina and Sir Philip and Brian and Clive and Penny and her sister and that taxi driver and the other Matt and Ranjit and Dr Adams and little Mac and Janet and Frank and Mand' and Charles and that jogger and Miss Marple and Alan and Doug and my mum and Tod and Claire and Paul and George and Lucy and Nigel and Ted and those fishermen and Connolly and Jules and Bill and those policemen and those people on the street…'

'I didn't kill them,' I protested.

'No, no you didn't did you? You "loved" them. You "loved" them all, just the same as you'll love Adelaide. You'll love her to death.'

'I won't. I love her.'

'Stop saying that. You don't know what it means.'

'I do.'

'You're going to fucking kill her and she'll hate you just like everyone else does.'

'No, she won't. I'll love her and show her…'

'Do you love me?' asked Rose.

'How about me?' said Janet.

'What about me?' Penny then joined in.

'Tell me you want me,' Katrina laughed.

'Tell me you want all of us,' Claire roared.

'My mate had five numbers and only got two grand,' George mused.

'Stop it! Stop it! Stop it!' I sobbed stumbling into the living room, but the voices just followed me.

I flopped down hard into my armchair and felt something hard stick into my back. It didn't hurt because I was so out of it but it did make it hard to get comfortable so I reached behind me and after some digging I pulled out a little snub-nosed .38 Special from down the side cushion. I'd locked all my guns away in the safe as I always did when I drank and had posted the keys to myself rather than risk finding myself drunk beyond sense in possession of a gun – like now. I checked to see if it was loaded.

It was.

Angela, Rose, Claire, Penny, Janet, Katrina, my mum and George all looked on with bated breath as I held the piece. Soon they had to make room for Lucy and Doug and Alan and Ranjit and all the rest of them as they filed in the room and stood round me in a semi-circle looking down at me. Before I knew it the room was packed with ghosts, all muttering excitedly to one another.

'It's easy,' Angela said. 'It doesn't hurt. I promise.'

'You can do it old boy,' Sir Philip said encouragingly.

'Go on, go on, do it,' Ted followed up.

'Please,' Rose said. 'Do it for me. Please. Do it and we'll be together for ever.'

'Take a drink,' Connolly said. 'One for the road then we'll all go together.'

I looked at the pistol and then at the bottle and I took a big swig.

'That's the spirit,' Ted said.

'Do this and we're quits,' Angela pleaded.

'Yes, and that goes for all of us,' one of the fishermen said.

'Yes,' they all said. 'All square.'

'Not as far as I'm concerned,' Breen objected, but they quickly turned on him and told him to shut up.

'Come on, you can do it,' Angela said. 'I believe in you. Show us that you're not selfish after all.'

'Yes, you reckon you love Adelaide? Prove it,' Rose said.

'It's the only way she'll ever be safe,' Penny said.

'You'd do it if you loved her,' her sister agreed.

I cocked the pistol.

'That's it!'

'Yes come on, over in the blink of an eye. You won't feel a thing.'

'It doesn't hurt.'

'Put it in your mouth!'

'Please, for us.'

'For Adelaide.'

'Come on, just do it.'

'Do it now.'

'You could've done it in the time you've been looking at it and it would all be over now.'

'No more pain.'

'No more killing.'

'You won't know anything about it.'

'What reason do you have for not doing it?'

'Put it to your temple.'

'Come on, just do it. Please do it. Please do it. Please do it. Please do it,' I sobbed over and over again as I held the gun against the side of my head. 'Please… Please! Do it…'

There was water.

Water was soaking my clothes, spilling down my face, getting into my mouth and into my eyes when I tried to open them. There was also extremely bright light and that was most unwelcome. I held up my hands to shield my face from both water and light but both just kept on coming. It was about then that I realised I was in the shower. I tried to reach up to turn the taps off but I couldn't get up, the pain in my head was utterly paralysing.

Oh God, had I shot myself?

I felt my face and head and both seemed to be intact, if a little tender. I tried to get to my feet again and suddenly became aware of the fact that I wasn't alone.

'… the fucking state of you,' someone was saying somewhere beyond my eyelids. I forced them open again and looked up to see Craig looking down at me and shaking his head.

'Uh…huh…ne water'off, please,' I said, then added, 'I'm getting all wet.' I must've still been plastered because it didn't even occur to me that it was probably Craig who'd put me in the shower in the first place. As far as I was concerned he was just passing by while I was finding myself in a bit of difficulty.

'You ready for the cold stuff?' he asked and twisted the shower setting. The water began to cool, then all too soon it became freezing. This was miserable. I was in so much pain and felt so overwhelmingly unhappy that I started to cry. I'd never known such utter desolation like it. In fact it was only when Craig turned off the shower that I suddenly remembered there were good things in life as well as bad things – like not getting pissed on by freezing cold water any more. That was a good thing. And there, just there at that moment, I felt grateful for that and my spirit lifted a few millimetres off the rocky bottom where it had lain the last few days.

I don't remember much about the following hours. Craig poured coffee down me and scotch down the sink as he set about straightening me out. I begged him for a quick glass before it was all gone but all he'd let me have instead was a fried egg sandwich – which he didn't manage to get within ten feet of me.

It was late afternoon before I was compos enough to hold a conversation with him.

'How is she?' I asked. 'Do you know?'

'Yeah. She's stable. Still unconscious and... you know,' he trailed off without going into further details. Adelaide had been completely busted up. She'd broken her arms, her legs and worst of all, her back and had sustained shocking head injuries that had left her in a coma and thankfully unaware of her condition.

Small mercies.

'Drinking yourself to death isn't going to solve anything,' Craig said rather patronisingly. 'You've just got to sort yourself out, try and be strong for her. And if the worst comes to the worst then you just have to deal with it and move on, otherwise that car would've killed two people instead of one. And that would be just pointless.'

'No, my life, that's pointless.'

'Whose isn't? I know mine is, but who cares? Life's not about having a point, it's about having a laugh. I know this isn't the sort of shit you want to hear right now but you've just got to be a bit more selfish. Don't take everything so personally and don't…'

'You're right,' I said, interrupting him.

'I know I am.'

'No, I mean about not wanting to hear this shit right now.'

Craig let out a long breath, furrowed his brow and bit his tongue.

'Sorry man,' he said, which I accepted with the nonchalant wave of a hand. 'You want another cup of coffee?'

'Fuck no!'

'How about some grub?' I just shook my head. 'Come on, I'll order us a pizza or get a Chinkies in. Even if you only have a little bit. You need your strength.'

'What for? I'm not doing anything at the moment.'

Craig couldn't answer that. Instead he just resorted to, 'Well I'm fucking starving. Why don't I order two big pizzas with everything on 'em and if you can't eat yours I'll have it?'

I couldn't make up my mind whether he was trying to mother me or whether he just wanted two pizzas. In the end I let him order what he wanted as that seemed the option with the least amount of discussion involved, though when the guy knocked on the door Craig found he didn't have any money on him so I had to pay.

I tried to eat a little of it but found I was still too choked up to be able to swallow, so I gave up.

My mind went back to Angela and those few long weeks after her mum had died (all right, after I'd killed her mum). She was utterly distraught as I remembered, same as how I felt at this moment, unable to eat, sleep or let an hour go by without bursting into tears. I'd had pizza with her back then too and it hadn't done much good on that occasion either. It made me wonder whether it was just a simple coincidence or whether pizza was generally viewed as cheering-up food. I thought about other take-away meals and tried to compare their spirit-lifting qualities in my mind… then I snapped back to the here and now and felt thoroughly ashamed of myself that I should be thinking about such trivialities when Adelaide was lying half-dead in the hospital.

I couldn't help it though. My mind was soon wandering off again and each time I caught myself and brought it back it was like hearing the news for the first time all over again.

I tried to concentrate on my grief as it was about the only thing that made me feel better but it got to be like trying to squeeze soap hard, especially when Craig turned the telly on.

'What are you doing here?'

'I thought I'd come round and make sure you was all right, that's all,' Craig said without taking his eyes off *The Simpsons*. 'Do you want that last hot wing?' he then asked.

'I didn't want the first one,' I replied. In the end I decided to just let my mind wander where it would as I figured it needed a break from itself. I tolerated Craig's presence also as he kept conversation to an absolute minimum and didn't try to get me to open my heart about anything that wasn't pizza-related.

'Phwoar, I'm fucking stuffed,' he said twenty minutes and two deep pans later. 'I don't think I could eat another thing.'

We sat in silence and watched the telly trying where we could to stick to the funnies. I thought about Angela again and *Only Fools and Horses* and felt like watching an episode, but none were on.

Angela? The thing about her grief though, it suddenly occurred to me, was that it lessened with time. Her mum died on such and such a date and time went by to separate her from that event. But that wouldn't happen with me. Adelaide wasn't dead, she was just injured. Badly injured, that said, maybe even crippled, but she wasn't dead, so she'd always be there (possibly) to grieve over. An unending nightmare of remorse and heartbreak.

I wondered if she'd be better off dead. Or more to the point, I wondered if I would.

It was a question I thankfully never got round to contemplating as I was disturbed at that moment by the phone. I picked it up. I was expecting it to be Jackie or the hospital or Eddie or even JB.

The last person I was expecting it to be was Logan.

'How are you boy?' I heard him say. 'Bit low at the moment I shouldn't be surprised.'

'Danny? Shit, where are you?'

'You mind if I don't tell you, only I'm hoping to die of old age one day and I'm concerned you might put the mockers on that?'

'Well, no. I suppose not.'

'Sorry I dropped you in it by the way. It was all a bit last minute and I didn't really have a choice. Glad to know you're still walking around.'

'Thanks,' I said, less than sincerely.

'I'm phoning you for a reason,' he said getting to the point. 'It's about your young lady friend, Adelaide I think her name was, wasn't it?'

'Adelaide? What about her?' I said then noticed Craig staring at me.

'Who's that?' Craig asked.

'Who's that?' Logan echoed.

I told them both and Logan told me to go to another room… and get a gun.

'What are you talking about?' I said. Craig suddenly looked extremely shifty and told me to hang up the phone. I looked down at the floor next to the chair and saw the .38 Special I'd been threatening myself with last night. If you ask me now why I did it I couldn't tell you, it was pure instinct; a sixth sense of something not right. My old self-preservation taking over and beating my brain to the jump. I ducked down and grabbed the gun and pointed it at Craig. Craig jumped back a couple of steps but was composed enough not to reach for his own shooter.

'Call me back in two minutes,' I told Logan and dropped the phone into the armchair. 'Live or die, it's up to you, but I want all of your weapons on the table now. And you'd better do it nice and slowly or else I'll blow your fucking head off. And you know I mean it.'

'Ian, wait...'

'No waiting and no thinking, do it now or die.'

Craig seemed unable to move at first and it was only when I cocked the hammer that he found the impetus. Craig placed his two pistols, knife, knuckleduster and cosh on the table and stepped back when I told him to.

'This had better be all of it. If I find any other weapon on you I'll kill you,' I said, calm as you like.

'I know that but listen. Don't believe anything Logan tells you, he's only trying to use you the same as...'

'Shut up!' I told him. 'No more talking, not a fucking word. Don't worry, you'll get your chance but for now I'll do the talking and you do the lying on the floor with your hands tied behind your back.'

A minute later Craig was doing his bit and I was doing mine as Logan painted me a picture.

'It was John who done your bird in Ian. Well, at least he would've had someone do her for him only they didn't do a very good job because she's still alive from what I hear.'

'John? I don't understand. What are you talking about? Why would JB want Adelaide done?'

'Same reason he wanted Rose done, and that other bird, what was her name? Her with the stupid leg.'

'Angela?'

'That was it, Angela, the cleaner.'

'Adelaide a grass? I don't believe it,' I told him.

'And you'd be right not to,' Logan replied. 'Adelaide weren't no grass, but then again neither was Angela.'

Logan didn't say anything for a moment. I guess he wanted to let that sink in before he went on. He had quite a wait.

'What do you mean? Angela was a police informant, you said so yourself. You ordered the hit!'

'It wasn't true. Oh we needed her dead all right, but it had nothing to do with her, it was all about you.'

'About me! I don't understand Danny, I don't understand any of this.' I looked down at Craig who was all trussed up on the floor and staring up at me in apprehension, but he didn't seem to be able to shed any light on the situation either. 'Danny, tell me. What are you talking about?'

'You have no idea what you are, do you?' he said. 'You have no idea just how special and how valuable you are to the organisation. Ian, you are the best killer I've ever known – ever! And it's not because you're some sort of shit-hot James Bond SAS superhero or nothing like that, it's because you ain't got a shred of guilt or regret about you. You're the perfect remorseless, clock-work psychopath that we could just wind up and point in whoever's direction we needed taking care of. No right, no wrong, no second-thoughts, no hesitation, you always got the job done – and no questions. You got to be so efficient at sorting out our problems that you became the easy option. Sure we could pay off this guy or blackmail that one, but why fucking bother, we'd just give you a call and that would be that. Problem solved.'

'What the fuck does this have to do with Adelaide or Angela or Rose?'

'You still haven't worked it out yet? Jesus, Bridges, I know I always said no questions but take a fucking day off. They got in the way. They threatened our investment. You know why you're such a good little killer? Because life ain't fair. You've been getting the shaft your whole fucking life from every cunt and his wife so why the fuck should you give a shit about anybody else, hey? Someone got to get their head blown off? That's too bad, shit happens. Someone got to disappear? Hey, don't go looking to you for sympathy. That's your attitude and it always was. I saw you for what you were the moment I met you in nick. You had a terminal case of the "not fairs". You were fucked off, you were miserable and life wasn't fair and as long as things stayed that way for you,

you could do the job with a clear conscience. Or rather, no conscience at all. So, when you got out and came to work for us, all we had to do was make sure things stayed that way for you. Don't worry, it wasn't a nine to five job or nothing, you did a pretty good job on yourself most of the time. But every now and then something would come along that threatened to rock the boat and take you away from us, but we couldn't afford to let you go easy, so we invented a few excuses and had you do the business yourself. No hard feelings Bridges, it was just business.'

I listened to Logan without saying a word. What could I say? It was all so fantastic (and I don't mean fantastic as in 'smart/superb/brilliant'). I even forgot about Craig tied up by my feet and almost tripped over him at one point as I paced backwards and forwards trying to associate what Logan was saying with me, with events from the past… with Adelaide.

'You still there Bridges?'

'What? Yeah, I'm still here.'

Logan continued.

'You have to understand, this is how John operates, this is how he's stayed in the business for thirty years. He doesn't give a shit about you, much as he doesn't give a shit about me… actually, that's not true. I think he gives a shit about me very much these days but that's another story. All I'm saying is, we were all just expendable assets to him, that's why I never felt too cut up about taking his money.'

'You're telling me that you killed Angela and Rose just to make sure I was unhappy.'

'Hey, you want a good attack dog, you don't let it sleep in silk sheets.'

At that moment, all too sickeningly, I knew Logan was telling the truth. I'd be lying if I said I'd always known because I hadn't, I hadn't a clue, but now, now that it was spelt out for me in black and white I couldn't believe how obvious it all was. How had I missed it? Had I been walking around with my eyes closed or something?

Conditioned. That was what Logan had said. Conditioned. I'd been conditioned to accept what Logan told me. I'd been conditioned to think life wasn't fair. I'd been conditioned to kill without question, even someone I knew – or loved.

I'd always said there was a conspiracy against me. It's a surreal fucking moment when you wake up and discover there really is.

'I'm going to kill you, you motherfucker!' I told Logan and Logan said why did I think he was using the phone instead of taking me out for a beer?

'I shouldn't think our paths'll be crossing again, my old mate, but I'll keep my eyes peeled, just in case they do. Anyway, you're missing the point, I'm not phoning to wind you up or nothing, I'm out of the game now so I don't really give a shit. But, and you can believe this if you want to, it doesn't matter to me, I always had a bit of a soft spot for you so I wanted to warn you: that little girlfriend of yours, she's still in danger.'

'Adelaide?'

'Yeah, her. And not only her, but anyone else you're ever likely to meet. The cards are stacked against you, sunshine, John's got the whole pack in his pocket, I just thought I'd chuck you an ace. Good luck,' and before I could say anything further the line went dead. I stared at the phone a little longer and thought about calling him back, then it occurred to me that I didn't know where he was or what number he was calling from.

1471, naturally, drew a blank.

That was the most frustrating thing. Okay, I believed him but it still hadn't sunk in properly and I had a hundred different questions and suddenly no one to ask.

I looked down at Craig.

'Okay, you may now speak,' I told him.

Craig did a reasonable job of convincing me that he had nothing to do with the attempted hit on Adelaide. He admitted as much as to say that he'd started to suspect something was amiss when JB called him over to his place a few days ago and Adelaide cropped up in the course of the conversation. Craig said that he hadn't even known JB knew who Adelaide was or why he should care, but when he started asking him about her Craig got a bit spooked. JB dressed it up as general chitchat but Craig read between the lines and got the uneasy feeling he was being sounded out about a job.

That was two days before Adelaide was knocked over.

Craig said that he'd wanted to warn me, or at least make me aware of JB's interest, but he never got the chance. At the end of the conversation JB packed Craig and Eddie off up to Newcastle to baby-sit a package for two days and that was that. JB obviously decided to entrust the job elsewhere and the package probably contained nothing more than an excuse to get Craig out of the way for a few days.

Craig baby-sits the package, Eddie baby-sits Craig and the job is done quick before any word can get back to me.

'I tried to ring,' Craig implored. 'I tried to ring you a dozen times but you never answered. Where were you?'

My machine. I'd only answered the phone to Adelaide.

'I'm sorry Bridges, I fucked up because I dithered. I didn't know what to do or even if it was all just in my head and it was only when I got back into town and heard… well you know, that I knew for sure. I'm sorry man, I'm so fucking sorry.'

'Why did you come round here Craig? You going to do a job on me?'

'No Bridges, no. I came round to make sure you were okay, that's all. If I was going to whack you don't you think I would've done it while you were out for the count when I first got round?'

'Maybe that's just your own fault and you couldn't. Maybe you ain't ruthless enough. Maybe Logan's right about me. Yeah, maybe that's why I'm the best, because I don't have a single iota of compassion or remorse for anyone… not even for someone I know.'

I stared down at Craig, all trussed up on the floor and staring back at me with fear in his eyes.

'Maybe that does make me a fucking psychopath,' I said, then I walked to the table and picked up Craig's knife. 'A little clockwork psychopath who butchers and kills without a second's thought. Even my friends. Even my lovers.'

I looked around the room and saw a dozen familiar faces staring back at me. 'Perhaps they're all right too, and I really can't love anyone, not anyone, except myself.'

Craig started to struggle against his bonds and pleaded with me as I knelt down beside him.

'No Bridges, no!'

'They made me into a monster did they? Okay. Okay. Now it's time they saw what a real monster can do.'

'No Bridges, please! Please…' I whipped the knife back once and Craig went quiet. I did it again and then again and then again, then stood back… and offered him my hand.

Craig hesitated for just a second, then kicked the loose ends of rope away from his feet and took my hand. He eyed me cautiously as I pulled him to his feet and almost jumped out of his skin when I offered him back his knife.

'I'm not going to kill you Craig. Not now, not next week. And I ain't going to kill Adelaide either. You're all wrong about me, all of you.' Craig looked around the room a little baffled.

'What are you going to do then Bridges?' he asked after pocketing his knife, gun and knuckleduster.

'I'm going to do what Logan reckons I do best. I'm going to take them out – every last fucking one of them.'

He thought about this carefully then said, 'I'll help you,' but I told him no.

'This is my job and mine alone. Go back to Newcastle. Look after another package. Open up your own package-minding shop because you ain't going to have a job when you get back to London. And listen, just so that we both know where we are, if I see you again I'll have to take it that you're coming after me and

I'll have to do you. You understand me?'

Craig said that he did.

'All right then, go. I've got things to do.'

27: Retribution

I took a couple of sleeping pills and made sure I got a good eight hours under my belt before setting out. It was dark by the time I left the house, though I felt alert and awake.

I knew where he'd be, of course. I'd phoned him earlier and told him that I'd had a bit of a break as regards Logan – which was sort of true. JB asked me what it was but I told him I didn't want to say over the phone so he told me to come down to his place on the docks around ten.

Perfect.

I parked up in a little quiet spot by some waste ground about half a mile away from the wharf. All the lights were on and the river sparkled beyond the line of warehouses.

JB had one of these. I didn't know if it was a legitimate business or a front for a smuggling or laundering operation or what. All I knew was that JB kept his offices here and the place was a long old way from anywhere. The nearest civilisation was some two hundred yards away on the opposite bank...

...and the sound from silenced weapons doesn't travel that far.

I stayed low and kept to the shadows as I approached the site. JB had three buildings here: a main hangar-type warehouse, a smaller storage unit and a couple of Portakabin offices stacked on top of each other in-between the two. These buildings were located on a small industrial park that also played home to baker's, print-maker's, double-glazer's and candlestick-maker's (probably), all of whom had the good sense to knock off and go home at the end of the day. There was also the main security office at the entrance to the park which housed two coffee, paperback and pornography enthusiasts.

That was my first target.

I was so quick that I doubt either guard had a chance to know they were dead before they were and by that time, there wasn't a great deal they could do about it. Chest shot, chest shot, head shot, head shot. It was all over in the blink of an eye. I had a twinge of regret at taking out the two guards as they weren't on JB's payroll (well, not directly) but then it wasn't me who started this thing. Besides, I was a psychopath, remember? So what were one or two innocents on top of all the killing I was to do tonight? I switched off the office light and checked the bank of monitors for any sign of movement about the park.

Two guys milling about by the side of JB's warehouse.

These were JB's own personal security guards and unlike the two uniforms by my feet I knew these guys would be armed. I cut all the phone lines in the security office, switched off the security cameras, holstered my pistol and brought my silenced Heckler & Koch MP5 around from behind my back.

Round chambered. Safety off.

Let's go.

I crossed the road and made my way via the shadows around to the men so that when I came at them they'd have the warehouse to the side of them and not behind them, so that if any of my shots missed they wouldn't rattle off the side of the unit and wake everyone up. I knew very few people in the warehouse would be armed but their numbers meant surprise was still my best weapon.

I darted out of the shadows and ran towards them full tilt with my thick silenced barrel already levelled. One of the men started raising a hand for me to slow down though neither saw the gun against my black combat gear until two quick muzzle flashes sent five pieces of hot lead ripping through each man's chest. I jumped over them without breaking stride and stopped dead by the side exit.

My heart was hammering away inside my flak jacket and the sweat was starting to break through the boot polish I'd done my face in.

By Christ I looked the dog's bollocks, I did!

Well, if you're going to do something like this you might as well go the whole way and tart yourself up like Steven Seagal. If only Adelaide could've seen me like this…

Adelaide.

I suddenly snapped back and remembered why I was here.

My poor little Adelaide.

I took a peek around the corner through the window in the door and saw that it was all business as usual. The door was an emergency exit and opened outwards so I blocked it off with the big industrial wheely-bins and the two dead guards to make sure no one could escape without getting past me. That just left the front door and the goods entrance beside it. The front door led to offices upstairs and the goods entrance to the main shop floor.

The goods entrance shutters were up, which would probably cause me problems, so I decided to block off the front door then close the shutters behind me so that we were all in there together and nobody could escape.

Before I did any of this though, there was the question of the Portakabin offices and the smaller unit next door. The unit was empty though the top Portakabin had a couple of collar and ties playing with their calculators. I burst through the door firing short bursts, knocking them both off their chairs and shattering the windows behind them. Instinctively I shifted the muzzle towards the ceiling and took out the strip lights with two more bursts, plunging the offices into darkness.

I'd been quick but noisy.

Glass tinkled down and my heart jumped inside my chest when I heard a voice call up to me.

'Are you all right up there? What's happened?'

'Bloody ceiling fell in,' I called back. 'Give us a hand with this will you?'

The footsteps made it to the top step but no further. I pulled the trigger and emptied the last couple of rounds into his neck and chest sending him tumbling back down the steps. By the time he reached the bottom I was right behind him, new magazine locked home and running.

I darted around the corner and saw a couple of lads coming out to investigate. I lifted my weapon and fired, dropping them to the ground, and carried on past them and into the warehouse.

I slammed myself up against the wall just inside the goods entrance and hit the red button. Immediately a warning siren started to echo around the vast warehouse and a yellow light began to flash as the heavy steel shutters descended behind me. Several heads poked out from behind packing crates and from the offices above when they heard the noise.

JB poked his head out of his office to see who was closing the door and stared at me for one second before his face turned to utter horror.

'Oh my God! It's Bridges, it's a hit!' he screamed at everyone and dived back into his office before I could get a shot off in his direction.

I aimed upwards towards the offices and fired. Three windows shattered with three silenced bursts and I dropped one guy off the mezzanine and hit at least one other. Screams of panic broke out all around me as I lowered my sights back down to the shop floor and started picking my targets with unflinching ruthlessness.

Logan would've been proud.

My Heckler & Koch might've been heavily silenced but the shrill whistle of dampened machinegun fire still echoed around the enormous hangar. Every time I put a short burst into someone's back the sound seemed to continue after I took my finger off the trigger to accompany the tinkle of spent cartridges as they bounced off the concrete floor.

The warehouse was basically rows and rows of shelves and containers on either side so I started systematically making my way down the central aisle forcing those in amongst the shelves to try and run or to try and hide. The runners were easy to pick off. And

I have no hang-ups about shooting men in their backs.

Not these men anyway.

Trigger – muzzle flash – shrill – tinkle – gasp – pick next target. Trigger – muzzle flash – shrill – tinkle – scream – reload – pick next target.

Some of them I recognised from The Aviary and other past meetings and some of them recognised me. Not that it did them any good.

Syd... can't remember his second name... pleaded with me, 'No Bridges, don't!' just before I took his head off and Tommy Leicester just stared at me in total pant-pissing fear and confusion when I cornered him down the third aisle and splashed his guts across the wall with a squeeze of my forefinger.

Each time I pulled the trigger I'd stop and wonder for a fraction of a second, was it you who was driving the car?

Trigger – muzzle flash – shrill – tinkle – thud.

It was just after Tommy that I heard the first cracks of retaliatory fire. Several bullets ricocheted off the shelving around me forcing me back up the aisle for safety. I'd barely had a chance to regain my bearings when there was a second blast from the catwalk above and the shelving around me exploded under a hail of lead shot. I dived in-between the shelves as blast followed on the heels of blast and glass, wood, lead and spent shells showered down all around me.

I hadn't even known there was a catwalk up there for fuck's sake.

Shoddy. Very shoddy.

I was relatively sheltered in-between the steel shelving from the pump action above but I was pinned down and all too soon reinforcements would be arriving to finish me off. From my vantage point I couldn't see the shooter above but I could see the suspension cables that supported the catwalk a little further down so I pulled out the shoulder rest, took careful aim and opened up at them. I used up a disturbing amount of ammo before I was able to sever the cable, but when I did the catwalk suddenly dropped twenty degrees on one side. The second it gave I fell out from in-between the shelving landing flat on my back and emptied the rest of the clip into the target directly above me.

Phil shuddered and screamed as the bullets ripped into his feet, groin and arse before toppling over the side and landing next to me with a thud and a splat.

The dust had barely had a chance to settle when I saw some-thing out of the corner of my eye whipping past the end of the aisle and making for the goods entrance. I was on my feet again in moments and after it, but again, when I got to the end of the aisle someone took a shot at me from the upstairs offices. I leapt back out of the line of fire, giving whoever was making a break for it precious seconds to get the shutters up once again.

I grabbed Phil's pump action, found a gap in-between the shelving and let rip in the direction of the top offices, killing windows and sending lead shot spraying in dozens of different directions until the gun was empty, but I was too late.

The siren began to wail and the light began to flash as the steel shutters started to roll up.

Desperate times call for desperate measures as they say, so I pulled out one of the four live grenades I'd brought with me, pulled the pin and lobbed it over the shelves and in the direction of the opening door. I'd primed the grenades to give them two-second fuses and there was a deafening explosion (made all the more deafening by the fact that we were inside) followed by a hail of shrapnel and a tinkling of glass.

The shutter never so much as paused.

It was disappointing but sometimes you have to know when to cut your losses. I could've gone after whoever was making a break for it but that might've meant some of the bigger fish getting away, so there was nothing more for it but to press on.

I pulled out another grenade and lobbed it in the opposite direction, blowing apart crates and upsetting shelving, and jumped out from cover firing. The two explosions in a relatively enclosed environment must've momentarily stunned the shooter up in the offices because I saw the target and had time to aim and fire long before he saw me. Not that, I guess, he ever did see me again. My line of fire cut across his midriff and dumped him hard against the back wall, though he still managed to get a couple of directionless, reflex shots out before dropping the gun over the side.

I couldn't risk anyone finding it so, still firing into the offices above, I quickly made my way towards where I thought I saw it land and found myself standing at the end of an aisle staring at two guys hammering against the emergency exit.

'Bridges wait…' one of them screamed raising his hands above his head. I wondered, for the briefest of seconds, how he knew me because I didn't recognise him. It was something that was to remain a mystery as I opened them up all over the emergency exit.

Never pause. Never check. Never think.

Just kill.

'Psychopath,' Logan kept whispering in my ear. 'You're a fucking psychopath,' while my mum stood by the two fellas and shook her head in disgust.

More, I replied. I want more.

I had a quick look for the gun though when I didn't find it I decided that it must've dropped one aisle up. I was just running around the central aisle when suddenly Felix was there.

The gun was in his hand…

He was pointing it at me…

He was pulling the trigger…

There was a sharp pain in my chest…

I was flat on my back…

Felix was standing over me…

The gun was still in his hand…

Shit!

This was it, I thought to myself. This is the moment I am going to die.

I tried to bring my Heckler & Koch around but there was no way I was going to make it. Felix already had the gun pointing at my head and his finger was on the trigger. All I remember is the end of the barrel. I could see right up it. I know it's my imagination because this is impossible but I swear, in that instant, I looked up the barrel and saw the actual bullet that was going to rip out my brain.

All this is probably no more than the product of overactive hindsight because the whole thing couldn't have taken more than half a second, but it's true what they say, time does slow right down just before the end. Maybe that's what death is like; time stopping and you left with a still picture to take away with you for all eternity.

I was all resigned to clocking out when three bullets whizzed past my ears...

... and into Felix's chest.

A great scarlet cloud erupted from the point of impact and Felix flew back headfirst into a stack of steel crates. I rolled on to my front and looked behind me but there was no one there, just a few dead bodies, a bit of mayhem and the blackness of the night out beyond the open goods entrance.

Not that it mattered. I couldn't see him out there and I wasn't even sure where he was but suddenly I knew I had a guardian angel watching over me.

I got to my feet and took a moment to look down at the mess that used to be Felix's chest. 'Nice grouping, Clarence,' I said and felt a warm glow of pride in my pupil.

My own chest felt sore from where I'd taken a bullet in the flak jacket from close range and I guessed I had a couple of fractured ribs, though I was thankful I didn't have Felix's problems.

I snapped back to the here and now and decided to go straight for the offices. Craig could take care of the stragglers in my wake. All I wanted now was JB. A steel spiral staircase twenty yards to the left led up to the mezzanine and I made it there in one piece and a hop and a skip. A few more faces greeted me on the way and I dealt with them the same as I'd dealt with all the others until my Heckler & Koch had fired itself dry.

I dropped it where I stood and pulled out my Glock and my Walther P5 and made my way up the staircase. There were three glass-fronted offices stretched out along the mezzanine and JB was in one of them. I dashed along the back walkway and stopped at the corner of the first office. The doors and windows were all smashed in and half the ceiling and fixtures were hanging down inside. I paused momentarily when I heard more shouting and screaming coming from the front of the warehouse followed by a volley of single shots and then a rat-atat-tat of automatic fire and silence before I got on with the job in hand.

My third grenade rolled through the broken door and came to a standstill in the middle of the office as I hit the deck. The blast ripped the guts out of the office and whoever was hiding in there under the desk because I didn't recognise him after that. Mind you, I'm not sure even his dentist would've recognised him after that.

Movement!

A figure jumped from the next office up and fired towards me three times. Two of the bullets hit my flak jacket sending me tumbling to my arse while the third ripped a crease in my skull. The guy must've been busy congratulating himself on a job well done because he didn't spot the flak jacket and he didn't go in for the head stopper and before he registered my arms lifting I'd fired a shot from either pistol; one plugged him straight in the chest, the other hit a little higher up and ripped out his throat.

Never pause. Never check. Never think.

Just kill.

I lobbed my fourth grenade into the middle office and cleared that of any further danger leaving just the final office. This one was JB's. I knew that as I'd been here before. It was where I was most likely to find JB and it was the one I'd planned to hit last.

I lobbed my fifth grenade in through the window.

Yes, my fifth grenade, you read right. Four live grenades.
One dud.

Two seconds later I followed it through the door and caught
JB trying to squeeze himself behind a heavy steel filing cabinet
along with a man I recognised as Forester, his warehouse manager.
I shot Forester dead where he lay and trained my guns on JB.

'Get out of there,' I told him, my teeth clenched together
through sheer fury and adrenaline. I fired a shot into his right arm
to demonstrate the seriousness of my intent and also to disable it
in case he was concealing a gun. JB screamed and clutched his arm,
though somehow he managed to roll over and look up at me.

'What's going on? I don't...' he started to say but I shouted him
down.

'You know fucking well what. I spoke to Logan yesterday and
he told me everything.'

'Logan? Logan? What are you talking about?'

'I'm talking about Adelaide. And Rose. And Angela. I just
wanted you to know before I killed you.'

'No Bridges, wait! You're being used! Logan's using you! I
don't know what...'

But I didn't want to hear it.

Never pause. Never check. Never think.

Just kill.

A bullet in each of his legs and then one in the stomach had him
squealing like a pig. I stood over him a little longer and looked over
at my mum who, for once, didn't say anything. She just shook her
head sadly and rolled her eyes.

'What?' I protested, then stuck one last one in JB's head.

Okay, so I'd paused and checked and thought a little bit right
at the end there, but that was just because I didn't want JB dying
without him knowing who'd killed him. I hadn't gone to all this
fucking trouble for nothing, you know.

This wasn't a hit.

This was retribution.

And with retribution, you've got to take the credit, otherwise what's the point?

I allowed myself a moment out on the mezzanine to survey the carnage and admire my handiwork. It would be this moment that I would return to again and again and again every time I felt anger and bitterness over what had happened to Adelaide, Rose, Angela and the rest of them so I took a few precious seconds to make the most of it and soak it all up.

That just left the C4.

I fitted one block downstairs to the mezzanine supports and one block to the forklift diesel drum and set the timers for ten minutes. Hopefully there would be plenty of other flammables in here to torch any evidence I may have inadvertently left behind. It would also burn up most of the bodies so that whoever was left over that I didn't get tonight couldn't very easily take a register and spot the missing names.

Talking of missing names, where the fuck was Eddie? I thought he'd be here tonight. How very disappointing! Oh well, never mind, you can't have it all your own way I guess. Besides, he was one bloke at least that I knew wasn't driving the car as he'd been up in Newcastle with Craig.

Ah bollocks to him, live and let live, that's what I say.

Or at least, I did from now on.

I dropped my Walther and my beloved Glock (I always hated getting rid of my favourite guns) down next to the diesel drum and made my way back to the goods entrance. Don't worry, I still had my .38 just out and in hand in case I ran into any trouble but there was no point in taking any of the others with me as they were about to become rather sought after by the Old Bill.

There were several bodies outside that had nothing to do with me and I guessed they were down to Craig. I was just wondering where Craig was when I noticed another body across the road in the shadows. I ran across to it and my worst fears were realised.

He'd taken a couple of bullets in the shoulder and torso and hadn't had the foresight to stick on a flak jacket like I had.

Craig looked up at me and rolled his eyes about in semi-consciousness.

'Come on, let's get you out of here,' I said picking him up and supporting him under the arms. Craig shrieked in pain suddenly, now only too awake but I ignored his protestations and dragged him across the waste land to where I'd parked my car and bundled him in the back. I'd half-hoped to hang around and watch the fireworks but Craig had taken a couple of good'uns so time was at a premium.

I crunched the car into gear, put my foot on the floor and pulled my mobile from the glove box.

Dr Ranjani cut Craig's clothes away and shook his head as he cleaned up the wounds.

'These are serious I'm afraid, my friend,' he said, not daring to look up at me or the gun I had tucked into my trousers.

'I know that Doc, that's why I brought him here.'

'You should've taken him to a hospital, there's precious little I can do for him.'

'Can't do that, not after tonight. He's in your hands.'

'I don't know what you want from me but this lad's as good as dead. I haven't got blood supplies, plasma or even half the equipment I'd need to give him a fighting chance.'

'Then get it,' I told him in no uncertain terms.

'Just like that. Get it!'

'You can do it. Call in all your old favours you're owed. Buy off who you'll need but just get it. Money's no object.'

'I'm sorry, but it's just not possible.'

'You're wasting time Doc. Get on the phone and get the stuff you need.'

'Please listen to me…'

'No, you listen to me,' I said calm as you like and pulled out my gun and stuck it in his face. 'It's really this simple – he dies, you die.'

Dr Ranjani went comically cross-eyed staring at the gun in his eye socket then picked up the phone.

So, what do I do now? Suddenly I find myself out of a job and at a loose end. Actually, that's not quite true. That bird from Craig's party's been trying to get ahold of me through Eddie. She wants her old man rubbed out or something, though I'll have to see about that. I think Eddie's trying to fix me up with some work to save his own skin. Be my agent, as he put it. Prove he's useful to me alive, in other words, though like I told him already, he doesn't really have anything to worry about because I'm all out of revenge. I don't know why, but I feel quite calm. Perhaps it goes back to what I said earlier about believing the world was against me, then suddenly finding out that, shit, the fuckers really were!

It's almost a bit of a relief to discover the worst because then at least you can go out and do something about it. And that's got to be better than sitting around hoping you're wrong.

Sure I heard what JB said about Logan using me and maybe he did and maybe he didn't, but that really doesn't matter. JB missed the point, and that was that you should never try and wind up a psychopath, clockwork or otherwise. Come on, I would've killed Logan as well if he'd been there but he wasn't so what was I going to do?

I know it's not fair, but come on JB, wasn't that the whole point of my existence in the first place? To get your way at all costs? To not be fair?

Who am I talking to? No one, that's who. No one's listening. Not JB, not Angela, not Rose, or Janet or George. I've finally managed to lay them all to rest, since I found out that it wasn't me who killed them, I was just being used. In fact, I was the victim as much as they were. Well, sort of.

Of course my mum's still here, worst luck, and I have started to wonder how many I'm going to have to bump off to put her to bed for good. There's just no getting rid of some people is there? But happily she doesn't come round half as often as she used to though, as I've got other things to occupy my thoughts.

Adelaide.

Adelaide's still in hospital but she's been downgraded from critical to just plain fucked up. She still hasn't regained consciousness though, but I'll be here waiting for her when she does. Imagine how much she'll love me when she sees that I stuck around. Imagine how much she'll care for me when I take care of her. Imagine the love we'll have for each other when she wakes up.

It took so long, almost half my life, but I finally found her.

Adelaide Harrison.

My love.

My life.

My coma girl.